ever Any Doubt, told from both the male and female point of .ew, is a story about the importance of friendship, the recog- .tion of strength, and realizing that sometimes first love re- .ly is forever.

eenage romances don't usually last. At that age, no one is .ertain where their next pimple will appear, much less if a .ouple will stand the test of time. Paige Turner and Carter .ullivan had a connection from the moment they met at age .welve. Paige thought her relationship with Carter was differ- .nt. Parting after graduation due to his obstinacy, she was dis- .llusioned and heartbroken.

.Carter let Paige go so she could chase her dreams. After end- lessly regretting his decision, he is determined to find her and win her back. Paige has never forgotten Carter either.

At their ten-year high school reunion, after a thousand miles and a decade of separation, they rekindle their love affair. Yet despite Carter's persistence and their undeniable chemistry, Paige questions her ability to commit to a relationship due to a devastating event that occurred while they were apart and now jeopardizes their future.

Never Any Doubt
Copyright © 2019 Diane Ziock
ISBN: 978-1-4874-2501-2
Cover art by Angela Waters

Published by eXtasy Books Inc or
Devine Destinies, an imprint of eXtasy Books Inc

Look for us online at:
www.eXtasybooks.com or www.devinedestinies.com

NEVER ANY DOUBT
NEVER SAY NEVER BOOK ONE

BY

DIANE ZIOCK

DEDICATION

To my husband . . . my biggest supporter who always had the faith and the confidence that I would succeed.

CHAPTER ONE: PAIGE

"I can't believe he showed up," Peyton mock whispered, looking over at the entrance.

"Who?" I craned my neck to try to see over the throng of bodies between our table and the door.

"Travis Harrington!" she hissed.

"Of course."

Travis was Peyton's sometime boyfriend from the ninth and tenth grade. Sitting at a table at our ten-year high school reunion, I found it hard to believe that much time had passed. After going to college and working in Chicago, I had recently moved back to Connecticut, about twenty miles from where I grew up. Though I had stayed in touch with a core group of friends, this reunion was the first I had been able to attend since graduation.

The event was at an upscale restaurant near the coast with gorgeous views of Long Island Sound. Our school colors of blue and white punctuated the room and a DJ played hits from the era. The crystal chandeliers and peony floral center-pieces provided a modern feel, though the dress code was more suitable for a cocktail hour than a formal reception.

In preparation for the evening, I chose a teal silk blouse, high-waisted black crepe pants, and four-inch black sandals. A thin black leather belt, a silver choker, and diamond hoops completed the look. The stylist at the salon highlighted my brown hair deep auburn. I left it down for the evening, reaching halfway down my back. I used slightly more make-up than usual, drawing attention to my light blue eyes and applying copper matte lipstick to my lips.

I looked around the room. Though some of my classmates had changed, they were still recognizable. Back then, I carried an extra twenty-five pounds on my five-foot six-inch frame. Though I'd lost the weight soon after I entered college, I wouldn't be considered skinny due to my hourglass figure. Overall, I was satisfied with my size eight body even though I continued to wish for longer — and thinner — legs . . . and, if I was being honest, smaller boobs.

"Why don't you go over and say hello?" I asked Peyton. I was rewarded with an incredulous glance.

"I can't do that. He's talking with Simone Plexer. Ooh, how I despise that girl."

I rolled my eyes. "First of all, she's not a girl. She's twenty-eight just like us. Secondly, it's been ten years. Do you really think they're still an item?"

Peyton frowned. "He dumped me for her. He's talking to her now. I know they aren't married or anything, but still . . ."

I looked at Peyton, assessing her tall, willowy frame, wavy brown hair cut into a fashionable bob that reached her shoulders, and her topaz eyes.

"You are smart, successful, and beautiful. Where is this coming from?"

"I feel like I am the short, shy girl with slight acne and glasses all over again. Being around these people automatically sucks you into a time warp."

Laughing, I nodded. "It's weird. I guess because we haven't seen these people as we've matured, our point of reference is associated with the past."

Nodding herself, she said, "Exactly."

We both paused and looked back over at Travis and Simone. It didn't look as though he was engaged in the conversation. Simone was trying hard, I'd give her that. She looked about the same as she had in high school. Same bleached blonde hair. Same heavy-handed make-up. Same close-to-inappropriate clothing.

"If you want my opinion, Travis doesn't look thrilled with her company. I bet he would welcome the interruption."

Peyton studied the pair across the room.

"You may be right. Look at the way she is hanging on him. Can she be more obvious?"

"I say go over there and show him—and her—how awesome you are."

She smiled at me. "Thanks, Paige. You are an ego boost."

"Just the voice of reason. And a friend."

"The best."

She stood and smoothed down the skirt of her navy wrap dress. "Here goes nothing."

I watched her make her way through the crowd on the dance floor towards Travis and saw his double-take upon her approach. I couldn't wait to hear the conversation re-cap later.

Chapter Two: Carter

I slid into the passenger seat of Jaxson's vintage Camaro and shut the door.

"Hey, gentle with her, man," he admonished.

I didn't think that I slammed the door, but maybe I did. Admittingly, I was a little on edge.

"Sorry."

Jaxson grinned. "Anxious?"

"Screw you." I frowned.

He had been my best friend for twenty years, since we were eight. Unfortunately, that meant he knew pretty much everything about me. Including how I was feeling about going to our reunion.

"It's going to be a great night. I can tell."

"Oh yeah, Merlin? How do you figure?"

"Just a feeling."

"Uh-huh. You said that before the last reunion."

"And we had a good time."

"Yeah, but . . ." I looked out the window.

"But, no Paige."

I sighed. "Yeah, no Paige."

While it was good to see people at our five-year reunion and catch up with those I hadn't talked to since graduating, I was hoping to see one person in particular. That hope wasn't realized. I was starting to get discouraged, but I had already made my mind up that if she wasn't there tonight, I would find her. Needing to see her was becoming as necessary as breathing.

Ever since the day Paige left for college, I had been kicking myself for letting her go. Sure, deep down I knew we were kids and not ready for any huge commitment. I felt strongly that she should go to school free to experience everything without being tied to home. She didn't agree. We fought about it for weeks, but I was adamant. I won the argument, but I lost her.

After graduation, I stayed home and worked for my dad's contracting business, which I took over two years ago when he retired. I loved my job and was proud of the expansions I'd made. Financially secure and surrounded by family and friends, I still felt something was missing. I had an active sex life and had even had a few long-term relationships, but no woman ever truly captured my heart. Probably because Paige took it with her when she left. In the back of my mind, I always compared how I felt for anyone I was dating to how I had felt for Paige. And everyone since her had come up lacking.

I turned away from the window. "Jax?"

"Yeah?"

"If she's not there tonight, I want you help me find her."

Jaxson was a police lieutenant. He had offered to help me in my search before, but I had always declined. I had wanted Paige to come back to me of her own accord. But after waiting all these years, I just wanted her back.

His smile flashed in the dark interior. "About damn time."

An hour later, we arrived at the reunion's oceanside location. As we got out of the car and approached the building, I felt my heart beat faster in anticipation, wondering if I would see her again. I took a deep breath and told myself to get it together.

After greeting a few folks, I scanned the ballroom. Not seeing Paige, I walked around the dance floor toward the tables overlooking the ocean. Spotting my brother Xander, I clapped him on the back. He turned.

"Little brother!"

We were fraternal twins. He was older by seven minutes. He rarely let me forget it.

"Old man," I greeted.

"What took you guys so long?" he asked as Jaxson sat down.

"This started at six. It's seven. We're not that late, *Dad*." Jaxson chided.

I shook hands with Grayson Bradley and Hunter Carlson, who were also at the table.

Xander and I had known Grayson and Jaxson since third grade. Hunter joined the group our freshman year in high school. We had all stayed somewhat local—within an hour of each other—and met every Wednesday morning for breakfast. We were also all on the same league baseball team. We were all single except Grayson, who was engaged to Angie. Problem was, Angie was a real bitch, and none of us could understand why Grayson wanted to spend the rest of his life with the woman.

Looking around, I asked Grayson "Angie?"

He frowned. "Not her scene, man. She's out with her girl-friends."

"Spending your money, no doubt." This from Xander.

"Stuff it, Sullivan," Grayson retorted, but didn't deny it.

He looked miserable. I felt bad for the guy and made a note to have a serious discussion with him soon.

"I'm going to the bar. Anybody need anything?" Jaxson volunteered.

"Beer."

"Scotch on the rocks."

"Beer."

"I'll go with you," I volunteered.

We headed up to the bar set-up and waited in line to order. Suddenly, Jaxson jabbed me in the side, hard.

"What's your deal?"

He was staring at the tables on the other side of the room. "She's here."

I felt my heart skip a beat. "Don't fuck with me, Jax."

"Not fucking with you. Look."

I followed his gaze and went still. All the noise from the room stopped as if I was in a vacuum. He wasn't kidding. Paige was here.

She was thinner than when I last saw her, but she was still very curvy in all the best places. She had the type of body that a man wanted to feel cushioned beneath him as he sank deep inside. Her brown hair was longer and reflected red in the lights. I couldn't tell from this distance, but I would bet that every one of the smattering of freckles she had across her nose was still there. Many times, I had traced them with either my finger or my tongue. Her blue eyes sparkled, appearing almost the same color as her shirt. I thought she was gorgeous in high school. Now, she took my breath away. I wanted her with a ferocity like I had never experienced. *Mine,* my brain screamed territorially. I headed across the room to claim her.

Chapter Three: Paige

A love song started playing from the DJ booth. As the slow melody began, it was intriguing to note who swayed like we used to in high school and who had evolved to actual dancing. It was equally interesting to see who was dancing with whom. There was an even mix of former school couples and new pairings, along with a handful of those who had married their high school sweethearts.

Immersed in my musings, I didn't notice the figure standing behind me until I heard a warm, masculine voice ask, "Would do you me the honor?"

I looked to my right, letting my eyes travel up past the waistband of dark gray suit pants, a black leather belt and a sage green button-down shirt paired with a green, black, and gray patterned tie. After noting the clothes fit a toned, muscular frame, I continued my inspection to the chiseled jaw, short, slightly wavy dark brown hair and piercing gray eyes. My heart beat faster as I recognized him and grinned.

"Carter Sullivan."

From the second Carter and I first met, there was a connection. I know that sounds silly, considering we were only twelve and hardly capable of processing what chemistry was, but the pull was instantaneous. We were a couple on and off between 6th and 12th grade. He was my first boyfriend, my first kiss, my first love, my first everything. What I felt was so overwhelming it scared me, so I kept pushing him away. We would take a break, then he would call me, or just look at me, and we would be back together again.

I stood up and noticed that Carter was a little taller than I remembered. Back in high school he was a little short of six feet tall. Now, I estimated he was about six feet, two inches. Even in my heels, the top of my head was just about even with his nose.

He held out his left arm and I slipped my right hand in the space, holding onto his upper arm. As a boy, Carter was fit, but lean. As a man, he had definitely filled out. A sucker for biceps, I almost stumbled as I registered the size and strength of his. Strangely, though I hadn't seen him for years, I was overcome by an instant sense of security.

Guiding me to the center of the dance floor, he pulled me into his arms. I felt his warmth and smelled the familiar spicy sent of his cologne. His solid, muscular chest lightly brushed against my breasts, and my nipples hardened in response. It was a struggle to keep my hand on his shoulder when my fingers itched to delve into the thick hair at the back of his head where it curled slightly over his suit jacket. I was also having a difficult time fighting the urge to lick the side of his neck.

I had taken some dance lessons with a former boyfriend, and it seemed as if Carter had experience as well. We moved together across the floor, completely in sync. He felt so good it scared me. Having gone through what I'd recently experienced, I was extremely wary. *Relax*, I told myself. *It's just a dance. You'll probably never see him again after tonight. Enjoy catching up with an old friend. And take advantage of how good he feels, if just for a few moments.*

I looked up and met his gaze. "How have you been, Carter?"

"I can't complain, Paige. How long are you back in town for?"

Trying to concentrate as his thumb started stroking the back of my hand where they were joined, I sputtered, "I actually moved back to Connecticut about a month ago."

A slow smile came across his face. "Where to?"

"West of the river. Are you still in the area?"

He looked at me curiously when I didn't give him an exact town name. "I live in Glastonbury."

"Still working at your dad's construction company?"

"I took it over a couple of years ago. You?"

"I am an interior designer."

"Is that why you moved back? The job?"

"That, and I needed a change of scenery."

Carter gave me a look as though he wanted to ask further, but then decided against it.

"Married?"

"No."

"Boyfriend?"

"No."

"Girlfriend?"

I grinned. "No. What about you?"

"No boyfriend."

I smiled at that.

"Seriously, not in a relationship now."

I tilted my head up slightly to get a good look at him. "You look good, Carter. Though I have to admit that I kind of miss the glasses."

"Really?"

"A little bit."

He leaned down, and I could feel his breath on my cheek as he spoke into my ear.

"You look . . . devastating." He gently moved his hand up and down my spine.

Even with the silk barrier, I could feel his touch on my bare skin.

"And, amazingly, you feel even better."

A bit dumbfounded, I could feel myself blushing. I could also sense other parts of me warming. My already stiff nipples hardened further. Apparently, wrong choice wearing silk.

How was it possible that he still affected me so much? Regardless of age, the magnetism I felt with him was stronger than anything I had experienced with anyone else. Reacting to him this way as a teenager was scary enough. Now, it was downright terrifying.

In an effort to return the conversation to a safer topic, I asked "How is Xander?"

"Still causing trouble. He's around here somewhere."

"And Jarrod?" I inquired about his older brother by three years.

"He returned from active duty last year. He's doing well."

"I didn't know he was still in the Army."

"Special Forces."

I raised my eyebrows and then thought about it. "I can see that. He was always very focused."

"Both he and Xander are partners in the business. Xander's VP of Sales and Jarrod oversees electric and maintenance."

"The three of you together..." I grinned, shaking my head. "That must be interesting. And not quiet."

I recalled being with his family for gatherings and dinners. There was always so much love, laughter, and noise. It was quite a contrast from my home life.

Carter grinned. "Yeah, it certainly isn't dull but, overall, we work well together."

"Do you concentrate on residential or commercial?"

"Mainly commercial, but we do have a high-end residential unit."

"And how are your mom and dad?"

"They're good. Dad is still tinkering around on classic cars and my mom has her own local cable access cooking show."

I smiled and nodded. "I remember what a fantastic cook she is. Though I can't blame it entirely on her, I know my lack of discipline at all those fantastic meals contributed to me being chubby in high school."

His brow furrowed. "You weren't chubby. You were gorgeous. And you made me hard every time I looked at you."

I chuckled. "Carter, you were a teenage boy. You had that same reaction to any female with a pulse."

His gaze locked with mine and held as he said, "That may be true to an extent, but you affected me like no other."

Chapter Four: Paige

Not sure how to respond, I tore my gaze away and looked around the room.

"Is Jaxson here?" Jaxson was Carter's best friend in high school.

"Yeah. We came here together."

"He still lives in the area, right?"

Carter nodded. "Yep. He's a lieutenant with the state police."

I couldn't hide my wry expression. Jaxson had not been one for rules when we were growing up. "I know. Lys told me."

Carter grinned. "Astonishing, isn't it?"

"That's putting it mildly."

The slow song was coming to an end. Preparing to leave the dance floor, I started to loosen my hold on Carter's hand and shoulder when *Waiting for a Girl Like You* by Foreigner began playing. I silently cursed God. Why did this song — our song — have to be next on the playlist?

Carter tightened his hold and brought me in a bit closer. I rested my head on his shoulder and breathed in his edible sent.

"Every time I hear this song, I can't help but think of you."

I was glad he couldn't see my face. "Even now?"

"Even now."

Truth be told, every time I heard the song, I thought of him, too.

"The pool incident crosses my mind."

I chuckled. "Incident? You make it sound like international espionage."

He pulled back and looked at me. "I shouldn't have pressured you."

Searching his eyes, I stated, "It was over ten years ago, Carter. We were young. Hormones were raging. All was forgiven."

His eyes turned a deeper shade of gray. "I don't feel guilty anymore. I just can't help thinking about it whenever I hear this song. You were so responsive. I didn't know how to appreciate what a gift that was then."

His seductive words brought me back in time. One night when Carter and I had just started our senior year, we met up with a bunch of friends at the pool. The guys were engaging in their usual horseplay and we all played Marco Polo, which was a favorite for the boys, but we really had to watch their hands. About an hour before the pool closed, Carter and I got out and went upstairs to the bleachers. If you sat back far enough, it was very secluded. He and I were sitting up in the top far corner benches making out. At seventeen and dating on and off for four years, we had done our share of kissing. Up until that point, it took a huge amount of my self-control to not go all the way. Carter never pushed and always respected my boundaries. Though I was curious, hormonal, and completely in love, fear of the unknown and fear of what others would say were holding me back. Back in those days, engaging in anything much more than kissing automatically labeled you a slut.

Things were getting very hot and heavy and Carter's hands touched me in places he never had before. Shame at having gone too far flooded over me. I practically sprinted from the bleachers in humiliation. Carter called after me, but I didn't allow myself to turn around. I grabbed Peyton from the pool and made her drive me home, telling her a lie that I had gotten my period in explanation for our hasty exit.

That night, Carter phoned me for two hours straight trying to reach me. I was so mortified that I didn't answer until about midnight. He apologized profusely and asked me to forgive him. He played our song to me through the phone. I felt horrible that he was blaming himself. I was a million times more embarrassed than I was angry at him. So I broke up with him, but I was just delaying the inevitable. We got back together a few months later. Carter was extremely conscious of not going that far again.

Not knowing now how to respond to Carter's last comment, I didn't answer him. I was having a very difficult time trying to control my body's reaction to being in his arms. I kept telling myself that it was nostalgia, but I knew I that wasn't the case.

CHAPTER FIVE: PAIGE

Over Carter's shoulder, I heard a deep voice question "May I cut in?"

I pulled back from Carter's hold, looked over, and smiled broadly. "Jaxson."

Carter barely succeeded in keeping a scowl off his face as he looked at his best friend. Jaxson smiled wider. Carter was clearly wrestling with himself to not be rude, and Jax was enjoying torturing him. After a moment, he reluctantly released me with a sincere "Thank you" and walked off the dance floor.

Jaxson hugged me and then gathered me into his arms with a flourish.

I laughed out loud at his antics. "How have you been, Jax?"

"Fantastic. Busy."

"I can't believe you are a cop."

He raised an eyebrow. "Carter told you."

"Actually, Alyssa did. Last I knew, you were headed down the path of being on the other side of the law."

He laughed. "I was. Stole one stop sign too many. The chief of police himself hauled me into the station. Let me sit in lock-up for eighteen hours. He called my dad and then offered me a proposition. Come every day and do work around the station or get arrested and have a permanent record. Luckily, I was smart enough to accept his offer. At first, I grumbled every second of working there, but eventually, I wised up and saw the character of the officers and staff. After three months, I enrolled in the academy. The rest, as they say, is history."

I smiled. "I'm so proud of you, Jax. Though I doubt you are completely reformed."

His brown eyes twinkled. "Nah. I'm an angel now."

I threw my head back and laughed out loud. "Right."

I looked him up and down. His tousled brown hair was still a little wild, as though he perpetually ran his fingers through it. He had always been tall. At about six-four, he towered over me. He used to be a beanpole, but clearly being on the force had bulked him up considerably. He was a mass of muscle. He had turned into a gorgeous man. How come when he held me in his arms, I didn't feel anything other than extreme fondness?

"Carter was pissed, huh?"

"What do you mean?"

"That I cut in."

"You and I are old friends. Why would he be?"

Jaxson looked over my shoulder and gestured with his chin. "If looks could kill, I would be six feet under right now."

I glanced to the spot where Jaxson was gazing. Carter was staring at us with stormy gray eyes. I felt a shiver go down my spine. The possessive look he had should have scared me. Instead, I felt turned on.

"Carter and I have not seen each other in years. So, we used to date? There's no reason for him to be upset with you for dancing with me for goodness sake."

He looked down at me, searching my face. "You really don't have any idea, do you?"

My brow crinkled as I met his gaze. "What are you talking about?"

"Let's just say that, at the last reunion, Carter was wondering if you were going to attend. Now that you're here . . ."

"He was specifically looking for me? After all these years?" I was flummoxed.

"How come you never contacted him after you went to

college?"

The question surprised me, and I frowned. I didn't know if Carter had shared what happened the night before I left for school, so I gave Jax part of the story. "When I left for Chicago, he said he didn't think a long-distance relationship would work. I didn't agree, but he was adamant. When I came back at Thanksgiving and went to the school football game, I saw him with another girl. I was surprised that he had moved on, but what could I do?"

"Another girl? At the football game?"

"Yes, a blonde. He had his arm around her and was smiling down at her."

I could still see them as they huddled together in the cold. I had thought about Carter every day and missed him with a physical ache. I was planning on insisting that I wanted to be with him, even if it was long distance. Despite the awful way things ended, I missed him. It decimated me to learn that he had moved on so quickly.

I went back to college heartbroken. After that, I worked in Chicago during all my summer and winter breaks. I came back for the Christmas holidays, but I never heard from Carter. Nor did I try to contact him. Over the years, I came to the realization that because I felt so much for him, I had assumed he felt that same. I didn't hold any ill will towards Carter. How do you fault a teenage boy for not wanting to get tied down? Or for not being the most delicate in his choice of words? The one niggling question that stayed with me was how I could have misinterpreted his feelings for me, believing they were so much stronger than they actually were.

Jaxson looked perplexed, then thoughtful. "A blonde?"

I rolled my eyes. "Yes, Jaxson, a blonde. It was so long ago. Do we really need to rehash it?"

"It's just—"

"Seriously, let it go okay?"

The song ended. I took a step back and saw Alyssa waving me over. I gave Jaxson a hug and thanked him before heading over to where Alyssa was sitting at our table with Caitlin and Peyton. Alyssa frowned as I approached.

Chapter Six: Carter

I'm going to kill him, I thought. Paige was finally in my arms again, and Jaxson cut in. What the hell? I watched the two of them talk and laugh and was again struck by both her beauty and my desire. She was back. After wanting her in my life again for so long, I couldn't wrap my brain around it. Knowing I could use Jaxson's skills to get her phone number but not wanting to wait, I spotted Caitlin at the buffet.

"Caitlin Jensen."

She turned around, and a smile broke out over her face. She launched herself at me. "Carter! How come you get more handsome every time I see you?"

I hugged her back. "Good genes." I released her and took in her blonde hair, sparkling hazel eyes, and petite curvy figure. "How come you look so damn cute every time I see you?"

She tossed her head back and laughed. "Lots of ice cream."

I grinned. Caitlin had always been feisty and outspoken. It was nice to see she hadn't changed.

"I saw you and Paige dancing."

"Yeah. It's good to see her."

She smirked. "Uh-huh, I bet. I had to fan myself just looking at the two of you."

Crap. Was it that obvious? "Caitlin . . ."

"Carter . . ."

"We were just catching up. I haven't seen her in years." Ten years and twenty-seven days, to be exact. "She told me she recently moved back."

"She told you that?"

Strange, Caitlin acted surprised that Paige had let me know she'd returned to the area.

"I didn't get a chance to ask for her contact info. Do you think you could give me her number?"

She bit her lip. "I don't know, Carter. I really shouldn't."

"It's me, Cait. You don't think she'd be okay with me reaching out to her?"

I watched Caitlin struggle with my request. That, too, struck me as odd. Granted, we hadn't kept in touch over the past several years, but it wasn't like I was a stranger. She knew me. What was there to consider? Caitlin looked at me, searching my face, and then nodded, almost as if she was verifying something.

Muttering something like "She's going to kill me, but I know I'm right," Caitlin held her hand out for my phone and programmed Paige's number into my contacts. She handed it back to me and held onto my hand for a moment, which caused me to look at her quizzically.

"Don't hurt her, Carter. Please. She's been through . . ." She broke off her words, took a deep breath and finished with "Just treat her the way she deserves."

I tried to decipher what she wasn't saying. I didn't really understand, but I heard the caring and the worry in her voice. "I'll treat her like the treasure she is, Caitlin. I promise." I had never seen Caitlin so serious nor so protective, but I knew how good of a friend she was to Paige.

"I'm going to hold you to that, Carter." With that, she walked away into the crowd.

Still feeling unsettled by the conversation, I walked outside onto the deck. Only a handful of people were milling about, as the night, combined with the ocean air, had turned cold. What had Caitlin been alluding to? It sounded more than just the usual warning a good friend would give to a prospective suitor. What was I missing? Again, I cursed myself for letting

Paige go. I wondered if she had forgiven me for not being strong enough to say no that night and the hurtful way I had reacted. Though it was a long time ago, I wouldn't blame her for still carrying around some bitterness.

After graduating, Paige and I spent all summer together. I was so in love with her. I also wanted her so badly it hurt. My dad had taught all of us boys to be respectful of a woman's wishes and let them take the lead. He treated my mom like gold and expected us to do the same in our relationships. But I was eighteen. It was a day-to-day internal battle for me to not make Paige mine in every sense of the word.

There was another battle going on inside me as well. I knew Paige was headed off to college. She had big dreams, and I didn't want to hold her back. Selfishly, I didn't want to say goodbye. I wanted to stay in her life, but I knew I had to let her go. I loved her too much to be the reason she didn't achieve her goals.

Three weeks before she was due to leave, we had a huge blowout at the park. I lied and told her that I didn't think long-distance relationships worked. I gave her all kinds of lame reasons. I threw every excuse I could at her to avoid telling her the truth—I loved her enough to let her go.

She fought me. She cried and told me that she loved me. Needed me. It killed me to see the tears streaming down her face and to act like hurting her wasn't ripping me apart, but I knew I was right. Seeing that she couldn't change my mind, broken, she finally left.

I walked home in a daze. As soon as I shut the front door behind me, my mom appeared in the kitchen doorway. She took one look at my face and held her arms open. I hugged her and did something I hadn't done since I was a little kid. I sobbed until I had no tears left. My mom never asked for an explanation. She just held me, stroked my hair, and just kept saying "I know, honey, I know." To this day, I'm convinced she really did know why I was so upset.

Chapter Seven: Carter

The night before Paige was leaving for Chicago, there was a thunderstorm brewing. Wanting to be alone, I was sitting up in the massive treehouse my dad, brothers, and I had built in the big maple tree in our backyard. I hadn't heard from her since our argument and had been walking around like a zombie. Xander, never one to pass up an opportunity to give me shit, didn't throw any insults my way, as if sensing the severity of my mood.

I had started to dial Paige's number hundreds of times, but never completed the calls. It was ripping me apart to not break down and beg her to come back to me. Doing what I thought was the right thing was killing me.

As I stood lost in thought, I heard footsteps on the ladder. To my utter shock, Paige appeared in the doorway. I was so grateful to see her, I took a couple of steps forward before I stopped myself.

"What are you doing here?" I asked, hoping she couldn't detect the emotion in my voice. I clenched my hands into fists in an attempt to keep me from pulling her into my arms.

Tilting her chin up and looking me directly in the eye, she stated "I heard everything you said to me, Carter, about why we shouldn't stay together. You know I don't agree with you."

Exasperated, and desperately afraid I would cave and tell her I changed my mind, I sharply said "Paige, we're not going to have this argument again. I'm right, and you know it."

Her blue eyes flashed fire. "You're not right, Carter, but I am not here to fight with you."

I was taken aback. "Then why are you here?" And what can I do to make you leave so I don't have to see you and be reminded of how much I love you and how much I want you?

For the first time, I noticed that she was wearing what looked like a man's raincoat. Her fingers went to the top button and started unbuttoning each one slowly, but with purpose, never taking her eyes off mine. When she was done, she parted the coat and let it drop to the floor. She stood before me in a white lace bra and matching bikini panties. I'd been hard since the second she climbed up the ladder. Now, I was downright steel.

My tongue caught in my mouth. "Paige?" I croaked. Did she know what she was doing to me?

With a determined glint in her eyes and a knowing smile on her face, she crossed the room until she stood inches in front of me. I stopped breathing. "Make love to me, Carter. I have always wanted you to be my first."

What could I say to that? My brain had stopped working the second I saw her. I ran my hands through my hair. "Fuck, Paige!" I responded in frustration.

She smiled. "Exactly." Then she kissed me with such ardor that we fell back against the wall of the treehouse. I tried to fight it, but I was eighteen. And male. And had wanted Paige with a feral hunger for as long as I could remember. I had always wanted to be her first. Hell, I wanted to be her only.

Though she was a virgin, I was not. I'm not particularly proud of it, but during a few of the times that Paige and I broke up in high school, I had sex with other girls. Not a harem or anything, but there were a couple of different girls and maybe a handful of times. The girls were willing, and I was horny. I felt like I was cheating on Paige, even though we weren't technically a couple when it happened. She was aware of my past, but I knew it hurt her, so I didn't talk about it. I never wanted her to feel like I had gone elsewhere because she wouldn't put out. I had gone elsewhere because I was miserable without Paige and I was a teenage boy with raging hormones.

The thunder crashed as Paige's hands moved from my hair to the bottom of my T-shirt. I helped her by grabbing the hem and pulling it over my head. She had seen me shirtless plenty of times, but this was different, and we both knew it. I had planned to sleep out in the tree house, so I had an air mattress, a pillow, and some blankets already set up. I gently lowered her onto the makeshift bed. There was nothing gentle, however, when I crushed my mouth back to hers. I mimicked what I wanted to do to her body using my tongue. I swallowed her moans and heard myself responding in kind.

Her bra had a front clasp and I flicked it open. I looked at her full breasts with their dark rosy nipples. I scraped my short nails over one, then the other. Her body lifted in response and she whimpered. I loved the way she responded to my touch. I bent my head and swiped my tongue across the beads, then sucked. She squirmed, frantic for more. Her hands went to the zipper of my jeans, pulled it down and reached inside to stroke me. Touching myself was nothing like her touch, and I knew if she continued, I would be done before we really started.

I grabbed her hand and pulled it away.

She looked up at me in confusion. "Don't you want me to touch you, Carter?"

I groaned. "I want it too much, baby. It feels so good, but I can't control myself when you do that."

I pulled down my jeans and underwear. She looked at me with a mixture of desire and a little bit of fear. I stilled at her expression. With superhuman effort, I said "We can stop anytime, Paige."

She bit her lip and hesitantly asked, "Don't you want me,

Carter?"

"Baby, I want you so bad, but I want you to be sure."

She smiled. "I showed up here in underwear and a trench coat. I've known what I wanted for weeks. I want you, Carter."

Her words fanned an already blazing fire. I kissed her again and again, touching her hair, her neck, her breasts, her belly. Her hands stroked me everywhere she could reach. I didn't know how long I was going to last, but I willed myself to concentrate and make it good for her. I reached down and felt between her legs. Her panties were soaked.

"Damn, baby, you are so wet for me."

Arching into my hand, she begged "Please, Carter."

The desperation in her voice was so raw. I ripped her underwear off in one swift movement. Knowing she needed to be as ready as possible to take me inside her, I stroked her, inserting first one finger and then two into her channel.

"You are so fucking tight."

Her head thrashed side to side.

I was about to lose control, and I knew it. I continued kissing her and fingering her. She moaned, "Carter, I can't take it."

"Come for me, baby."

I felt her breath catch, and then she spasmed around my fingers, crying out my name. I quickly rolled on the condom I'd grabbed from my wallet and positioned myself above her. I gazed down at her face, flushed with her orgasm.

"Paige, look at me."

She opened her eyes, the blue darkened to almost the color of midnight with desire.

"I am going to go slow. I don't want to hurt you."

I eased the head of my cock into her heat. The feeling was so unreal, I almost came right then. I felt her body stretch to accommodate my size. I clenched my teeth to stop myself from plunging in and taking her with the ferocity I was feeling. She dug her fingers into my ass. Then, she did something completely unexpected. She pulled me completely into her with one huge tug, and I felt the last barrier break away. Her body jerked in response to the moment of pain. Sweat beaded on my forehead and I held myself still.

"Are you okay?"

She gazed directly at my face in wonder and beamed. "I am more than okay." And then she started to move. The last of my control snapped and I pounded into her over and over. I could feel how close she was and wanted to wait but couldn't. I reached my release with her name on my lips, vaguely noticing as she spasmed around me once again.

I rolled over and laid next to her. Both of our breathing was ragged, and we were covered in sweat. My previous sexual encounters didn't come close to what I had just experienced with Paige. And now I had to let her go. What was I thinking? Clearly, I wasn't thinking. Shit! I felt so selfish for taking her virginity knowing that she was leaving in the morning for a life that most likely would not include me.

"We shouldn't have done that." I said quietly.

She sat up and looked at me incredulously. "Are you kidding me?"

"No, I'm not. I'm sorry, Paige, but you're leaving tomorrow. And we may never see each other again. I was selfish to take that from you."

I had seen Paige mad before, but the angry look that came over her face floored me. The fury was quickly joined by hurt. She stood up and put on her coat, not bothering with her undergarments. She started down the ladder. "You're wrong about us. You love me. I love you. Your sense of *doing the right thing* is so misplaced, but I know you well enough to know that you aren't going to change your mind. You did take something from me tonight, but it wasn't my virginity. I *gave* myself to you because I wanted to. No matter how much of a jerk you're being, I don't regret it. Goodbye, Carter."

I sat up, my chest tight from both her pain and mine. I wanted to say so much, but I felt frozen, unable to speak. I watched her run across the back yard with the thunderstorm raging around her. When daylight broke, I was still staring out the window of the treehouse, and it was still pouring rain.

CHAPTER EIGHT: PAIGE

Eyes narrowed, Alyssa asked "Were you dancing with Jaxson Mancini?"

"Yes. And that is a problem because . . ."

"It's Jaxson."

"Ah."

Alyssa and Jaxson had always had a contentious relationship. She was a goody two-shoes growing up. His wild ways bugged the heck out of her. He was forever telling her to loosen up and she was perpetually annoyed that he didn't straighten out.

"Cut him a break, Lys. He's a good guy. You're the one who told me he's a cop now."

Glancing in his direction, she nodded. "That doesn't make him a good guy."

"Just because he continues to push your buttons whenever you see him doesn't make him a bad guy either."

Caitlin chimed in. "Oh, there's more to it than just their run-ins at the courthouse. Remember that self-defense class she signed up for?"

"Yeah . . ."

"Guess who was her instructor when she walked in the first day of class?

Unsuccessfully stifling a snort of laughter, I turned to Alyssa. "And how did that go?"

"She took one look at him and walked out of the class," Caitlin responded.

My gaze swung back to Alyssa. "Lys!"

She looked at me a bit sheepishly. "I did sign up for a different class that same day. I've been going for three weeks now."

"You honestly couldn't have stayed in that class? He's a friend."

"He's not a friend. He's a menace."

"A hot menace." This from Peyton.

"Oh, yuck," responded Alyssa.

"That statement is not believable if you are turning five shades of red, Lys." I smiled.

Caitlin nodded in agreement. "He is a fine-looking man, Lys. That's really not up for debate."

Alyssa, still blushing, mumbled unconvincingly, "To each their own."

"Speaking of fine-looking men, we saw you dancing with Carter, Paige."

"Yes, I did."

"And . . ." Caitlin implored.

"And, what? He asked me to dance and I said yes. Just two old friends catching up."

Alyssa scoffed. "Two old friends, huh? I got a sunburn from the heat between the two of you. And I thought your chemistry was explosive in high school!"

Now it was my turn to blush. "Knock it off. You're exaggerating. Yes, he's attractive—"

"Attractive? That's an understatement. And the two of you are like magnets, drawn to each other," Caitlin interrupted, smirking.

"You guys are nuts. It was a high school romance. It's our reunion. We danced. After tonight, I will most likely never see him again. End of story." Maybe if I kept saying things like that, I would convince myself too.

"Yeah, right" Alyssa scoffed.

Maybe not. Trying to change the subject, I turned to

Peyton.

"What happened with Travis?"

She grinned. "He asked me out to dinner on Saturday."

I winked at her. "Told you so."

"Seems everyone's hooking up with old flames." Caitlin sighed. "Of course, my old boyfriend is now happily married with two kids. Just my luck."

"Then you'll just have to look at who else is here tonight," responded Alyssa. "Anyone catch your eye?"

"Not really. I was hoping there would be."

"The right one is out there for you, Cait. I know it." I chimed in.

"I'd settle for *Mr. Right Now* at this point. I am seriously missing having a hot guy in my bed. A battery operated significant other only goes so far."

We all laughed at that.

"I wish Sarah was here," Alyssa sighed.

"Me too." Caitlin and I agreed at the same time.

Sarah was working for a high-end jewelry store in New York City as a Director of Communications. Currently, she was on an overseas trip to their London office. The five of us had known each other since middle school. We were all located in the northeast—me, Alyssa, Caitlin, and Peyton in Connecticut and Sarah in New York. When Sarah returned, we were hoping to get together monthly for lunch, and once a year we took a girl's vacation.

The rest of the night was spent dancing and catching up with old friends. I knew I was driving home, so I had limited myself to two glasses of wine earlier in the evening. A little before ten, the four of us went to the ladies' room and then the coat check. As I slipped on my coat, someone grabbed my arm. Instinctively, I recoiled and wrestled my arm away. Stepping back, I realized it was Jaxson, who was standing talking to Carter.

"Are you all right?" Jaxson asked, concerned.

Trying to brush off my overreaction, I replied "I'm fine. You just startled me."

Both Carter and Jaxson looked at me like they didn't quite believe me. Perceptive. My overreaction *was* caused by something deeper.

To cover my embarrassment and stop any questions, I hugged Jaxson. "It was great to see you."

I looked at Carter. His eyes were troubled. Knowing I couldn't bring myself to hug him even though I desperately wanted to do more than that, I nodded in his direction and said, "Thanks for the dance." Not giving either of them a chance to respond, I hurried out the door to catch up with my friends.

CHAPTER NINE: CARTER

I turned to Jaxson. "What was that about?"

"I don't know, man, but from Paige's reaction, she is certainly wary of being touched. My gut says she's had some trouble in her past."

My stomach tightened at the thought of anyone putting their hands on her. "Fuck."

"I don't know to what extent, but I think something happened to her. I've seen enough of it to recognize the signs."

Irrationally, I blamed myself for not being there for her. Again, I cursed my younger self for letting her walk out of my life. "I'll be back," I told Jaxson, heading towards the parking lot.

"I thought so," Jax said to my retreating back.

I went through the glass doors and out into the cool night air. I looked around at the rows of cars, trying to spot Paige. I finally heard her over to my left, calling out her goodbyes. As she hurried to her car, she looked around as if she was watching for something or someone. I also noticed she clutched her keys in her right hand almost like a weapon. I thought about what Jaxson said. Maybe she was mugged? That could explain her behavior. I wanted to believe that was all it was. Not that a mugging was anything to be taken lightly, but compared to the other scenarios I was considering, a mugging was preferable.

She reached her SUV hybrid and used a fingerprint entry to unlock the driver's side door. Trying not to startle her, I called out "Paige!"

She whipped around and I could see the worried look on her face. When she realized it was me, her expression changed from fear to perplexed. I reached her in a few strides and stood a few feet away.

"What do you want, Carter?"

A loaded question. Her, I wanted her. Lust raged, but luckily concern interceded as I looked into her eyes. I could see her trembling.

"Are you okay?"

She looked away from me and then down at the ground.

"I'm fine."

"You said that before, Paige. I don't think I believe you. Look at you. You're shaking."

"I'm fine, Carter," she stressed, now looking over my shoulder.

"Paige," I cajoled.

She looked at me defiantly, though I could still see the fear in her beautiful blue eyes.

"I'm *fine*, Carter."

Hoping not to scare her further, I pulled her into my arms. She resisted for a few seconds, but then I could sense her body melting into me. It was heaven and hell at the same time. She felt incredible, and I had to hold back from turning her around and taking her from behind against the car. I retreated enough that she could see my face, trying to implore her to tell me the truth. I saw the wall come up, masking her true emotions.

"You were that jealous that I gave Jaxson a hug, so you followed me out here for one?" she teasingly asked.

I knew she was covering up what she was really feeling by joking. Not wanting to push her to talk about what was really going on, I tried a different approach to take her mind off things.

"Yes, I was jealous when you hugged Jax," I confirmed. "I

don't like to see any other man touch you."

She looked at me incredulously. "Carter, it's been over a decade. You can't possibly feel that way."

"I don't care how damn long it's been. I can. And I do."

My declaration brought heat into her eyes. I welcomed the sight. "Let's see if I can make you tremble for the right reasons."

Before she had a chance to answer, I closed the distance between us and captured her mouth with mine. I tried to be gentle as my lips touched hers. For just a moment, she stiffened, but then she wrapped her arms around my neck and clenched her fingers in my hair. I nibbled on the corners of her mouth and swiped the crease with my tongue. When she sighed a moan, I took the opportunity to slide inside. She tasted of wine and Paige. Paige alone was intoxicating.

When she stroked my tongue with hers, I couldn't prevent the growl that came from deep within me. The two of us always had incredible electricity. As adults, it was downright explosive. Before I could stop myself, I devoured her as if I couldn't get enough. Not wanting to frighten her with my intensity, I forced myself to end the kiss.

I looked at her flushed face and her rosy, full lips and needed so much more. For me, it was exactly where I was meant to be. I wanted to believe she felt the same. Now that we'd found each other again, there was no way in hell she was going to be out of my life.

I leaned down, touched her hair, and whispered in her ear, "I like the red. It suits you."

I opened her car door, helped her inside, then reached over and buckled her seatbelt and kissed her cheek. I watched her drive off, still worried, but also hopeful.

CHAPTER TEN: PAIGE

As I drove home, I was in a haze from Carter's mind-blowing kiss. I was having a difficult time wrapping my brain around everything. Why did I let him kiss me? Why did my body respond so intensely to him? Granted, I was aware that the chemistry between us had never been replicated in any other relationship I had since the two of us were together years ago. And, strange as it may sound, though Carter made me burn hot, he also made me feel safer than I had felt in a long time. I both missed and craved that feeling.

Part of me was scared to death of the way I had reacted to Carter. Another part of me was encouraged that I had reacted to him at all, considering I hadn't felt stirrings of any kind for the past year. I hadn't been sure I would ever be capable of wanting again. Though it was disconcerting that Derrick was roaming around free somewhere and not locked up like he should be, I was slowly learning to trust again, knowing that I couldn't let one person change the way I viewed the rest of the world. Yet even though I had taken self-defense classes and carried pepper spray, it still upset me anytime someone touched me when I wasn't expecting it. Hence my reaction when Jax grabbed my arm.

I also knew that my physical scars continued to affect me emotionally. I had never been a vain person, but seeing daily the marks that stood out on my otherwise smooth skin was a constant reminder of the trauma. No one was perfect, but the scars — and where they were located — made me feel less attractive and also angry that I hadn't been able to prevent them.

By the time I arrived home at my townhouse and punched in the security code to disable the alarm system, I was exhausted. After resetting the alarm for the night, I walked upstairs to my bedroom and removed my clothes on the way to the bathroom. I stood in front of the mirror and took a good look at my reflection. Honestly assessing my naked form, my gaze traveled up my toned calves and slightly plump thighs, my relatively flat belly, my very full breasts, and my slim arms that showed some muscle definition. Then I focused on the three raised puckered four-inch slashes that extended from my strip of pubic hair to my left hip and the four similar looking marks radiating out from my right nipple towards the right side of my breast. Their bright pink color had faded to a much lighter tone, but still they stood out garishly against my fair complexion. Logically, I knew I could've fared much worse and was lucky to have survived the assault. Physically, though, it still made my sick to look at them.

Shaking off the negative thoughts, I washed my face and brushed my teeth. After smoothing on both face cream and body lotion, I grabbed a tank top and silk pajama bottoms from my dresser drawer and crawled into my queen size bed. I turned the TV to ESPN to check out the world of football and turned off the lights. Well, not every light. I slept with one small corner lamp on. I wasn't comfortable surrounded by pitch black. Five minutes later, my phone buzzed with a text message. Who would be contacting me at midnight?

I saw it was from Caitlin. *You're going to be mad.*

That was never a good leading sentence, but I was used to surprises from Caitlin. She was forever signing all of us up for crazy adventures and speaking before thinking.

What did you volunteer me for now? I typed.

Well, I did tell Grayson that you would help at his clinic during the animal adoption event two weeks from now, but that's not what you're going to be mad about.

Yeah, I wouldn't be mad at that. You how much I love animals. What did you do? Silence. *Caitlin???*

I gave Carter your phone number.

My body immediately flooded with panic and anger. *You did what?!*

I gave Carter your phone number.

I took a deep breath and tried to avoid texting something I would regret. *Why would you do that, Cait? You know not to give anybody my number. Ever.*

I know, Paige. But its Carter, for gosh sake.

I don't care who it is. You promised.

After what happened with Derrick, I obtained an unlisted cell phone number and I made my best friends vow to never reveal it to anyone unless it was a life or death situation. Up until now, everyone had kept their word. Why would Caitlin break it now?

I know that I promised. I would never have broken your trust if I didn't think it was worth it.

That stumped me. *Worth it how?*

I saw Carter look for you at the last reunion. And I saw the two of you together tonight, Paige.

You are reading far too much into this. It was just a dance. We have history, that's all.

From the way you two looked at each other and the way he looked at you when you weren't aware, you don't just have history. You have a future. I love you, Paige. What you went through with that monster makes me so mad. You deserve to be cherished and treated with respect. Carter will do that. I know it.

A bit stunned at the certainty of her words, I answered back. *I love you too, Cait. I don't know how you can really believe what you just said. I think you may have had too much wine, but you have always been a romantic at heart. I forgive you, but please don't do it again. Ever.*

I won't. I have no need to. Giving your number to Carter was the right thing to do. You just don't want to admit it. But you'll thank me when you hire me as your wedding planner.

I laughed out loud. *Good night, Caitlin.*

Good night, Paige.

Assuring myself that Carter would most likely not contact me, I put my phone under my pillow and turned on the sleep timer for the TV. As I was drifting off, I felt the buzz of an incoming call. I reached for my phone, proclaiming aloud, "I swear, Caitlin. If you are calling to tell me you have booked my wedding venue, I am going to kill you." Looking down at the caller id, I saw an unfamiliar number on my screen. I considered not answering, but then hit the Accept button.

"Hello?" Even to my own ears, my voice sounded breathy. Just sleepy, I assured myself.

"Paige? It's Carter." His deep tone made my toes curl.

"Carter?"

"I know it's late, but I wanted to make sure you got home okay."

Feeling warm all over from both his concern and his sexy voice, I responded with "Yes. I got home a little while ago. I was just about to doze off."

There was a moment of silence. "I wish I could have been there to tuck you in."

Need slammed through me. I started imagining him beside me, and I definitely wasn't thinking about sleeping. "Carter, I'm not five. I am perfectly capable of settling into bed on my own."

He chuckled softly. "I am extremely aware you're not a child, angel."

A tingle went down my spine — it was the endearment he used to call me.

"And the thoughts I am having are not parental in the least. Would you like me to elaborate?"

Yes, please. "Not necessary, Carter, but thanks for offering."

He laughed again. I wondered if he could tell that I was

desperate to hear him tell me exactly what he was thinking? In detail. And then perhaps show me?

"How's ESPN tonight?"

I almost fell off the bed. "You remembered?"

"I remember everything about you, Paige."

His words were like a caress. I needed to end this conversation before I was in too deep.

"Then you must recall that I get annoyed at anyone disturbing me while I am watching news about the Cowboys. And Steve Levy just started talking about them. So, goodnight Carter."

"I used to know just how to divert your attention, but that will have to wait for another day. Sleep well, angel."

I ended the call and pulled the covers around my shoulders knowing two things. One, I had no idea what the announcer was saying. And two, my dreams were going to be anything but sweet. Hot and X-rated most likely, but definitely not sweet.

CHAPTER ELEVEN: PAIGE

"I can't believe I am up at this ungodly hour," Alyssa grumbled from the elliptical machine next to me.

"You say that every time we're at the gym together, and yet you always meet us to work out," Peyton commented while smirking.

It was the Wednesday morning following the reunion. Every Tuesday, Wednesday, and Thursday morning Caitlin, Peyton, Alyssa, and I met at the gym at 6 a.m. to work out for an hour. Meeting as a group provided accountability and made the exercise fun. Well, the company was fun. The exercise was . . . exercise.

"If I didn't show up, you guys would probably drive to my place and physically drag me here."

"You're probably right," Caitlin panted. "And we wouldn't let you change into your workout clothes first."

Alyssa looked incredulous. "But I sleep naked."

Caitlin smirked, "Exactly."

Peyton and I laughed out loud.

Alyssa narrowed her eyes at Caitlin. "You're evil."

Looking affronted, Caitlin replied "Hey, if I make myself come here with you three days a week to put myself through torture just to try to maintain my less-than-skinny figure, you can haul your ridiculously perfect ass to suffer in solidarity."

Peyton looked in the mirror behind us. "She does have a perfect ass, doesn't she?"

I nodded. "Pretty much, yeah."

Alyssa rolled her eyes. "Admittedly, my ass is pretty nice,

but I would love to have your boobs, Paige, your long legs, Peyton, and your waist, Caitlin."

"Put us all together and we'd be the ultimate woman." This from Caitlin.

Peyton shook her head. "There is no perfect woman. We always want to change something about ourselves. It's the nature of the female mind. Just be thankful we're here and healthy."

The three of them looked at me. I knew they were thinking of how far I'd come in recovering. After the attack, all of them, plus Sarah, flew out to Chicago. They cried at the severity of my injuries and threatened to personally kill Derrick for what he had done. I don't know how they arranged it, but no one left my side for two weeks while I healed enough to take care of myself. They took shifts changing my bandages, driving me to doctor's appointments, cooking, cleaning, and holding me when I cried. Being an only child with parents who had never been nurturing, my friends' support during those horrific first few weeks meant the world to me.

After showering and changing into a red peplum top, a tan pencil skirt, a black blazer and black heels, I drove to the office. Every day when I walked through the front doors of Perlman Designs, I felt blessed. Parker Perlman, VP of Design, and I had been close friends in college. Parker joined the multi-million-dollar company, owned by his Uncle Mike, as an architect straight out of college. He had been begging me to come on board for the past five years. Four months ago, wanting to put some distance between me and Chicago, I accepted their offer. After getting everything squared away and finishing up some projects at my previous job, I began working at Perlman six weeks ago. I really liked the people and I loved what I was doing.

"Good morning, Paige!" Gail, the fifty-something executive assistant to the Design department called out as I walked to my office.

"Hi, Gail!"

"You have a nine o'clock initial briefing with Parker in the Flutie Conference Room." Mike was an avid Patriot's fan. Various rooms around the office were named after former players. Being a Dallas Cowboys fan, I was forever teasing Mike about belonging to the dark side.

"Who's the client?"

"Parker didn't tell me. Just that it was a bigwig. Coffee and bagels are already set up."

"Thanks, Gail."

I turned on the lights in my office, answered a few e-mails, grabbed a notepad and headed for the meeting. I was the first one to arrive, so I poured myself a cup of coffee and grabbed a wheat bagel. I was just about to take a bite when Parker rounded the corner followed by a handsome, tall, well-built man with sandy hair and green eyes.

Parker led the guest over to me. "Paige, I want you to meet —"

"Hunter Carlson," I finished Parker's sentence and stood up and walked up to Hunter. Enveloping me into a huge bear hug, Hunter smiled. "Paige Turner. You are as gorgeous as I remember."

"And you are just as sweet as ever." I smiled. We all took seats around the table.

Parker looked between the two of us. "I take it you have met before?"

"Hunter and I went to high school together. We were part of a group of kids who often hung out." Turning to Hunter, I asked "Were you at the reunion on Saturday? I didn't see you there."

"Yes, but I didn't stay long. I'm sorry I missed you. I didn't know you were back in the area."

"I moved back a month and a half ago after I accepted the

job at Perlman."

"Funny, when I was researching the firm, I didn't see your name listed."

I shot a worried glance at Parker. The Perlman website included biographies of all the staff. One of the things I insisted upon hire was that mine not be included. I didn't want to risk being located.

Parker covered for me, "Since Paige is new, her information hasn't been uploaded yet."

A crease formed between Hunter's eyebrows. "Hmmm."

Wanting to change the subject, I asked "What did you come to see us about today, Hunter?"

"Carlson Enterprises just bought one of the historic buildings overlooking the Connecticut River. We want to gut the place and make it suitable for our video and photography division."

Carlson Enterprises was the largest supplier in the world of all things communication and media. The company had been in business for over a hundred years and was worth billions of dollars. I knew that Hunter himself was a millionaire several times over. Though his family was extremely rich, Hunter never flaunted his wealth. From what I knew, he routinely volunteered both his time and money for a variety of charitable causes. As a kid, he'd been quiet and thoughtful. He was also the first one to offer you the shirt off his back or a shoulder to lean on.

He went on, "Being that it is on the historic registry, there are a number of guidelines we need to adhere to when planning and constructing the site. I'm looking for someone to not only come up with the design, but to oversee the construction and guide us through the whole process."

Parker nodded. "We've handled a number of historic properties. Why don't you give us the parameters of what you are looking for in terms of style and function? We'll put a proposal together."

For the next two hours, we went over details. Parker and I agreed to have our bid to Hunter on Wednesday of the following week. As Hunter stood up to leave, I offered to walk him out. Ever the gentleman, he offered me his arm. Though he was built and had shoulders the width of a football field, I didn't feel any of the shockwaves I had experienced when I had walked the same exact way with Carter onto the dance floor.

"Congratulations on your engagement. I saw the announcement in *Town and Country*."

His expression darkened slightly. "Thanks."

His lackluster response confused me. "You don't sound very excited about finding the love of your life, Hunter."

He shrugged. "It's complicated."

I turned to face him as we reached the lobby. "Love sometimes is, but you should still be looking forward to spending the rest of your life with the person you're going to marry."

He sighed but remained silent.

"Look, Hunter. I know I haven't seen you in a while, but I don't believe you have changed that much. You were always fiercely loyal, and when you cared about something, you threw yourself in with so much passion. Correct me if I'm wrong, but I am not sensing that now. Instead of looking exhilarated, you look defeated. And I have never known you to settle."

He searched my face. "How do you know if you're settling?"

"If you're even asking yourself that, then you know."

With an almost imperceptible nod, he leaned down and gave me a quick kiss on the cheek. "I'm glad you're back, Paige. I'll see you soon."

I watched my old friend walk away, concerned over the torment he was going through. I hoped he would come to a decision he could live with. He deserved someone who would unleash his passion.

CHAPTER TWELVE: CARTER

Thursday night. Five days since I had last seen and spoken to Paige. Having willpower sucked. I was trying not to crowd her by coming on too strong. Throughout the day, I thought about how I wanted to see her, talk to her and touch her. Between replaying our dance, the kiss we'd shared, the seductive sound of her voice over the phone, and the image of her in bed, I had been walking around with a perpetual hard-on. Every morning and every night when I showered, I found myself jerking off just to take the edge off. I hadn't masturbated this much since high school. The irony was not lost on me.

Xander, Grayson, Jax, and I were meeting Hunter at his place to watch the Thursday night football game. Throwing on jeans and a long-sleeved NY Giants T-shirt, I hopped in my Ford F-150 to make the twenty-five-minute drive. Along the way, I stopped and picked up a case of beer and a variety of chips.

As many times as I had been there, the sight and size of Hunter's house never failed to amaze me. Made of wood, river rock, and glass, the two-story mansion had sweeping views of a large lake. The guys and I had spent many an early morning or late afternoon there fishing off the dock. We also spent a lot of time acting like idiots trying to outdo each other, seeing who could do the most outrageous waterskiing tricks while being pulled by Hunter's thirty-five-foot speed boat. I parked my truck in the circular driveway and let myself in the front door. Walking back to the kitchen, I put the beer in the fridge and headed towards the family room.

"Brady is the all-time best. No contest," I heard Xander say as I entered the large, open room furnished with two huge couches and a couple of chairs.

Grayson scoffed. "You're out of your mind. He's so over-rated."

"He's won five Superbowls. Five. How can you argue with that?"

"And he did that all by himself, right?"

Xander and Grayson had been having this same argument for years.

"Hey, man. Thanks for the chips," Hunter welcomed as I set the food on a large dining table on one side of the room.

"No problem. I brought beer too. It's in the fridge."

"Suck-up," Xander joked.

"Fuck you," I retorted.

Jaxson had just finished racking the balls on the pool table. "Kick your ass?" he asked me.

"You wish." I grabbed a pool cue and chalked the tip.

"Usual wager?" We bet twenty dollars a game.

"You're on."

"I call winner," Hunter yelled.

"This won't take long," I asserted.

"Cocky bastard," Jax muttered.

I wasn't really cocky, just confident. Although he was pretty good, I could count the times he had beaten me at pool on one hand. Tonight was no different. After I demolished him, I re-racked as Hunter joined me by the table. I broke and sunk a solid.

As I looked over the felt deciding on my next shot, Hunter asked, "Do you think I should marry Angie?"

Since the reunion, I had been planning to have a talk with him about his fiancé, but his question surprised me. He didn't talk about Angie much. Probably because he knew we couldn't stand her. The two of them had been together for about two years and engaged for six months. She was from a wealthy family, just like Hunter. But, unlike Hunter, she was very materialistic and into appearances. She rarely showed up when we hung out. I think she believed we were beneath her, even though we were all successful in our own right, though not in the same financial stratosphere as Hunter. Granted, she had a hot body and she always dressed impeccably, but she didn't strike me as sexy. She was too cold. And I hated the way she treated Hunter. Generally, she liked to try to get him to do whatever she wanted which included only fraternizing with people she thought were worthy of her social status.

I lowered my cue stick to my side. "I think the more important question is do *you* think you should marry Angie?"

He took a deep breath and let it out. "I don't know, man. I have been thinking about it a lot. I know that I haven't been really happy for a long time."

"Probably not a good sign."

"No, but then Paige said something to me this week that made me think."

Holding back my question of how and when he talked to Paige, I asked "What did she say?"

"She said she had never known me to settle for anything. And she's right. I don't like to settle. If I am not certain that I want to do something, I don't do it. I'm an Executive Vice President of a global company. I got where I am because I am driven, thorough and decisive. I've always wondered why I don't have that same intensity in my relationship with Angie. Granted, she's from a good family and it would be a good merger . . ."

"Merger, really?" I interrupted. "You think of marriage as a business deal?"

"Stupid, huh? On paper it works."

"Love isn't about facts and figures, Hunter."

"I don't know any different. I've never had that feeling of not being able to live without someone. Not to sound like an asshole, but Angie is just . . . there. Don't think I'm unaware of how mean or demanding she can be. The sex — rare as it is nowadays — is okay, but I keep thinking there has to be more. Where's the overwhelming desire and the friendship? In my world, that hasn't existed in any relationship that I've had."

"At the risk of sounding like a girl, passion exists in everyone's world. You just haven't found the right woman yet." I couldn't help thinking about Paige. "When you do, she will be all you think about, and you'll want her with an all-consuming need. You'll be completely fucked, but in the best way possible."

He grinned at me. "You didn't ask where I saw Paige."

"Shit. That obvious, huh?" I cringed, looking sheepish.

"Yeah, pretty much. I'll put you out of your misery. She's working for Perlman Design in Greenwich. I had a meeting with them yesterday about our new building and she was there. She looked good, Carter."

I felt rage boil up at his comment, even though it was Hunter. "Don't even think about it, man."

He grinned. "Not going there. Just messing with you."

I flipped him off.

"You want to know something odd though?"

"What?"

"When I was doing research into the firms I was seeking proposals from, her info wasn't listed on the Perlman website."

"What's so weird about that? Didn't she just recently start?"

"Perlman is a multi-million-dollar company, Carter. You're telling me that they don't have a marketing department that can get a bio up within a month?"

I thought about that and realized it was a little odd.

"Hey, girls!" Xander shouted. "The game's starting."

I went over to join the others just as the doorbell rang, signaling the arrival of the pizzas. Turning back towards the front door, I said over my shoulder, "My treat this week. How fortunate that I have Jax's money to help cover the tab."

This time I was the one who got flipped off.

Chapter Thirteen: Paige

Friday morning, after another restless night of sleep thanks to very vivid dreams about Carter, I arrived at the office early. I figured if I couldn't sleep, I might as well get some work done. I had the finishing touches to put together for a restaurant in Old Saybrook and specs and price points to research for the Carlson bid. At seven a.m., I was the first person to arrive in my department. After unlocking my office, I sat down at my desk and delved into my tasks. Concentrating, I was vaguely aware of the other staff members arriving. Several hours later, I was ready to take a break. I stood up from my chair and stretched. Looking at the clock that read eleven-thirty, I figured it was a good time to grab a cup of decaf. As I opened my door, I almost ran over Gail, who was carrying a huge bouquet of white calla lilies in a tall vase.

"Oh, Gail. I'm so sorry. I didn't mean to run into you."

"I'm fine, Paige. I'm just lucky I didn't drop these."

"They're beautiful."

She smiled. "They were just delivered. For you."

"Me?"

"Yes. I was just bringing them to you."

"Thank you." I took the flowers and went back into my office. My heart was racing. Could Derrick have found me? His flowers of choice had been blood-red roses, so I doubted it, but ... Angry at my reaction, I looked and saw the card tucked into the blooms. My hand was shaking as I opened the envelope. *I couldn't find anything as beautiful as you, but these will have to do. Carter.* I let out the breath I had been holding and smiled despite my residual anxiety. I hadn't heard from Carter since his phone call the night of the reunion. While part of me was relieved to have not heard from him, another part of me was disappointed. Both feelings bothered me.

Just then, my cell phone rang. Glancing at the caller id, I smiled in spite of myself.

"Hello, Carter."

"Good morning, Paige." His voice was like a caress. I instantly imagined him saying those same words in person. In bed.

"They're gorgeous."

"Not even close to how stunning you are."

The rich timber of his voice made the corny line feel sincere. Instead of arguing, I decided to be gracious. "Thank you. How did you know where I work . . . ah, Hunter, right?"

"It pays to have friends in high places."

I smiled. "It was good to see him, though I got the feeling he is struggling with something."

"He told me you and he talked about Angie. Some of the things you said really got to him."

I frowned. I hope I hadn't spoken out of turn. "I didn't mean to upset him."

"No, not at all. From what he told me, you helped bring clarity to things."

"He's such a good guy, Carter. I really want to see him happy."

"Me too. I think he's getting there."

"I'm glad to hear that."

"Have you had lunch yet?"

He caught me off guard with the abrupt change in topic. "Not yet, no."

"Great. Meet me out front."

"What?"

"I'm waiting outside by the front door. I'll see you in a few minutes."

"Wait, Carter, I don't know . . ." I frowned as I realized he had disconnected. I wasn't sure it would be smart to see him again, but it would be rude to just not show up. I grabbed my sky-blue cardigan from the back of my door and took a quick look in the mirror over the small loveseat in my office. Noting the flush in my cheeks, I fluffed my hair and applied a quick coat of lipstick. Fridays were casual days at Perlman. I wished I had worn something a little dressier than a pair of navy slacks, a white button-down blouse and gold strappy sandals. Oh well, maybe it was for the best. I didn't want to look like I was trying too hard.

About ten minutes later, I reached the lobby. Carter was talking with Al, the front desk security guard. When he noticed me, his face broke into a wide grin. Damn the man and his one dimple. He looked sexy as sin in jeans and a forest green Henley. The jeans were somewhat worn and molded to his powerful thighs and tight butt. The long-sleeved T-shirt highlighted his broad chest and muscular arms. Why couldn't he have a beer belly? Oh, who was I kidding, even that wouldn't detract from his appeal. I took a deep breath and walked over to the desk.

Al smiled at my approach. "Good day, Miss Paige."

I grinned in response. "Hi, Al. How are you?"

"Can't complain."

"And Marla and the grandkids?"

His eyes sparkled with pride at the mention of his family. "Marla's the sunshine in my world and the kids are as rambunctious as ever."

"Let me know the next time Marla sends you in with another batch of cookies. Thought my hips still haven't forgiven me for the last time, I can't resist."

Al laughed. "I'll tell her to make some for the office next week." He nodded at Carter. "Nice to meet you, Carter."

Carter reached out to shake his hand. "Back at you, Al."

As we walked out into the fall day, Carter leaned down and whispered "I think Marla's cookies must be magic. Your hips are perfect."

Between his nearness and the feel of his breath on my cheek, I shuddered. "If Al keeps bringing them in, they are going to be perfectly huge."

"Whatever size, they'd still be perfect."

I glanced up at him to give him an incredulous look. Bad choice. One glance into his gray eyes caused me to stumble slightly. He grabbed my waist to right me. I felt his touch in every part of my body. Even after I regained my footing, he kept his arm around me. Knowing I should pull away, but enjoying how it felt too much, I didn't say anything. We walked over to his truck and he opened the passenger door to let me in. I put on my seatbelt as he rounded the front and got in beside me. After buckling up himself, he started the engine and pulled out of the parking lot.

"Where are we going?"

"It's such a nice day. I thought I'd take to you a place by the water."

"That sounds great."

Between the electricity in the air and my nervousness, I was on edge. Looking for something to focus on besides his delectable scent and his gorgeous body so close to mine, I reached out for the radio. "May I?"

"Sure, go for it."

I turned on the volume and immediately recognized the metal song blaring. I smiled. "Still a headbanger, huh?"

He grinned. "Always. Still listen to classic rock?"

"As any true music lover should."

He laughed. We turned down a gravel road.

"Just where are you taking me, Carter?"

"Trust me."

Not an easy thing to ask from me, but strangely, I did. I knew that Carter would never hurt me. At least not physically. We came to a clearing and he eased to a stop. Spread out before us was a grassy area overlooking the ocean. I hadn't realized that we were ascending a hill, but evidently we had, as the flat land clearly was the top of some kind of cliff. Carter got out and came around to open my door. I climbed down as he walked to the back of the truck and grabbed a blanket and a picnic basket from the truck bed. As a teenager, Carter was forever surprising me with sweet, romantic gestures. I always appreciated his thoughtfulness. Today was no different. He led me down to about twenty feet from the edge and spread out the blanket. Taking off my shoes, I sat down facing him and looked out over the water.

"This is spectacular."

CHAPTER FOURTEEN: CARTER

Not tearing my gaze away from Paige's face, I agreed. "Yes, it is."

She turned back towards me and caught me looking at her. I noticed her cheeks flush.

"How did you find this place?"

"I was working on a job in the area and the owner mentioned it."

"It's breathtaking and calming at the same time."

I opened the picnic basket and spread out the sandwiches, fruit and sparkling cider.

"I was going to bring wine, but since you have to go back to work, I thought this would be better."

"It looks delicious, Carter."

She looked delicious, sitting out here with me in the sunshine. Her hair blazed fire when the light hit it. She had taken her sandals off when we sat down. Even her toes, painted a bright pink, were sexy. Though I never had a foot fetish, I wanted to take each one in my mouth. Granted, there was a lot more of her that I wanted to lick as well. Slowly and thoroughly.

I poured each of us some of the cider. Nodding towards the sandwiches, I asked "Turkey, veggie, or ham?"

"Turkey, please."

I handed her the sandwich on a plate and took the ham for myself.

"How are your mom and dad?"

She looked off into the distance. "They're doing well. Dad

is still working as an accountant, and Mom is busy with her various charitable organizations."

"How about Riley and Jordan? How are they?" I asked, referring to her cousins who were two and four years older than she. The three of them had spent a lot of time together growing up and acted more like sisters than cousins.

She smiled. "Fantastic. Riley is traveling the world as a photojournalist. And Jordan is working at the DA's office as a prosecutor in Boston. We get together every couple of months. And I spend every Thanksgiving at Aunt Pam and Uncle Henry's."

"How's the new job going so far?"

Her eyes sparkled. "I love it. I am doing exactly what I have always wanted to do. Everyone has been very welcoming too."

"I remember how you used to come over and work with my mom to rearrange rooms in our house. I think you and she must have changed every room in our house at least five times."

She smiled brightly at the memory. "Yeah, I knew I wanted to be a designer even back then. Your mom was so nice to indulge me."

"She loved your company. You were like the daughter she always wanted."

"And she was like the mother I always longed for." Paige's mom and dad had given her a roof over her head and fed and clothed her, but they weren't very loving. They pushed her to succeed and were extremely stringent about grades and how she presented herself. In contrast, I know she used to relish spending time at my house, because it was always full of love and laughter.

"Would you like to come over to Mom and Dad's on Sunday for dinner?"

A concerned look crossed her face. "I don't know if that's

a good idea, Carter."

"Why do you say that? Everyone would love to see you."

Clearly conflicted, she sighed. "It would be great to see them again too. I've . . . missed them."

Had she missed me? I had yearned for her since the moment she left. Even though I was sitting across from her, I still missed her. I missed not holding her, not touching her. Luckily, I had placed my napkin over my lap almost immediately after we sat down, hoping to hide the erection I'd had since I picked her up for lunch.

She chewed on her lip. "I just don't want them to get the wrong idea."

I had all sorts of ideas about Paige. None of which I felt were wrong. "What idea would that be?"

"That we're seeing each other."

"And why would that idea be wrong?"

She rolled her eyes. "Because we aren't, Carter. We can't just meet up after ten years and pick up right where we left off."

"I don't want to pick up where we left off. Where we left off was you leaving."

Her eyes flashed. "Where we left off was you telling me you didn't want to be with me."

I was taken aback. Did she really believe that? Did my lame excuses lead her to believe that it didn't kill me to let her go? Didn't she realize that I had to let her go so she could achieve her dreams?

"I always wanted to be with you, Paige. Don't doubt that for a minute."

She stood up and started pacing back and forth on the grass. I could practically see the steam coming out of her ears. She looked so damn beautiful, I ached.

"Really, Carter? *Really?* You told me that our relationship would never last when I went away to school. That we couldn't survive the distance. If you really loved me, if you truly wanted to be with me, you would have fought to keep us together. You wouldn't have let physical distance keep us apart."

Now I was pissed at her questioning my feelings. I stood up and faced her, gently talking her wrist so she would stop moving. "I wasn't going to be selfish, Paige. You were heading off to work on reaching your dreams. Can you honestly say that you would have been able to achieve everything you have if we had tried to stay together? If you always had to be concerned and tied to someone who was halfway across the country? How could I live with myself if I knew that I was the reason you didn't succeed?"

She shook her head side to side as she softly said, "Oh, Carter. Do you remember when I told you that you took something from me that night and it wasn't my virginity?"

I had always wondered what she had meant by that. "Yes . . ."

She stepped out of my hold. "What you took from me was choice. You decided that I needed to be without you in order to succeed. You decided that you would hold me back. You decided that I would be better off without you. When had our relationship ever prevented me from being my own person or going after and achieving goals? Why did you make the decision that I would turn into a needy, clingy female incapable of being with you and making it through college? It made me furious, Carter. What you should have done was let me decide for myself and let us work it out. Together."

Stunned, I sat back down on the blanket. She was right. I had always thought I was being noble by letting her go. Turns out I was being an overbearing idiot. But then something occurred to me.

"If you were so sure of us, then why didn't you ever try to see me again? To tell me what you just told me now?"

Paige lowered herself to the blanket. Again, she glanced at the ocean, then whispered. "I did."

Now I was really shocked. Until the reunion, I hadn't seen her again after that night in the treehouse. Of that I was certain. "What? When?"

She turned back and looked at me. I could see the hurt reflected in her eyes. "I was miserable without you. I knew you were wrong about us. I was certain of how I felt about you, and I thought I understood how you felt about me. But I also knew how stubborn you were, and I wasn't going to change your mind before I left. I didn't want to have that conversation over the phone, so I made up my mind to make you see things clearly when I came home for Thanksgiving. I wasn't going to return to Chicago without knowing you were mine. So I showed up at the football game because I knew you would be there. I saw you with another girl and I realized that I had completely overestimated your feelings for me. How could you be with someone else so soon after I left? I ached for you, Carter. And you had moved on. I knew then that it was truly over."

My head was spinning trying to process what she had just shared. I had always been completely sure of my feelings for Paige. I thought about her constantly, yet I wouldn't let myself contact her because I needed her to come to me out of want, not obligation. I knew she loved me, but I don't think I ever let myself believe she cared for me with the same intensity I had felt for her. To find out that she did floored me. And to learn that she had attempted to reach out? I was seething inside for the time we lost. However, I had no clue what other girl she was talking about. I certainly hadn't even thought about anyone else for months after she left for school.

"You saw me with another girl?"

"Yes. A blonde. You had your arm around her."

I racked my brain to think back. When it dawned on me

what she had seen, I swore at what she had obviously misinterpreted. "Shit."

CHAPTER FIFTEEN: PAIGE

"Mad at yourself for getting caught?"

Carter's eyes were stormy as he shook his head. "No. Pissed that you were so hurt over a misunderstanding. Angry that we have wasted so much time."

Completely confused, I asked "Misunderstanding?"

He nodded. "That girl you saw me with? She was Jarrod's girlfriend at the time. She was excited because I had just told her he was coming back to town for two weeks on leave."

Stunned, I repeated, "Shit." I didn't doubt him. From the regret on his face, I knew he wasn't lying.

Carter leaned over and gathered me into his lap, my back against his chest, his strong arms wrapped around my front.

"There was never anyone but you, Paige. Since the moment I laid eyes on you, you were it for me. I wanted you with every breath. I still do."

His low, sincere voice penetrated my heart. I had felt so much for the boy he was, and I was starting to feel even more for the man he had become. I had never connected with another male on every level. The sexual attraction was off the charts. More than attraction, it was a need. But more disconcerting than that was the emotional bond we had. Even in the short time since we had reconnected, I found myself wondering when I would talk to him, when I would see him next. I was really scared and didn't know if I could be intimate with him given my scars. He remembered me as a young woman, not a flawed adult.

Despite my fears, I couldn't stop my hand from reaching

up behind me and stroking his face. He bent down and kissed the side of my neck in response. Heat flooded me as I felt the sizable bulge beneath my rear end. Before I had time to think, Carter turned me so that my breasts pressed into his chest and I was straddling his lap. His gray eyes connected with mine before he cradled my face in his hands and lowered his mouth to mine. He kissed me gently at first, but it quickly became urgent. I slid my tongue along the seam of his lips and felt him groan as he opened and let me inside.

Quickly taking over, he licked and ravaged my mouth. Shamelessly, I ground myself against his erection, craving the contact. He tore his mouth from mine and nuzzled, licked, then nipped at the side of my neck. The touch sent bolts directly to my womb, which was already wet with need. He started unbuttoning my blouse, revealing the top of my nude sheer bra. Immediately I froze, knowing that if he went much farther he would be able to see the marks on my skin. Panting, I pushed on his chest and hurriedly buttoned up, eager to cover up any glimpses he may have seen.

Face taught with desire and his gray eyes deepened to almost slate, he was the most gorgeous man I had ever seen. I wanted him so much, but shame won out over my desire. Needing to put some distance between us and to do something with my hands that didn't involve stripping him naked, I stood up and started to gather up our lunch. Carter stood as well and gently laid a hand on my arm.

"I am not sorry for kissing you and touching you. I *am* sorry if it was too much, too fast."

Not quite meeting his eyes, I murmured "There's nothing to be sorry for. I just need to get back to work."

He looked at me intensely, and I could tell he wasn't convinced at my excuse for ending our kiss. He quickly recovered and smiled. "Of course. I wouldn't want to get you in trouble with the boss."

Grateful that he let me off the hook by not questioning, I let him take my hand and lead me to the truck. I was fairly silent on the ride back to my office, not trusting myself to speak. When we arrived at our destination, he opened my door and walked me to the entrance.

"So, dinner Sunday?"

No. No dinner Sunday. I wasn't about to torture myself by continuing to see him when I wanted him the way I did and I knew I couldn't let him see what had become of my body. "Okay." Where the hell did that come from?

"I'll pick you up at five. What is your address?"

Still shocked that I had agreed, I retorted, "I'll meet you there." This way I could leave anytime I wanted to. Plus, I wouldn't be tempted being alone with him in the car to and from his parents' house.

He frowned but didn't push. Slowly lowering his head, he sweetly brushed his mouth with mine.

"See you then."

God help me.

Chapter Sixteen: Carter

"If you keep jumping up at the sound of every car that passes by, you're going to blow out a knee," Xander joked.

I shot him a look and sat back down in the living room by the front bay window.

"Seriously, man, you are such a girl. Take it down a notch."

He was right. I was nervous and acting like a woman waiting for her prom date to show up. It was a few minutes before five on Sunday, and I was anxiously looking forward to Paige's arrival. Given her reluctance to accept my invitation for dinner, I was concerned that she had changed her mind about showing up.

Jarrod clapped his hand on my shoulder. "She'll be here."

I looked at him gratefully. Where Xander was the jokester, Jarrod was quieter. When he said something, he meant it. Now that he was back after being in the Army for eight years, I realized how much his presence was perfect fodder for Xander's personality. I think that was why the three of us worked so well together. Where Xander schmoozed, Jarrod was methodical. I was somewhere in the middle, though I had nowhere near my twin's overt charisma.

At five o'clock on the dot, the doorbell rang. I jumped out of my chair to open the door, but Xander beat me to it. He swung open the door to reveal Paige. Even from where I stood, I could sense her hesitance. Xander grabbed her by the hand and pulled her inside. Immediately, enveloping her in a huge hug that lifted her off the ground, he gave her an exaggerated kiss on the cheek. My blood boiled at someone else touching her, even if it was my brother.

Meanwhile, Paige broke into a grin and started laughing at Xander's behavior. "Xander! Put me down."

"Maybe I'll just whisk you away with me," he threatened, eyebrows wagging.

"Maybe I'll let you," she retorted, smiling.

I growled in their direction. Xander reveled in pushing my buttons. He took Paige's coat and smirked as he brushed past me to hang it up in the hall closet. I barely refrained from taking a swing at him.

Jarrod approached Paige next. He enveloped her in a soft embrace. Again, my jealousy flared.

She reached up and touched his cheek, then stood back and took a look at him.

"My gosh, Jarrod, look at you. The last time I saw you, you were a boy headed off to boot camp."

Jarrod smiled fondly down at her from his full height of six-three. "I've grown up bit since then." He grinned. "And you have become even more beautiful with age."

Another involuntary growl came from deep in my throat. Logically, I knew that Jarrod had no interest in Paige other than as a big brother, but I still did not appreciate his comment. As I looked at her, his observation was certainly accurate. Dressed in casual black pants and a pink sweater set that outlined her curves, she was breathtaking.

Paige blushed. "You're sweet, Jarrod. Thank you."

Hearing the noise coming from the foyer, my dad joined us. His face lit up at seeing Paige. "Paige, darlin'. Aren't you a sight?"

Taking a few steps towards him, she was wrapped up in yet another hug. "Mr. Sullivan. You look just like I remember. How have you been?"

He tucked her arm through his and let her into the dining room. "What's with the Mr. Sullivan? It's Patrick," my dad blustered. "I can't complain. The boys have taken over the business, though I like to check into things every now and again. It has freed me up to spend more time with Colleen and work on my cars."

At the mention of her name, my mom stepped out from the kitchen carrying the last of the meal and set the dish on the table. She turned to Paige and opened her arms. "Paige, honey, it's so good to see you." Then, stepping back, she looked Paige up and down. "You are stunning. After Carter told us you were back, I can't tell you how much I have been looking forward to seeing you."

I noticed unshed tears of emotion in Paige's glorious blue eyes.

"Oh, Mrs. Sullivan—"

"Colleen, please."

Paige nodded. "Colleen. It is so good to see all of you. It has been too long. This is for you." She held out the small package she had been holding. "I remember how much you love your tea."

"Thank you, Paige. We have missed you, sweetie. And my poor house probably looks exactly the same. Without my own personal decorator, I was afraid to change anything."

Paige tipped back her head and laughed. "We did do a number on this house, didn't we? I think you managed just fine on your own." She looked around. "Everything looks exactly as it should."

My mom beamed and motioned for all of us to sit down. She and Dad took their seats at each end of the table, with Xander and Jarrod sitting across from Paige and me. As I held out the chair for Paige to take her seat, I caught a whiff of her perfume. She still wore the same fruity sent. And it still made me hard as a rock. Thankful for the barrier of the dining room table that would hide my current state, I placed a napkin in my lap for added security.

My mom leaned forward, nodded to my dad and said "Patrick, will you please lead us in grace?"

We all joined hands. As I grasped Paige's smaller one in mind, I stroked my thumb across hers. God forgive me, I asked as my mind reacted to feeling her soft skin and my thoughts were decidedly less than holy. With pure male satisfaction, I felt her breath hitch at my touch. As soon as Dad finished prayer, I reluctantly let her go.

"Everything looks fabulous, Colleen. Carter told me you have your own cooking show."

My mom's eyes sparkled. "Yes. I love it. It's weekly, every Tuesday morning from ten to eleven. There's a small studio in Hartford that it's broadcast from."

"She's always trying out new recipes on us," Xander offered.

"And I'm sure you hate that, right?" Paige joked.

"It makes it tough to maintain my girlish figure."

We all laughed. Xander was not quite as tall as me and Jarrod, but he was a little over six feet and didn't have an ounce of fat on him.

"You seem like you are maintaining just fine, Xander. Me, on the other hand . . . If I was one of your mom's guinea pigs, I would probably gain all the weight back I lost when I went to college."

I looked at her. "And you'd still be gorgeous."

Paige blushed. Xander and Jarrod grinned. My mom and dad looked on, amused.

Sensing her discomfort, Mom said, "Catch us up on what you have been doing over the years, Paige."

Looking relieved, Paige answered, "Well, I got my undergraduate degree in Design from Northwestern and then my master's in Business from Loyola. After I graduated, I was lucky enough to land a job with a top interior design firm in downtown Chicago."

"And what brought you back here?" my dad inquired.

A shadow crossed her face and she hesitated. "My good friend from Northwestern, Parker, had been bugging me to come work with him at his uncle's firm. After five years, he finally wore me down. I moved back about two months ago."

"Well, we're certainly glad you're back." This from my mom, which earned a smile from Paige.

"Some of us are *really* glad you're back." Xander grinned. Jarrod elbowed him. I gave him a dirty look, but without much behind it, as he was just telling the truth.

Ignoring Xander, my mom commented, "I bet the girls are happy you're here."

Paige nodded. "Yes, we're still very close. I don't know what I would do without them."

"I ran into Caitlin at the TV station a few months ago. That girl is a whirlwind, isn't she?"

Paige laughed. "She is. Always has been and probably always will be."

"I saw Peyton at the recent car and truck show at the XL Center last month," my dad chimed in.

Jarrod choked on his drink, coughing.

"Are you okay, son?"

"Fine. Just swallowed wrong. I'm okay."

"Is Peyton still working at her dad's trucking business?"

"Yes," Paige responded. "She's vice president of commercial vehicles. And I'm not surprised you saw her at the car and truck show. She is forever researching the latest equipment."

"Hey, Mom? Have you given any more thought to getting a new dog at Grayson's next weekend?" Jarrod asked.

"I don't know, honey. While I miss having a pup around, your dad and I travel more than we used to, and I'm not sure it would be fair to board him all the time."

"Oh, I remember Kodak. He was such a love," Paige remarked.

"That he was," my dad said. "Got him figuring he would be a great watchdog for Colleen while I was working. He didn't have an aggressive bone in his body. Probably could've licked a burglar to death, though."

We all laughed.

"We'd take turns watching him for you, Mom," offered Xander.

"You can barely take care of yourself," I said.

Xander grinned. "When I said *we,* I meant you and Jarrod."

Jarrod laughed. "Of course, you did."

"Well, we're all helping out at the adoption event Saturday, Mom. Feel free to come down and take a look," I suggested.

Paige turned and faced me. "You're helping out next Saturday?"

"Yeah, why?"

"Caitlin volunteered me to help out as well."

"You always were a complete sucker for animals. Hunter used to call you *Doolittle.*"

She smiled.

"I'm surprised you don't have at least one pet of your own by now."

A look of hurt crossed her face. "Just have been too busy, I guess." She stood up and started to clear her dishes. "That was delicious, Colleen. Let me help clean up. It's the least I can do after such a wonderful meal."

"This one's a keeper, Carter," Xander offered. "I can't remember any of your other girlfriends ever offering to help clear the table after the family meal."

I watched Paige flinch slightly at the mention of other women in my life. It warmed me to think she was jealous. Before I could respond with an insult, Mom chimed in.

"Carter's never invited any other girls over for Sunday dinner, Xander, and you know it. Stop giving him a hard time."

Paige whipped her head around to look at me. "You've never . . ."

I looked into her eyes and shook my head. "Only you, Paige. Just you."

CHAPTER SEVENTEEN: PAIGE

Blown away at Carter's admission, I almost dropped the plates I was carrying. Quickly trying to recover and ignore the heat that spread throughout my body from the way he was looking at me, I grabbed a few more dishes and followed Jarrod into the kitchen. Between the six of us, we made quick work of clearing the table, washing the pots and pans, and loading the dishwasher.

"I have a fresh peach cobbler for dessert if anyone's interested," Colleen offered.

"As delicious as that sounds, Colleen, I am stuffed from dinner." And I needed to leave. Being around the Sullivans brought back a lot of old memories. It was evident that from the moment I walked in, it felt like coming home. Overwhelmed by the enormity of my emotions, all I could think about was escape.

"Why don't you show Paige the koi pond, Carter?" Patrick suggested.

Despite my eagerness to get back home, I couldn't help but be intrigued. "You have a koi pond?"

"Yep. Me and the boys just finished putting it in this summer."

Carter held out his hand and I slipped mine into it. "Lead the way."

We stepped out onto the back patio. The night had turned cool and I shivered involuntarily. Carter frowned and noted, "You're cold. I'll be right back."

As he ducked into the house, I looked around at the

backyard. Colleen had a green thumb, and the yard looked like a magazine, bursting with a variety of flowers and bushes. Flagstone surrounded the covered in-ground pool. I looked towards the back corner of the yard and noticed they had added a horseshoe pit underneath the big maple tree that held the treehouse. Memories of that night came back with a rush. I had meant what I said to Carter. I still didn't regret giving him my virginity. Despite how it ended and how much his words hurt, I never would.

After our discussion on Friday, I mourned the loss of the years we had been apart but recognized there was nothing that could be done about the past. As for the future, I was scared and unsure. How could I let things go any further when I knew an intimate relationship couldn't happen? He deserved someone who could fully give herself to him, not a woman with a scarred body. Yet the thought of not being with him made me sad. And the thought of someone else being with him made me sick to my stomach.

"Here you go," Carter stated, slipping a heavyweight sweatshirt around my shoulders. I fit my arms into the sleeves, rolling them several times so they didn't cover my hands. The length hit me mid-thigh. I took a deep breath, noting and loving the scent of him on the garment. Taking my hand again, he led me over to the corner of the yard opposite from the treehouse. There, nestled in between a few large bushes, was the koi pond complete with a small waterfall. He reached into his pocket and handed me some morsels so I could feed the fish. I bent down and scattered the food into the water, laughing when the white, orange, and black fish came rushing over to feed.

"They're beautiful," I commented.

"They are, aren't they? My mom always wanted a koi pond. We surprised her for Mother's Day this year."

As we watched the fish in silence, Carter wrapped his arms

around me from behind and laced his fingers together at my waist. I had been very aware of him from the moment I stepped through the front door of his parents' house. Sitting next to him at dinner, I could feel the heat from his body and the strength of his thigh against mine. Even the man's breathing turned me on. Now, with his arms around me, I leaned back into his chest, feeling the definition of his pecs and the hardness of his abdomen. Against my lower back, I also felt the rigid length of him. Even though we weren't engaged in any kind of sexual activity, it was gratifying to know the effect I had on him.

"Are you glad you accepted my dinner invitation?" he asked in the rich, low voice that never failed to make me shiver.

"Yes. I am. It was so good to see everyone. You know how much I always loved being here. Your parents used to welcome me with open arms. Tonight was no different."

"They adore you, Paige, which is very easy to do."

I shivered again.

He tightened his hold in response. Turning me around to face him, he looked down at me and frowned. Slipping a lock of hair that was blowing in my face behind my ear, he said, "You're cold."

I closed my eyes, wanting to lie to him and agree. Instead, I admitted the truth.

"I'm not cold."

"You're shivering."

"I am shivering because you're touching me. The tremors I'm having are in response to you, not to temperature."

A slow, sexy smile of pure male satisfaction appeared on his face. "Nice to know I have that effect on you."

I rolled my eyes. "Like that was ever in doubt, Carter."

"I notice how your body responds to me, angel, but every man likes to hear he can turn his woman on."

The feminist inside me bristled at him calling me his woman, but the woman inside me reacted to his possessive tone with pure joy.

His eyes darkened. "I have been wanting to feel that sexy mouth on mine since the moment you walked in the door."

With that, he framed my face with his hands, bent down and kissed me behind one ear, nipping the lobe and then soothing it with his tongue. I moaned because his touch went directly to my womb, making me wetter than I already was. He sweetly kissed me, lightly licking one corner of my mouth, then the other.

"Let me in, baby. I need to taste you."

Whimpering, I opened my mouth under his as my arms clutched his biceps. He slowly tasted me, stroking my tongue with his. It was the most sensual kiss I had ever experienced, and I couldn't get enough of his thorough exploration. Wanting to be even closer to him, I reached underneath his shirt and ran my hands along his broad, strong back. He growled at my touch and the kiss turned from sweet and seductive to hot and frantic. His large hands cupped my ass and pulled me tight against his erection.

His right hand moved from my behind to cup my left breast. He plundered my mouth while he kneaded its fullness and brought my already aching nipple to an even tighter point. Shafts of pleasure shot directly between my legs and I whimpered. Lifting my shirt up, he took my nipple in his mouth through my pink lace bra. I moaned his name as he bit down, then soothed the point with his tongue. I was so close to coming, with him using only his mouth on me and feeling his body against mine.

Breathing heavily, he implored, "You're driving me crazy. Let me drive you home so I can be inside you where I belong."

His voice awoke me from my sexual haze. I became acutely aware that my sweater had been pushed up to reveal my bra.

Thankful that it was very dark outside and most likely Carter couldn't see well enough to make out the scars on my skin through my bra, I pulled back and fixed my clothing. I closed my eyes and forced myself to take a few deep breaths. When I opened my eyes and saw the desire on his face, I almost agreed to his request. But then I thought of the look on his face if he were to see me naked. The image served as a bucket of cold water.

Still shaking with need, but trying desperately to hide it, I spoke, "I'm sorry, Carter. I shouldn't have let things go this far."

Perplexed, he looked at me. "What's going on, Paige? I felt how you responded to me and I know that you want me. Did I do something wrong?"

Desperately wanting to tell him the truth, but not wanting to reveal details of the attack, I explained, "Not to sound cliché, Carter, but it really is not you. It's me. I'm just not ready to get involved on that level."

His brow furrowed. "Is there someone else? Is that it?"

"No, Carter. There's no one else."

He took a step closer to me and touched my face. "Then what, Paige? Talk to me."

Instinctively, I knew that his questioning was not just a way to get me into bed. I felt his concern and how much he wanted me to share my reasons with him. I just couldn't. To have this man reject me would be crushing. Aware that I was being unfair to him by acting like I wanted him and yet holding him at arm's length, I looked straight at him. "If you don't want to see me again, I understand, Carter. It's probably better that way."

He shook his head vigorously and I saw the anger in his eyes. "Better for who, Paige? Certainly not better for me. I let you walk out of my life once before. It's not happening again. If you can honestly say that you don't want me the way that I want you, then you're going to have to make the decision to end it."

I wanted to be able to lie to him and tell him that I didn't want him, but I couldn't. "I can't tell you that, Carter. You must know how much I want you. But I am not prepared to give you all of me. I wish I could, but I can't. And you deserve more."

He pulled me into his arms, and I could feel his strong heartbeat. "Weren't you the one who told me that I was wrong to make your choices for you? Are you really going to do the same for me?"

I chuckled despondently. "Not fair, Carter. I don't want to hurt you." A few tears had started to run down my cheeks, signaling my exasperation at what I felt was an impossible situation.

Wiping the droplets with his thumbs, he insisted, "The only thing that would hurt me is if I didn't have you in my life, angel. Other than that, I will be fine."

At that moment, I knew I had no hope of not falling for this man. I felt so frustrated at the enormity of the situation. Right now, I just needed to go home and try to sort out my feelings. I took off his sweatshirt, mourning the loss of his fragrance enveloping me. Holding it out to him, I stated, "I think I am going to call it a night."

For a second, he looked like he wanted to argue, but then he nodded. "Okay. I'll walk you out."

As we crossed the backyard and headed for the house, I dried my face and tried to put on a smile to hide my inner turmoil. Everyone was gathered in the den, watching the Sunday Night Football pregame. I didn't want his family to notice and ask any questions.

"Well, it's getting late and I have work tomorrow so I'm going to say goodnight. Thank you so much for having me."

Patrick, Xander, and Jarrod each gave me a kiss on the

cheek. Colleen gave me a hug and said, "You're welcome any time, Paige. I hope to see you again soon."

I smiled in response and headed for the front door. I grabbed my coat from the hallway closet and Carter helped me into it. "Carter, I—"

He brushed my lips with his. "I'll talk to you soon, Paige."

Grateful that he was giving me some space and the time that I needed to process what had happened, I whispered "Goodnight, Carter."

CHAPTER EIGHTEEN: PAIGE

Wrestling with my emotions, I called Peyton on my way home.

"Hello?"

"Hey, it's me."

Immediately concerned at my tone of voice, she asked "What's wrong?"

"Oh, Peyton. I don't know what to do."

"About what, sweetie?"

"Carter."

"Ah. Well, that's easy. Have you seen the man? What should you do? Do *him*."

In spite of my mood, I laughed. "If it were only that easy."

"He's gay?"

I chuckled again. "No, Peyton, he's not."

"Married?"

"No."

"Involved?"

"Nope."

She sighed. "Okay, then I'm confused. What's the issue?"

"You know that I went over to his parents' house for dinner tonight right?"

"Yes . . ."

"Well, his parents welcomed me like I had never been away. Xander was . . . Xander. And Jarrod was his usual sweet self."

"Jarrod was there?"

"Yes. He is Carter's brother."

"Mmm-hmm. I know."

Her voice sounded weird. "Oh, that's right. You had a crush on Jarrod way back when, didn't you?"

I could hear her blushing through the phone. "Not really, no. I mean, sort of. But we're not talking about me. We're talking about you. What happened?"

Knowing she was deliberately changing the subject and sensing there was more going on with Jarrod than she wanted to admit, I let it go for now. I sighed. "He kissed me."

"And that is bad how?"

"The actually kissing part is not bad. In fact, it was unbelievably hot and parts of me that have been dormant since . . . what happened are very much alive."

"That's fantastic, Paige. So, what's the problem?"

"I have scars, Peyton."

"You're still healing emotionally, but if there is anyone you can trust, it's Carter. You know what a fantastic guy he is. He always treated you with respect."

"I have *physical* scars, Peyton."

"Oh," she said as if a lightbulb went off in her head. Back when they were taking care of me in Chicago, all four of my friends had seen the vicious cuts.

"Sweetie, do you really think that Carter is that superficial? That he would care about some marks on your skin?"

"I don't know. I don't think he's superficial, but what man wants to have sex with a woman who has slashes on her breast and her pubic area? How sexy is that? To have these puckered scars on the areas that are supposed to be the most alluring parts of a woman?"

"I saw the way that Carter looked at you at our reunion, Paige. You could have scars all over your body and he wouldn't care."

"How do you know, Peyton? He may pretend it doesn't bother him, but how could it not? And even if he acts like it doesn't bother him, it bothers me. I see them every time I look in the mirror. I haven't felt attractive naked since that bastard branded me!"

I was crying now, and angry at the same time.

"So, he wins, then, huh?"

"*What?*"

"Derrick stabbed you in those places deliberately, Paige. You know he did. He wanted you to think of him every time you saw yourself. He wanted to mark you to punish you for not wanting anything to do with him. If you keep seeing your body as just the marks he left you with, then he has control over you. Why can't you see your body for what it truly is — strong, beautiful, and *alive?*"

I was silent for a moment, then responded. "I want to not see the scars as ugly, Peyton, I really do. I wish I could think of them as a badge of honor. As a reminder of how I survived and he didn't break me. I'm trying, I really am. But I'm not there yet. And if I see even a hint of disgust from Carter if he were to see me naked, I don't think I can handle it. Every woman wants the man she is involved with to see her as desirable."

"I understand how you feel, but maybe you can try looking at yourself through Carter's eyes without letting your feelings about the scars bias you."

"I'm scared, Peyton."

"I know, honey, but wouldn't you be more scared to let Carter go without trying?"

When I didn't immediately answer, she said "Think about it, Paige."

As if I could think about anything else.

"Hey, how did your date with Travis go?"

She was silent for a moment. "Let's just say once an asshole, always an asshole."

"I'm sorry."

"It is what it is. Not all of us were meant to resume our high school romances."

"His loss."

She laughed. "Damn straight."

"Goodnight, Peyton. Thanks for listening."

"Anytime. I love you, Paige."

"Love you too."

Reaching my townhouse, I pulled into the garage and parked. I entered and turned off the alarm, then reset it after locking up. In the bedroom, I took off my clothes and went into the bathroom to take a shower. As I washed my body, all my nerve endings were alive with unfulfilled desire. As I was towel-drying my hair, I caught my reflection in the mirror. My skin was flushed, and my breasts looked fuller than usual. I appeared like a very aroused woman ready for her lover. For the first time in a long time, I noticed my curves and the flush of my skin before my scars. Was Peyton right? Could Carter really look past the marks, not notice them as we made love?

After putting on a fitted T-shirt and cotton pants, I climbed into bed. I turned on the TV, settling in to watch the football game. My cellphone buzzed.

"Hello, Carter," I greeted a bit nervously.

"Paige." His voice was like a caress. "Just checking to make sure you arrived home okay."

His concern for my welfare was comforting. But the warm, masculine sound of his voice did nothing to tamper my arousal. "This is becoming a habit."

He emitted a low chuckle. "I like talking to you before bed-time."

My breath caught. I liked talking to him before I went to sleep too. And I wanted to do more than talk to him.

"Did you make it home okay?" I asked.

He laughed again. "Yes, thanks for asking."

I pictured him lying in bed, and heat flooded my core.

"Watching the game?" he inquired.

My body was on fire with need. What game? "Yes." My voice sounded breathy, even to my own ears.

"Are you okay, Paige? You sound out of breath."

I could feel myself blushing. "I'm fine. I'm just . . ." Not wanting to admit the state of my arousal, I couldn't finish the sentence.

"Still turned on from earlier?" he finished my statement for me.

His not being able to see me made it feel safe to admit it. "Kind of."

"Me too, sweetheart." His voice deepened. "Do those beautiful breasts of yours feel heavier?"

Because I wasn't concerned about his reaction to seeing my scars, I felt free to respond. I took turns cupping first one than the other in my hand. They did feel larger, swollen with desire.

"Yes," I admitted.

"And are your nipples drawn, begging for my hands and for me to take them into my mouth and suck?"

I slowly circled the tight points with my fingers. They were drawn tight, painfully sensitive.

"Yes," I breathed.

I could hear the desire in his voice as he continued. "Are you wet for me, baby?"

I knew I was, as I could feel the moisture dampening my pajama bottoms, but I reached down and cupped myself through the material. "Practically dripping." I admitted.

"I wish I was there to lick every drop," he growled. "Is your clit begging for my mouth and my teeth?"

His sexy words inflamed me. Reaching underneath my pants, I parted my legs and touched the sensitive bud. At the first stroke, my hips jerked upwards in response. "Oh yes, Carter."

His breathing had become harsher as well. "And when you put a finger inside yourself, is it hot? Does it grip you like it would grip my cock?"

Squirming uncontrollably, I inserted a finger inside myself, pumping in and out. I was so close, my body straining for release. "Oh, god, yes." I panted, lost in the sensations.

"You are so fucking sexy, baby. I can picture exactly what you look like, touching yourself."

His sensual words, combined with the way I was touching myself, were a dual onslaught to my senses.

"Just thinking about what you must look like right now has me so hard, baby. My cock is like steel at the thought of your tight, wet pussy clamped down around your fingers."

Through my haze, it occurred to me to ask, "Are you touching yourself too, Carter?"

Something between a chuckle and a growl came through the phone. "Damn right I am. You have me so worked up, I'm going to explode."

The image of him, naked, with his cock in his hand, stroking, was enough to put me over the edge. My orgasm slammed into me and I screamed his name. I heard him shout my name as he reached his own release. My body sated, I removed my hand and adjusted my clothes.

"I can't believe we just did that." I was a little embarrassed, but I also felt a sense of power at his reaction to me.

He chuckled. "You've never had phone sex before?"

"No. I've never wanted to before," I admitted. "Have you?" I asked, not really wanting to know the answer.

"No, but you make me so hot, baby. When I heard the need in your voice, I couldn't help myself. You are the sexiest woman I have ever known."

I flushed at his praise, wanting to believe it. "And you are the sexiest man I have ever seen."

I could feel him smiling across the line. "Good to know you

feel that way, sweetheart. I love to hear that you want me like I want you."

Knowing that this potent man wanted me with such a vengeance warmed me somewhere deep inside. Would it be enough to help him overcome my physical imperfections? Would he still want me after he saw the slashes? The thought sobered me. Between the emotions of the day and my recent physical exertion, exhaustion swept over me. Not knowing how to delicately end the conversation, I simply said, "Thank you for a wonderful night. Goodnight, Carter."

"Goodnight, Paige," he responded.

The last thing I remember before falling asleep was disconnecting the call and my head hitting the pillow.

CHAPTER NINETEEN: CARTER

The week after Paige joined me for dinner at my parents' house was busy. I had several jobs I was overseeing and numerous meetings at the various sites, ensuring that all the projects were on schedule. Xander and I touched base every day to discuss future opportunities.

I called Paige every night. While there was no repeat performance of Sunday night, we talked about our days and generally got more familiar with each other. I was extremely aware of her, however. Just the sound of her voice aroused me and any thought of her breathy moans or my name on her lips as she came had me almost constantly erect. But I meant what I said to her about letting her decide the pace, even if it killed me.

Wednesday morning, Jarrod popped his head in my doorway.

"Got a minute?"

"Sure." I motioned for him to come in.

He shut the door and sat down in one of the chairs in front of my desk.

"What's up?"

"Something strange happened at the Vesper site this morning."

The Vesper project was a strip mall that we were building in New Haven. Laid out in an L shape, it would consist of fifteen retail shops and was scheduled to be complete in about two months. The foundation had been poured and the framework for the walls was almost done.

"What happened?"

"A handful of the girders were damaged. Almost like someone took a sledgehammer to them."

"What?"

"Yeah, and the oil line on one of the bobcats was messed with. There was a puddle of oil underneath it. I was able to repair the line and get it back up and running. I also put sawdust down over the oil spill to absorb the mess."

"Thanks for taking care of it. That area is pretty open, right? It was probably some kids messing around."

"Maybe," Jarrod said cautiously.

"I'll call up the security firm and have them put a couple of guys on night watch. Do we have enough replacement materials to replace the girders?"

"We should."

"How much will it put us behind?"

"Maybe half a day, but we can easily make up the time."

"Anything else messed with? Anything missing?"

"Not that I could find."

"Okay, good. Keep an eye out and let me know if you come across anything else."

"I will."

"Thanks."

He got up to leave. As he reached the door, he turned around. "It was great to see Paige the other night."

A smile spread across my face. "Yeah."

"She looks really good, man."

I frowned, instantly possessive, even towards my older brother. "You really don't need to notice how good she looked."

He threw back his head and laughed. "Oh, you've got it bad."

I couldn't deny it. "Yeah," I admitted.

"Don't let her go this time."

Staring straight at him with what I knew was a determined look on my face, I stated. "Not happening."

He nodded. "Good."

Thursday at noon, I met Jaxson for lunch at our favorite burger place. I arrived first and slid into a booth near the back. I asked for a coffee as I waited for him to join me. About fifteen minutes later, I saw him enter and look around. I raised a hand in greeting. He smiled, made his way over and sat down. Almost immediately, our waitress, Kelly, appeared.

"Hi, guys. The usual?" Kelly asked.

"Sure, Kelly, thanks." I responded.

She looked at Jax. "Coffee?"

"Definitely, thanks."

"Coming right up."

Glancing at Jax, I noted he looked a bit frazzled. "What's with you? Tough case?"

He sighed. "I wish. Nothing that easy. I just had a run in with my favorite defense attorney."

I laughed, asking "And how is the lovely Alyssa?"

"Lovely, my ass. The woman is a barracuda."

"Only to you, Jax. And maybe to prosecutors."

Jax nodded his thanks as Kelly put his coffee down on the table.

"Why does she have it in for me?"

I arched an eyebrow. "Do you really not remember what an asshole you were to her when we were younger?"

He scoffed, but grinned. "She needed to loosen up, man. I was just trying to help her have a little fun."

"By putting itching powder in her cheerleading uniform? By filling her car with ping pong balls?"

His grin grew wider. "Exactly."

I laughed. "You were relentless. Why didn't you just ask her out and be done with it?"

He looked at me incredulously. "Ask her out? What are

you talking about?"

"Come on, Jax. You've always had a thing for her. Why else would you go to so much trouble? And why else does she still get you all worked up?"

He shook his head. "You are fucking delusional, man. I never had a thing for her, and I certainly don't now."

"Keep telling yourself that, Jax. Maybe you'll start to believe it."

He scowled at me. "Fuck you."

I laughed as he continued to scowl. Just then, Kelly arrived with our burgers.

"Thanks, Kelly."

"Can I get you anything else?"

"I think we're good, thanks."

I took a bite of my cheeseburger. "Can I pick your brain about something?"

"Sure."

"Remember the night of the reunion when you said you thought something had happened to Paige in the past?"

"Yeah . . ."

"I think you're right. Each time we have been close to having sex, she shuts down."

"Maybe you've lost your mojo."

I gave him a look. "Seriously, man. Her body responds, but if I go to take the next step, she ends it."

"What do you mean by *the next step?*"

I frowned at him. "You want a play by play of my sex life?"

"Dude, get over yourself. You asked for my help. Spill."

I sighed. "She fine with the kissing and even touching, but only over the clothes. As soon as I make a move to reveal any . . . personal areas, she freezes."

He looked at me, concerned. "I hate to say this, Carter, but she may have been sexually assaulted."

My stomach clenched and I felt a wave of pure anger wash

over me.

"Raped?"

He nodded. "Maybe. Or at the very least sexually assaulted in some way."

"Shit."

"I can't say for certain, but the signs are there. Have you asked her?"

"I don't want to push. I am hoping she'll tell me when she's ready."

He thought for a moment. "If you want, I can pull sexual assault cases from the last few years in Chicago. Her name probably wouldn't be mentioned, because usually they aren't. And if it was never reported, there wouldn't be any record of it."

I was tempted to take him up on his offer, because I wanted to know if my instincts were accurate. I also wanted to find out everything I could to be understanding and help her through any residual effects. Deep down, though, I felt like I would be invading her privacy. I wanted her to trust me enough to open up. It was her story to tell.

I shook my head. "Thanks for the offer, but I think I should hear it from her. Any advice on how to let her know she can talk to me about it?"

"My dealings have been in an official capacity. I haven't dealt with this kind of thing from someone I know on a personal level, which I am sure changes the dynamics. The only advice I can give is to keep doing what you are doing. Build trust and don't force anything."

I took a deep breath. "It's killing me, man. The thought of anyone hurting her . . . Plus I want her so much."

"Blue balls, huh?"

"At this point, black."

He chuckled, then turned serious again. "I hope I'm wrong."

I looked him square in the eyes. "Me too, Jax."

CHAPTER TWENTY: PAIGE

Friday night, arriving home after a long week of work, I put my briefcase in my office and kicked off my shoes. It had been a busy week. Happily, Perlman had been awarded a contract for an office redo in Greenwich and another in New York City. I would be taking lead on both interior designs. In addition, Parker and I had finished the Carlson proposal and Gail had it messengered over to Hunter on Wednesday morning. Now we waited to see if we were awarded the bid. Hopefully, we would hear something soon.

Ascending the stairs, I put my shoes in the closet and undressed. Walking naked to my bathroom, I turned on the water in the soaking tub and added some bubble bath. I wound my hair into a bun on top of my head and turned on the radio. I sank down into the warm, fragrant water with a sigh. Closing my eyes, I felt myself relax. My thoughts went to Carter and our conversations over the past week. I had truly enjoyed learning more about his work and his life. I had known the boy, but it was enlightening to learn how he had matured as a man. He was invested in his work and loved his family. His relationships with his friends were important to him. He was still a NY Giants fan, poor guy, and loved the Boston Red Sox. He was sweet and impossibly sexy. His voice never failed to arouse me, and when he used endearments in his warm, masculine voice, I instantly flooded with heat.

We hadn't seen each other since dinner at Patrick and Colleen's. I missed his smile. I missed the way he held me. I missed the way he touched me. I knew that I was in a heightened state of arousal but had refrained from pleasuring myself, as it would have just made me yearn for more. The growing ache would only be satisfied with Carter himself. My defenses were slowly crumbling, but my fears were still real, though they seemed to be fading with each passing day.

As if he knew I was thinking about him, my phone rang. I put in on speaker. "Hello, Carter."

"Hi, Paige."

"Happy Friday."

"Back at you. Did you hear back on the Artisan bid?"

"Yes. We found out this afternoon that we were awarded the contract."

"That's great news. I know you were excited about that one."

"Definitely. They're redesigning their administrative offices in their building on Park Avenue. I can't wait to get in there. The budget is pretty expansive."

"You'll make it spectacular."

Appreciative of his confidence and praise, I responded "Thanks, I plan to. Did you finalize the plans for the Shivley complex?"

"I met with their VP this morning. What are you up to?"

"Currently, I am enjoying a bubble bath and decompressing after the long week."

My admission was met with silence.

"Carter?"

"Sorry, just thinking about you in a bubble bath," he said in a low rumble.

I flushed. "Carter . . ."

"Paige . . . You know what that image is doing to me? Thinking of your gorgeous body. Naked. Warm. Wet."

Immediately, my nipples tightened and I was wet in places that weren't touched by the bath water.

"Carter . . ." I breathed.

He growled. "Baby, when you say my name like that, it is such a turn on. I love to hear my name on your lips."

"You are a bad man."

He chuckled. "Not bad, just horny. And wanting you."

I wanted him too. Desperately. "I'm sorry to keep you waiting. I just—"

"Don't apologize, sweetheart. We'll make love. When you're ready."

Tears sprung to my eyes at his tenderness. What had I done to deserve this man?

"I'll see you at Grayson's clinic tomorrow?"

We were both volunteering at the animal adoption event. Grayson was a veterinarian for the counties in southern Connecticut. From what Caitlin told me, he put on this event yearly in early October. It attracted prospective adopters from all New England and placed hundreds of rescue animals in their forever homes. Being a huge animal lover and having volunteered at a shelter in Chicago, I was excited to attend.

"Yes, I'll be there before ten."

"I wish I could pick you up, but I have a meeting until eleven. I should get there about noon."

"Is your mom coming?"

"She's been saying no, but I have a feeling she'll be there. She has really missed having a dog around."

Thinking of my own loss, I murmured, "Me too."

"What?"

Trying to cover my admission, I said "I know how much she loved Kodak. Maybe she just needed some time before she was ready."

"Possibly. And as much as my dad complained about Kodak, he was just as attached as she was."

I smiled. "I know. That dog used to follow him around everywhere."

"He sure did. I hate to cut this short, but I better get my ass moving if I am going to make it to the game on time."

Carter played baseball in a league and usually had games a couple of times a week.

"I'd love to come watch you sometime."

"Anytime, Paige. We have games Tuesday and Friday next week. Tuesday is in Marlborough and Friday is in New Britain. Both at six-thirty."

"I'll check my work calendar and let you know."

"Great. Goodnight, angel. I'll see you tomorrow."

"Goodnight, Carter."

At this point, my bathwater had turned cold, so I got out of the tub and dried myself off. Slipping into a silk, floor-length nightgown, I went downstairs to make myself some dinner. After crafting a grilled cheese sandwich and heating up some soup, I wandered out to my living room. Deciding I was in the mood for a romantic comedy, I searched the TV stations until I found one. I lost myself in the movie, and by ten o'clock I was ready for bed. I fell asleep rather quickly.

It was pitch black and I was running down a long hallway. My feet were bare, and my clothes ripped and bloody. I tried every door, but they were all locked. Towards the end of the hall, I finally got lucky and the knob turned. Rushing into the room, I looked for somewhere to hide. Suddenly, I heard the door shut behind me and the click of the lock. I whipped around to see Derrick standing in front of the door with a horrible, sadistic grin on his face. I backed up and felt a jolt of fear as I noticed the long carving knife he held in his right hand. His brown eyes looked almost black and appeared soulless, like death. His short dark hair stood on end in different places. At just under six feet, he wasn't extremely tall, but he seemed to loom over me. His muscular body advanced towards me as he said, "Did you really think you could get away from me, Paige? We're nowhere near finished yet. There's so much more fun we're going to have." He reached out and grabbed me by the hair while he ripped off my bra and held the knife up to my chest. I screamed in pain as the blade slashed across my skin.

I was still screaming as I woke up, covered in sweat. The nightmares had been coming less frequently, but they still occurred about once a month or so. Forcing myself to breathe deeply and slow my heart rate, I threw off the covers and walked over to the chaise lounge in the corner of my room. The perspiration had started to evaporate, leaving me shivering. I grabbed a throw from the end of the chaise and wrapped it around myself. Knowing my subconscious was still working through the harrowing attack, I wished I didn't relive it so vividly. I sat thinking of how far I had come and how much I had healed in the past year. Derrick had physically changed me that night, but I was determined to not let him be in control of my mind. After about an hour, I forced myself back into bed, though I didn't turn out the lights.

Chapter Twenty-One: Paige

Still feeling a bit groggy from lack of sleep, I was up and out of bed at seven Saturday morning. I threw my bedding in the washing machine and changed into leggings and a long T-shirt. Grabbing my bike from the garage, I strapped on a helmet and took off for a nice, long ride to stretch out my limbs and clear my head. It was a crisp fall morning. The sun was shining and the leaves had begun to change. I headed towards Bryant Park figuring I would ride the trails. I nodded to the other bikers, walkers, and runners who were also out enjoying the day. After about an hour, I headed home.

Grabbing a bowl of cereal and switching the laundry to the dryer, I headed upstairs to shower and change. Standing in my closet in a robe, I decided on a long-sleeve lavender T-shirt and a buttery soft pair of jeans. Despite my casual attire, I selected a purple lace bra and matching lace bikinis that featured a bow on each hip. Even as a teenager, I favored pretty lingerie. I liked feeling feminine even if the rest of me wasn't dressed up. Fashioning my hair into a fishtail braid, I stepped into a pair of beige slip-on sneakers and grabbed a black cardigan sweater to ward off the morning chill. I put on minimal eyeshadow, mascara, and swiped a light pink gloss across my lips. I grabbed the clean linens from the dryer and quickly remade the bed. Forgoing my usual larger purse, I put my wallet, keys, sunglasses, and lip gloss into a smaller crossbody and headed to the garage.

Caitlin had texted me the clinic's address which I programmed into my GPS. Noting that it was about a half hour drive, I turned the radio to my favorite classic rock station and sang along. I made the final turn according to the directions and headed up a long driveway. A large, one-story building sprawled before me surrounded by at least a couple of acres of flat land. I parked towards the middle of the large parking lot and headed to the side of the building, following signs that read "Pet Adoptions This Way." As I rounded the corner, I saw about fifty volunteers working on the final stages of setting up. Numerous crates were set up in both the designated dog and cat areas. Wire pens littered the grassy area, each filled with a variety of puppies and kittens. I bent down to pet some Labrador puppies, giggling at their sweet faces and nipping mouths.

"Paige!" I recognized Caitlin's voice and turned around smiling.

"Hey, Cait," I responded giving her a hug as she reached where I stood.

"Isn't this awesome? I want to take every one of them home with me."

I laughed. "Me too. It's overwhelming. I didn't know there would be so many."

Grayson joined us. "Three hundred and eighteen, to be exact."

"Wow." I commented.

His blue eyes twinkled as he smiled. "And today we're going to find homes for each and every one of them."

Caitlin grinned and looped her arm through Grayson's. "Darn right we are."

He smiled down at her. Grayson stood about six feet tall and Caitlin was all of five foot three. They had been great friends in high school and acted like brother and sister.

"More than happy to help out, but first, where is the coffee?" I heard someone grumble from behind me.

Knowing who it was without even turning around, I said

"Hi, Lys," over my shoulder.

"Yeah, yeah. Hello. Seriously, where is the coffee?"

Grayson laughed and pointed to a table that had been set up with coffee, water, and juices along with a variety of muffins, pastries, and fruit.

She hugged Grayson saying, "Bless you," before making a beeline for the refreshments.

Aware that Alyssa did not like to rise before eleven on the weekend, I headed after her and told Grayson as I passed, "You really might want to set her up with a portable IV bag of caffeine. At least until noon."

I heard Grayson and Caitlin laugh out loud at my comment. I joined Alyssa at the table and grabbed a water. I chuckled as she made herself a cup of coffee, took a drink and sighed in pleasure.

"I'm surprised you made it."

"I said I would be here and here I am. Even at this ridiculous hour."

I looked at my watch. "It's nine-thirty, Lys. Hardly the crack of dawn."

"Close enough," she muttered.

"Ladies!" a voice boomed.

Turning around, I saw Xander, Jarrod and Jaxson approach.

Noticing Jax, Alyssa commented "Oh, great. Look who's here."

"Play nice, Lys."

"I swear one of these days, I am going to need to hire Robert to defend me for killing that man." Robert was one of the partners in Alyssa's law firm.

I choked down a laugh as I accepted greetings in the form of a kiss on the cheek from each of the guys. While she was fine accepting the same type of hello from Xander and Jarrod, she narrowed her eyes at Jax. "Don't even *think* about it."

Sparks shot from Jax's deep brown eyes. "The thought never crossed my mind. I would like to keep my balls just as they are, thanks."

Alyssa snorted. "Watch it. I've learned a lot in my self-defense class."

"Not as much as you would have learned in my class," he retorted. "If you hadn't been to chicken to see what a real teacher could show you."

Alyssa sputtered. I honestly thought I was going to have to hold her back from attacking him in some way.

"Now, kids. Let's play nice," Jarrod warned with a smirk on his face.

Luckily, Grayson chose that moment to call all the volunteers over to outline our assignments for the day. As I walked over to join the group of people, I noticed Peyton walking towards me. She gave me a quick hug and stood next to me. For the next fifteen minutes, Grayson outlined everyone's responsibilities. Along with Jarrod, I would be greeting folks, taking down their information, and directing them to the appropriate area depending on the type of pet they were looking for. A few minutes before ten, Jarrod and I sat down behind the welcome table.

"Where's Hunter?" I asked him, knowing that he wouldn't miss helping Grayson out.

"Last minute business trip to Austin. He was really bummed to miss it."

That was the last opportunity we had to talk to each other as the stream of potential adopters started arriving. For the next hour and a half, the two of us were bombarded with an onslaught of folks looking for a new pet. A little after eleven forty-five, I saw Colleen and Patrick approach.

Smiling, I greeted them. "Hi, you two. Decided to come check it out after all, huh?"

Colleen grasped my hands in greeting and Patrick leaned

down and gave me a peck on the cheek.

Looking up, Jarrod grinned. "You caved."

"We thought we would just come look," Colleen insisted.

"Right," Jarrod said, winking at his dad.

I heard a voice come from behind the Sullivans. "Mom caved, huh, Dad?" Carter asked, eyes twinkling.

Colleen turned to face him. "Carter Sullivan. I did not *cave* as you call it. We're just looking." In a bit of a huff, she put her arm through Patrick's and headed towards the dog section.

Jarrod, Carter, and I burst out laughing.

"She told you, didn't she?" Jarrod asked.

Carter smiled. "Oh yeah, put me right in my place."

"You're just lucky she didn't go all out and use your middle name too." Jarrod commented.

Carter shuddered. "Then I would've *really* been in trouble."

They both laughed. Turning to me, Carter bent down and brushed a kiss across my lips. "Hi, baby."

My body responded to his touch. "Hi," I returned softly.

Grayson approached us with a couple of people following. "You guys deserve a break. Go grab something to eat from inside. We have a table set up, buffet style, for the volunteers. Rachel and James will relieve you for the next half hour." He turned to Carter. "And you, slacker, come with me. There are some dogs that need walking. I'll set you up with a harness and some poop bags."

I reached out and touched Carter's cheek. "I'll see you later."

His eyes darkened at the touch of my hand. I could feel his gaze following me all the way until I entered the clinic, disappearing from his sight.

Chapter Twenty-two: Carter

I didn't have a chance to talk to Paige for the next three hours as I was too busy walking dogs and doing whatever else Grayson needed. I was very aware of her presence, though, as I always seemed to be if she was anywhere nearby. She would forever be the most gorgeous woman I had ever seen. Even dressed casually, her T-shirt outlined her full breasts, and her faded jeans cupped her curvy ass and thighs. With her hair in a braid and a few loose strands having escaped, her slim neck drew my attention. Almost as if she felt my gaze periodically throughout the afternoon, our eyes would lock, and I could feel the heat between us.

At three o'clock, the event ended. Grayson called all the volunteers together to thank us and let us know that two hundred sixty-five out of the three hundred eighteen animals had been adopted. It took another hour or so to clean everything up and get the remaining animals settled in the clinic. As we headed out to our cars, I wrapped my arm around Paige's shoulder, needing to touch her in some way. She leaned against me in response. Alyssa suggested we all head over to Pepé's Pizza for dinner. I wished that Paige and I hadn't driven separate cars. All I could think about was getting some alone time with her. I was going to suggest I follow her home and see if she was up for watching a movie after we ate.

"Looks like there is a new sibling in the Sullivan family," Caitlin commented.

"Yeah, how about that? Just coming to look, my ass," Xander responded.

"How they are going from an eighty-five-pound chocolate lab to a twenty-pound Corgi, I have no idea," I commented, shaking my head in disbelief.

Jarrod laughed. "Did you see Dad's face when Mom insisted that was the one?"

"Yeah, like what the hell am I going to do with this little ball of fur?" Xander chuckled.

"I think she wanted a dog that could travel with them," Paige offered.

"You may be right, but still . . ." Jarrod conceded.

Suddenly I felt Paige stop in her tracks and gasp. I looked down at her as her face drained of color. "What's the matter, Paige?"

She pointed at the side of her SUV where four long, thin scratches marred the front quarter panel. Not letting go of her, I walked over to take a closer look.

"Some idiot must have parked too close and scraped your car when they got out." Caitlin commented.

Jaxson bent down and examined the marks. "Maybe, but it almost looks like someone took a key to it."

Paige swooned. I didn't understand why she had such a severe reaction. Her skin paled, a thin bead of sweat broke out on her forehead. She looked as though she was going to faint. I picked her up in my arms and carried her over to my truck, setting her inside. Her teeth were chattering and she was shaking. I reached into the back seat of my cab and pulled out a blanket, wrapping it around her. I put my arms around her and rubbed her back in soothing strokes. I took a look at Peyton, Caitlin, and Alyssa and noted the fear in their eyes. I could understand being upset over Paige's car being vandalized, but I had the feeling something else was going on.

Jarrod pulled out his cell phone. "I'm going to call Dale and have him come pick up Paige's car and bring it to the body shop. He should be able to fix it and have it back to her early next week."

"I can drive Paige home," Peyton offered.

"I will drive Paige home," I stated.

"But . . ." Peyton started to argue.

"Really not a question, Peyton," I practically growled.

"I can drive myself home and bring the car in on Monday," Paige whispered.

"Not happening, baby. I'm taking you home and staying until you are okay," I insisted.

She looked up at me, still rattled, but some of the color had come back to her face. "I'm fine, Carter."

"Bullshit, Paige. Don't argue with me. Not now." I knew that I was coming across like a caveman, but I didn't care. All that mattered was taking care of her.

Apparently sensing the finality in my tone, she acquiesced. "Okay, thank you."

One by one, the women came over and gave Paige hugs and told her they'd call her later.

Jaxson pulled me aside as I walked around to the driver's seat. "I don't know what's going on, Carter, but I'm going to look into this in case it was deliberate. Take care of her."

"You know I will. Call me later."

He nodded. I started the truck and headed down the long driveway. I grabbed Paige's hand and stroked the back of it with my thumb. She stared out the window. I could practically hear her mind working.

"Paige, honey, what's your address?"

She looked at me blankly and then answered softly, "531 Lakeland Terrace. Avon."

I programmed the address in my GPS. I didn't want to push her to talk about what had happened or her reaction to it, but I did want to see if I could get her talking to make sure she didn't focus too much on it.

"Did you have a favorite today?"

"What?"

"Did one of the pups catch your eye?"

Refocusing on me and the question, she answered, "The German Shepherd puppy. The one with the black muzzle and the one floppy ear."

Remembering the one she was referring to, I said "Yeah, he was a cute one. Shepherds are good dogs, very loyal."

"Yes, they are. And very sweet."

I looked at her curiously. "Sweet?"

"Yes," she confirmed. "I know most people think of them as big watchdogs. They can be that, but they are also very loving."

"Really?"

"Uh-huh."

"And just how do you know this?"

She looked out the window. "I volunteered at an animal shelter for five years back in Chicago."

"Of course you did, Doolittle."

She smiled — my use of Hunter's childhood nickname must have tickled her.

"I'm still surprised you never got a dog of your own."

A shuttered look came over her. Looking out the window again, she asked softly, "I'm a little tired, Carter. I think I am going to just close my eyes for a little bit."

Not knowing why she'd suddenly shut down, I didn't want to push, so I replied. "Sure, sweetheart." I watched her eyelids flutter close and the rise and fall of her chest. I didn't know if she was faking sleep to get out of any conversation or if she was really tired. We drove the rest of the way in silence. I turned onto Lakeland and came to a security gate. I gently touched her shoulder.

"Paige?"

Her eyelids fluttered open. "Yes?"

"We're at the gate to your complex. Can you give me the

code to get in?"

"Five-six-nine-one."

I entered the numbers on the keypad, and the gates parted. I drove down the street until I came to five thirty-one. It was a two-story townhouse made out of stone and vinyl siding. I parked in the driveway in front of the one-car garage. Walking around to the passenger side of the truck, I opened her door and scooped her into my arms.

"You don't have to carry me, Carter. I'm perfectly capable of walking," she protested.

"Maybe I just want to hold you. Is that okay?"

She didn't answer, but I could feel her relax in my arms. Reaching the front door, I loosened my hold, and her body slid down mine. Locating her keys from her small purse, she unlocked the front door. As soon as I entered behind her and shut the door, she punched a code into the keypad, disarming the alarm system. Then she locked the door behind us. I followed her from the foyer to the open living room — kitchen — dining room area.

"Are you hungry?"

"A little," I admitted. "We could order out."

"I have some lasagna I made the other day. I can heat it up, if that's okay."

"Sounds great. What can I do?"

"You can cut up some cucumbers and carrots for a side salad if you'd like."

"Sure. I think I can handle that."

Paige handed me a small knife and a cutting board for me to get to work. I sliced the vegetables and put them into the two small bowls she provided. In the meantime, she cut portions of the lasagna and put them in the microwave. She then sliced some Italian bread, spreading it out on a small platter. Grabbing some spices from the cabinet, she sprinkled them over the cucumber and carrot mixture. Reaching in the refrigerator, she drizzled some balsamic vinegar on top as well.

"What do you want to drink? I have water, juice, wine, beer . . ."

Wanting to keep a clear head, I answered "Water would be good."

She grabbed a bottle for each of us, along with silverware and napkins. After setting our places at the dining room table, she started back toward the kitchen to get the meal.

"Why don't you sit down? I'll bring everything in."

"Thanks."

I made a few trips back and forth, placing our lasagna plates, salad bowls, and the bread platter on the round glass table. I bowed my head and reached for her hand. After placing her hand in mine, I said grace, thanking God for the meal and thanking God for Paige. When I opened my eyes and raised my head, I saw her eyes were shiny with unshed tears.

"Carter, I—" she began.

I interrupted her. "We don't have to talk about what happened this afternoon or what else is bothering you right now, sweetheart. We'll talk when you are ready to talk. No pressure."

"Thank you. I just . . . can't right now. I'm sorry."

I looked into her beautiful face so full of emotions. All I wanted to do was wrap her in my arms and keep her safe. Every part of me wanted to take away her worry and fix any concerns she was struggling with. Stroking the side of her face with my fingertips, I asserted, "No apologies necessary. You never have to be sorry for how you are feeling. I just want you to know that I am here for you. Whatever you need."

A single tear made its way down her cheek. As I wiped it with my thumb, she took my hand in hers and laid a gentle kiss on my palm. "What did I do to deserve you, Carter? I appreciate you so much. Thank you for making me feel safe and cared for."

"Never doubt that, angel. You know I would take on an army for you."

She smiled. "My very own Superman."

I shook my head. "I'm no Superman, Paige. Just a man who cares for you very much and would do anything to protect you. I do wish I had superpowers to make everything better and bring the light back into your eyes."

Still holding my hand in hers, she placed my palm against her cheek and closed her eyes. "No superpowers needed, Carter. You're doing just fine."

CHAPTER TWENTY-THREE: PAIGE

After dinner, Carter and I worked together to clear the table and clean up the kitchen. My initial fear at seeing the damage to my car had subsided somewhat, but I couldn't help wondering if it was just an accident. Why four scratches, the same number as on my lower body? What if Derrick had found me? The possibility chilled me to my very core. I hadn't felt warm since walking out to the clinic's parking lot. I tried to tell myself that the chance of him looking for me, never mind actually locating me, was remote.

I knew I was going to have to explain my reaction to Carter, but I couldn't bring myself to talk about it. All I wanted was for him to hold me. I needed to feel his strong arms around me and breathe him in. Just being around him soothed me. I craved his presence as I didn't want to be alone. I wanted to ask him to stay, but I didn't want to take advantage of his protective nature and come across as a tease. Aware of the attraction between us, but given my current mental state, I was not prepared to make love with him. I ached to have him inside me, but my brain was taking precedence over my body.

After loading the last plate into the dishwasher, I turned to face him. "Do you want to stay for a little while longer?"

He pulled me into his arms and held me tightly against him. "Did you honestly think I would leave you alone tonight, Paige?"

"I didn't want to assume anything. I also don't want to give you the wrong idea."

He pulled back and smiled down at me. "I always have

ideas when I am around you, sweetheart. I'd have to be dead not to. But tonight I just want to hold you in my arms and make you feel safe."

"I'd like that. A lot."

"I'm going to run out to my truck and grab my gym bag. I have a couple changes of clothes for after baseball games."

I nodded. He leaned down and kissed me on the forehead and then headed out the front door. While he was gone, I texted the girls to let them know that I was okay and that Carter was spending the night. They must've realized how upset I was, because not one of them insinuated anything sexual would happen between the two of us. I promised I would contact them the next day. A soft knock on the door announced Carter's return. I opened the door and locked it behind him before setting the alarm. I led him up the stairs to my bedroom, turning off the downstairs lights on the way.

"So, this is where all the ESPN-watching happens."

I laughed. "Not *all* the ESPN-watching, but a good part of it."

"Nice. It's very you."

I looked around at the light wood bed and dresser, the art deco-inspired nightstands, and the taupe chaise lounge. I had outfitted the bed with both European and standard pillows in shades of chocolate and pink. The plush comforter was a cream color and there was a faux mink throw on the end of the bed in shades of brown and cream.

Carter set his bag on the brass-and-linen bench at the foot of the bed.

I walked over and drew the curtains closed. Then I grabbed a baby blue silk T-shirt trimmed in lace and a pair of matching silk pajama pants from the dresser drawer.

"I'm just going to go in and change," I explained, gesturing towards the master bathroom. Nodding in response, he sat down on the edge of the bed and began taking off his shoes and socks. I entered the bathroom and shut the door behind me. Trying not to concentrate on the fact that Carter was on the other side of the door and that I was going to be sharing my bed with him, I jumped in the shower and quickly washed my body to get rid of any lingering animal odors. After putting on lotion, I washed my face, brushed my teeth, dressed and freed my hair from its braid. Normally straight, the long strands had a distinct curl as I released them. I ran a brush through them to get out any remaining snarls. The brushing diminished the curls somewhat, but soft waves framed my face. I pulled on my pajamas and swiped some Chapstick on my lips. As ready as I would ever be, I took a deep breath and opened the door.

As I stepped into the room, I saw Carter's eyes appraise me from my toes to the top of my head. His eyes darkened with desire and appreciation. I flushed with the knowledge that he liked what he saw.

"Your turn," I said. "Do you need a toothbrush?"

He patted the side of his gym bag as he approached the bathroom. "I have toiletries in here, so I'm all set."

"Fresh towels are in the linen closet."

"Got it. Thanks."

I pulled down the covers and climbed inside. I heard the shower turn on. Even in my anxious state, I found myself imagining Carter standing underneath the spray, water sluicing down his sculpted chest and powerful thighs. My body warmed, my nipples tightened, and I felt a dampness between my thighs. Did I say my mind was winning the war over my body? The scale seemed to have tipped in my body's favor. After another five minutes, the sound of the water stopped. A few minutes later, the bathroom door opened. As he entered my line of sight, I almost gasped. He wore only a loose pair of sweatpants, and my eyes devoured his muscular chest lightly covered in dark hair, his sculpted arms, and his six-pack abdomen. I had never seen a more gorgeous male body. My breath quickened.

Noting my reaction, he offered, "I can put a shirt on if you'd like."

My eyes like saucers, I replied, "Now that would be a shame."

He chuckled softly. Moving towards the bed, he placed his bag once again on the bench. He then went over and turned off the overhead light. When he made a move to turn off the small light on the table next to the chaise, I stopped him. "I leave that one on."

He nodded in compliance and got into the bed beside me. Without a word, he pulled me next to him, wrapping one arm around my shoulder and one around my waist. I laid my head on his chest. As my hand stroked the muscles of his middle, I felt his abs tighten and his heartbeat quicken. I also couldn't help noticing the covers around his waist tenting in response to my touch. Again, I was flooded with desire. I moved my hand away and placed it at my side. He reached for it and put it back where it had been.

"Don't ever think you can't touch me, Paige. Your hands on my body are the stuff that dreams are made of. I can't help my body's response to you. My cock gets hard the second we are in the same room together. I'm counting the minutes until I can bury myself inside you, but I know it's not going to be tonight. When I make love to you, it will be when you want me as much as I want you. Not when you are vulnerable and I would be taking advantage of you."

His honest, sensual words made me burn from the inside out. I wanted to argue with him, but deep down, I knew what he said made sense. I needed him tonight to feel cared for and safe. I wanted to be able to come to him with a confidence in myself and an overwhelming desire. Currently, though my body definitely yearned for his, my thoughts were still otherwise occupied.

He reached over me for the remote and tuned the television to Netflix. "I know what you need."

Closing my eyes and wrapping myself even closer to him, I whispered, "Besides your arms around me, I can't think of a single thing."

Tipping my chin up so he could brush his mouth against mine, he said "That is a given. But I can think of one other thing."

I heard the beginning notes of the Indiana Jones theme song and turned my head to look. As the opening credits for *Indiana Jones and the Last Crusade* flashed on the screen, I laughed. "My favorite movie."

He chuckled. "You always had a thing for Sean Connery."

"As every warm-blooded female alive does."

He laughed again. "Hell, I am in no way playing for the other team, but even I can admit he is one sexy guy."

He's got nothing on you, I thought. As I snuggled against Carter's hard, warm body, the events of the day faded to a distant memory. I don't even think I made it through the opening scene before I fell asleep.

Chapter Twenty-Four: Carter

I was jolted out of sleep by a loud, petrified scream. Paige was thrashing wildly in bed, pushing to get out of my arms. I quickly turned on the light and hauled her against my chest.

"Paige, wake up. It's me, Carter."

She continued to fight me. And to scream.

A little louder, I said "Paige, it's me, Carter. Wake up."

Snapping awake, she looked at me, her blue eyes dazed. "Carter?"

"Yes, baby, it's me. You were having a nightmare."

I ran my hand up and down her back in an effort to comfort her. Practically panting, she forced herself to take some deep breaths. Unable to meet my eyes, she answered, "I'm sorry. I don't usually have them so close together and since I just had one the other night . . . It was probably brought on by what happened today.

"There's nothing to be sorry for. Everyone has bad dreams sometimes. Do you want to talk about it?"

She got out of bed, shivering, and wrapped a throw blanket around herself. I started to get up and go over to her, but she stopped me by holding her hand up and shaking her head. She sat down on the chaise and took another deep breath. Looking fragile, she began talking.

"I met Derrick Walters about two years ago. His family's company hired the firm I worked for in Chicago to build their new corporate offices on the seventh floor of their downtown site. My boss, Peter, put me in charge of implementing the décor. Once the space was constructed, I met with some of the chief officers to go over their selections. Derrick was a Vice President. At thirty-five, he was being groomed by his dad to take over the business when he retired. He was good looking in a slick kind of way. After that first meeting, he called me and asked me to lunch. To discuss design ideas, he said. I had no reason to think he wanted anything else. When I showed up, he started off talking business, but it slowly morphed into him laying on the charm. I let him know I wasn't interested and thought that would be the end of it.

"I didn't hear from him for a couple of weeks, but then he started calling the firm on a regular basis, requesting constant meetings. Each time I met with him, I always made sure it was at a public place or in my office so he wouldn't get the wrong idea. I started getting more and more uncomfortable at the frequency of his calls and the inappropriate attention. I tried discussing it with Peter, but he told me that I was just being sensitive and that I should toughen up and learn to get along in a man's world. So I sucked it up and tried to deal with it as best I could.

"This went on for four months until the project was finished. To celebrate the unveiling, the company had a huge party in the new space. Towards the end of the evening, I was coming out of the women's restroom when Derrick cornered me. He grabbed me and tried to force a kiss. I could smell the alcohol on his breath. I slapped him and was able to get away. I chalked it up to him being drunk. I figured since the project was finished, I would never see him again.

"Then the flowers started arriving. Every week at both my office and my apartment. Blood red roses. At first the cards were rather benign. Bad poetry, date requests, that kind of thing, but they became increasingly desperate and almost threatening. He started showing up at different places that I frequented—my grocery store, my gym, the dry cleaners. He would call my office several times a day. I had the receptionist block both his office number and his cell phone number. I changed my personal number to an unlisted one. I instructed my doorman and the receptionist to not accept any deliveries for me. He switched tactics and started sending me cards and letters via the mail."

Paige stopped for a moment and walked over to the window, pulled back the curtain and looked outside into the night. It was taking all my will to not comment. I felt the rage bubbling up inside thinking about this asshole not knowing how to take no for an answer and for scaring her. I forced myself to sit up in bed and try to control my breathing. My hands were clenched tightly into fists, clutching the comforter.

"After dealing with Derrick's pursuit for another few months, I was becoming increasingly frightened. At this point, because I had effectively cut off all telephone conversations, he intensified the in-person run-ins. I never knew when he would show up, or where. Beyond shadowing me, he became bolder and would approach me with suggestive, lewd comments about my appearance and what he wanted to do to me."

"Asshole." I unsuccessfully tried to hold back the curses that were on the tip of my tongue. Paige smirked in my direction before continuing.

"Being a lawyer, Alyssa had been encouraging me to go to the police and file a report. I finally agreed and went down to the station. I brought all the cards from the flowers, the letters and voice-mail recordings. I also explained the stalking behavior. They told me that legally he hadn't done anything wrong. He hadn't threatened to harm me in any way. Sexually explicit correspondence wasn't against the law. I think they took pity on me, though, because they offered to pay him a visit and warn him to stop. Disappointed, but grateful for at least that, I agreed and left the station."

I made a mental note to talk to Jaxson regarding stalking

laws in Illinois. I wanted to know if the cops had mishandled the situation in any way.

"I didn't see or hear anything from Derrick for a month. I relaxed slightly, thinking that the warning from the police had done its job. Then, one Sunday afternoon, I let my dog out onto the balcony as I usually did, because he liked to look over all the action on the streets below."

Surprised, I interrupted. "I thought you said you never had a dog."

She shook her head. "Whenever you commented about it, I evaded, not ready to go into detail."

I nodded in understanding.

She smiled sadly, her eyes bright with unshed tears. "I had adopted him from the shelter and named him Landry — after the greatest coach of all time, naturally. He was a yellow lab mix and my constant companion." She shook her head of the happy memories, then continued. "After I let him out, I proceeded to clean the apartment. The balcony was safe, he couldn't fall off or anything and I had put him out there plenty of times before. After about an hour and a half, I opened the door to let him in and found him lying prone on the floor. At first, I thought he was just sleeping, but when I bent down, I noticed he wasn't breathing. I immediately picked him up, hailed a cab, and made it to the emergency vet. They tried everything they could to save him, but it was too late. He was only five years old, but I knew that sometimes there are congenital defects that haven't been diagnosed. Imagine my shock when the vet told me he had been poisoned."

I looked at her in disbelief. "Oh, baby, I'm so sorry."

She nodded in response to my utterance. "There was no evidence to prove it was Derrick, but I knew he did it. Naturally, being Chicago, there was a fire escape ladder that connected all the balconies. To realize that he probably climbed up and offered Landry some type of treat containing the poison while I was right inside scared the hell out of me. I wanted to go to the police, but I had no proof. I made plans to change apartments, but my lease wasn't up for another three months so I had to wait. But I did go down to the courthouse and filed for a restraining order.

"A week before the court hearing, Derrick's father's secretary called and requested that I come to their offices because they wanted to tweak some of the design elements. I didn't want to be anywhere near Derrick, so I discretely ascertained that he would be out of town at their Milan office when I was scheduled to visit. I arrived at their location about six thirty in the evening and signed in with the security guard. I took the elevator up to the seventh floor and made my way through the space, jotting down ideas and verifying dimensions. At about seven fifteen, I was wrapping things up and heading towards the elevator when I heard it ding announcing someone's arrival. I didn't think much of it as it was a large high-rise and thousands of employees worked there. The doors opened, and I was horrified to see Derrick standing in front of me."

Paige again sat down on the chaise. Her breathing started to quicken. She wrapped her arms around herself tightly to try to stop shaking. I again started to rise to go over to her, but she stopped me with a look.

"You don't have to continue, sweetheart. You can stop talking any time," I stressed.

I couldn't stand to see her in so much turmoil. Though I wanted to hear the whole story, her pain far outweighed my curiosity.

Her gaze locked with mine. "I want to tell you, Carter. I need to tell you." Trembling, she took a deep breath, and I could tell she was back there in that office building. "Derrick looked deranged. His eyes were almost black, and he had the most horrific grin on his face. He turned off the overhead lights, plunging the space in almost total darkness. Before I could react, he grabbed me and threw me down on the loveseat in the reception area. He told me he had enough of me playing hard to get and that he was tired of my games. I tried to fight him off, but he had about six inches in height and over sixty pounds on me. He tore my shirt and ripped the waistband of my skirt. I raised my leg to knee him in the balls, but he was too quick. He punched me in the face so hard that I almost blacked out.

"Don't ask me how, but I was able to reach a large metal bowl that was on the table next to us. I swung it down on his head with all my strength. Dazed, he loosened his grip. I made a dash for the stairs, but he was too quick. He grabbed me by the hair and dragged me down the hall to his office. I was screaming at the top of my lungs in the hope that someone would hear me. He tried to cover my mouth to muffle my screams, and I bit his hand. He punched me in the mouth and I tasted the blood.

"When we got to his office, he threw me on the couch and shut the door. Taking some tape from his pocket, he bound my hands above my head. Then, he reached into his other pocket and withdrew a large knife. I froze. He stood over me and told me that he was going to tame me. He said he was going to ruin me for any other man. I screamed over and over, pleading with him. He slapped me several times until I quieted down. Taking the knife, he cut off my clothes."

At this point, I was in such a state of rage at what she was telling me, it took superhuman strength for me to not punch a hole in wall next to me. I felt the bile rise up in my throat as a combination of anger and nausea overtook me. I wanted to hunt this shit of a human being down and kill him with my bare hands. Realizing the last thing that Paige needed to see while telling me her story was an out of control man, I forced myself to try to remain outwardly calm, though I could feel my jaw clench and the cords in my neck pull tight from the effort.

"He lowered his zipper to free his penis, which he then put in my face. I clenched my teeth shut, but he squeezed my cheeks so that I was forced to open my mouth. I gagged as he attempted to shove himself in my mouth. He let go of my cheeks, and I took the opportunity to bite down, hard. He roared back in pain and withdrew. But my action earned me a punch in the eye and then another.

"Changing tactics, he bent over me and put the knife to my chest. Slowly and painfully, he slashed my breast repeatedly. I felt the blood trickle down my abdomen. Then, he took the knife and repeated the process in the area next to my pubic bone. I cried out from the pain, which only made him smile wider. He told me no one would ever want me again. That I was his because he had branded me. Due to the pain and exhaustion, my screams had softened to cries. He kept telling me he knew how much I liked it. With a demonic look, he wiped his fingers across the cuts and licked off my blood.

"He took the knife and ran it over my body from my neck to the top of my thighs. Then he told me that he knew I wanted it rough. That he was going to do things to me that I had only dreamed of until I screamed and begged him for more. Just then, the doorknob to his office rattled. I could barely see through my swollen face, but I could make out a cleaning woman standing there. I screamed for her help and she turned around and fled down the hallway. All I could hope was that she was going to tell someone. Probably figuring that he was going to get caught, Derrick quickly pulled his clothes together. He leaned down and, holding the knife against my throat, whispered that he wasn't done with me yet. Then he fled. What seemed like hours later, the security guard and police arrived to find me naked and bleeding, almost unconscious."

Paige stood up and walked towards the window again, tears streaming down her face. I didn't care if she waved me off again, I needed to be near her. Yearning to comfort her, I got up from the bed and walked over and sat down on the chaise.

CHAPTER TWENTY-FIVE: PAIGE

Turning from the window, I saw Carter sitting on the chaise. I could see the concern on his face and the rage in his body. I sat down next to him. He pulled me into his arms, cradling me from behind.

"I spent five days in the hospital. I had a variety of cuts and bruises. My cheekbone was broken, I had two black eyes, and my face was swollen to the point that I was almost unrecognizable. Peyton, Caitlin, Alyssa and Sarah flew out and took care of me for a couple of weeks until I could get back on my feet. Derrick was arrested, but since the cleaning lady never clearly saw his face, she couldn't swear it was him. It was my word against his. I did have the evidence I had previously shown the police, but Derrick swore that what happened was consensual and just rough sex that got a bit out of hand. His father hired him an expensive team of attorneys and was able to plead him down to simple stalking and battery. He was sentenced to probation, community service, and they issued a no-contact order.

"Alyssa was outraged, but she knew since it was his first offense, the plea wasn't out of the ordinary. I was enraged as well. I knew that not only would he have raped me that night, but most likely, he would have killed me. I enrolled in self-defense classes and bought pepper spray. I filed a civil suit against both Derrick and his company and was awarded a modest judgement. After looking over my shoulder for three months after the assault, I called up Parker and asked him if the offer of a job with his uncle's company was still available.

Luckily, it was.

"I packed up my things and moved here. I used part of the civil suit money for the move and to put a down payment on this place. The rest of it was donated to sexual assault victims. I moved to a secure location. I made Parker promise that my name and photo would not be included on their website. I never told my mom and dad because I knew they would be embarrassed. It has been six months since I have had any contact with Derrick, but every day I wonder if a piece of paper can really stop him from coming after me again."

Carter held me tight against his chest and I could feel my shaking lessen and my breathing slow down. I sensed he was putting together all the puzzling events that had occurred over the past month. It would certainly be evident to him why I'd been reluctant to give him my address. My story also explained my overreaction to Jaxson grabbing my arm and my nervousness in the reunion parking lot. It also shed light on my reaction to my car being vandalized.

"I know that the chances of Derrick being behind the scratches on my car is small, but . . ."

"Jaxson is looking into it. Do you mind if I fill him in?"

Sensing my hesitation, he added, "I don't have to go into detail, but I would like to give him an overview."

"Okay," I agreed softly.

I was exhausted from the emotional unburdening, but I also felt relief at being able to share everything with Carter. He hadn't acted disgusted at what I had told him. Outraged and caring, but not disgusted. Still, I had to ask him to be sure so I turned around, crossed my legs, and faced him.

"Do you look at me differently now that you know what happened?"

With stormy gray eyes, he looked at me and shook his head. "I want to kill that son of a bitch for what he did. For putting his hands on you and cutting you. It makes me sick to think that you had to go through that. I'm pissed at not being able to protect you. I'm angry that the police didn't take it seriously enough. I'm sickened that the justice system let him off with a slap on the wrist. I hurt for the pain that you went through. I want to take away every worry and replace it with a feeling of safety. I want to wrap you in my arms and never let you go."

I smiled at words, but he didn't answer my question. "But do you find me less appealing? Are you repulsed at the thought of being with me now that you know?"

He gently took my face in his hands. "I want you to hear me when I say this. You are the most beautiful woman I have ever seen. Your sexy body was made for me. The way you respond to my touch gets me so hot. Every day I think about how I can't wait to kiss you and taste your sweet mouth. I walk around with a constant hard on at the thought of making love to you. I jack off every morning just to take the edge off, and even then it doesn't dampen my desire for you."

I wanted to believe him. "But that was before I told you, right?"

"Before, now, and always."

"What about my scars? They are ugly. Won't they remind you of what I have been through every time you see them?" I hesitantly asked.

He leaned down and gently kissed me. "Nothing about you is ugly, sweetheart. Any scars you have will only remind me of what a survivor you are and of how thankful I am that you are still alive and back in my life."

His acceptance of me—flaws and all—caused tears to stream down my face. "Are you sure?"

He kissed me again. "Positive."

Feeling emboldened by his assurance, I stood up and took off my T-shirt and pulled down my pants. Granted, it wasn't daylight in the room, but with some of the lights on, I knew he could see the scars. After a few seconds of silence, shame rushed through me and I bent to pick up my things.

Not wanting to see the disgust in his eyes, I looked down. "I told you they were ugly."

He stuck his arm out and lightly grasped my wrist to stop me from gathering up my pajamas. His breath caught. His eyes traveled up and down my body. I swear I could feel him caressing me, even though he had yet to make a move to touch me.

"You are exquisite," he said in a low, almost reverent tone.

He stood up and lifted me into his arms. Crossing the room in a few strides, he gently placed me on the bed and lay down next to me. Gently, he leaned down and kissed me behind my ear before nipping at the lobe. Kissing his way across my cheek, he nibbled on one corner of my mouth and then the other. Finally, he put his lips on mine. His tongue swept along the seam. I moaned and he gently licked the inside of my mouth. When he stroked my tongue with his, I moaned again and so did he.

For several minutes he made love to my mouth until I was quivering with need. He looked at me and whispered, "Not yet, baby. I have so much more to explore."

I whimpered, marveling at how close I was to orgasm from just his kisses.

He released my mouth and ran his tongue over my collarbone. Kissing his way to the tops of my breasts, he cupped the left one in his large hand. Gently squeezing, he plumped the already full flesh.

Mouth hovering over my nipple, he said "I've been wondering if these taste as sweet as I remember." Then his lips closed over the tightened bud.

My hips came up off the bed in response to his licking, biting and sucking.

"Mystery solved . . . they are even sweeter."

I moaned in response. His mouth left me and I cried out in protest.

He chuckled. "Relax, baby. I'm just trying to be fair." My body tensed as he cupped my right breast in his hand, knowing he was getting an up-close view of the slashes. Very gently, he slowly ran his tongue along each scar. Nerve endings that I had thought were deadened awakened in full force. He treated my right nipple to the same attention he paid to the left.

I moaned again and begged, "Carter, please."

"Soon, baby, soon." Again, I doubted I could take much more as the sensations were overwhelming. He kissed his way down my abdomen and circled my belly button with his tongue. Raising his head slightly, he whispered, "So pretty," as he gazed at my pubic hair trimmed into a thin strip. He nuzzled the curls with his nose. "You smell so fucking sweet." My body jerked at his touch and his words. He gently kissed the scars down there as well, his mouth the best balm I had ever felt.

Parting my lips with his thumbs, he licked me from top to bottom. I moaned.

"You taste so good. My fantasies didn't even come close."

I whispered his name.

"I have been dreaming about tasting you."

I looked down at him, dazed with desire. "Yes," I moaned. Rewarding me with a smile full of intent, he proceeded to do just that. He licked me up and down repeatedly before his mouth closed over my clit. My lower body thrust towards him over and over again as he alternately licked and nipped the swollen bud. My head thrashed side to side at the onslaught and I reached a peak of arousal.

"Come for me, Paige." His words opened the floodgates as my orgasm crashed over me.

Carter picked me up and carried me into the bathroom

where he took off his pants and turned on the shower. Placing me under the warm spray, he gently washed me. My body was still sensitized and, incredibly, I felt my desire start to rise again. As I moaned at his touch, he chuckled.

"I love how your body responds to me, angel, but you are almost asleep on your feet, so we will continue this another time."

Opening my eyes, I admired at his gorgeous, muscular body. Glancing down, I saw his large, erect cock. Wrapping my fingers around him, I asked, "What about you?" He tipped his head back against the tile and groaned before removing my hand. "Tonight was about you, baby, and how much I wanted to love your body."

"And while I appreciated it—immensely—how is that fair to you?"

"I'm not keeping score, Paige. And I am not taking advantage. You have been through a lot tonight and you're exhausted."

I smiled. "I'm not that tired, Carter. You had your meal. I want mine." I looked down at his erection. "Suddenly, I'm famished."

His face was taut with desire, but I could tell he was fighting it. "Paige, you told me what that asshole did to you. You don't have to . . ."

I realized he didn't want to pressure me as he thought it would trigger bad memories of Derrick trying to force himself into my mouth. I hadn't been with anyone since the attack. In fact, I hadn't been with anyone for about a year before that, either. I didn't have an extensive sexual history. I had only been with a handful of men. I enjoyed oral sex, but with Carter, I craved it. It turned me on as I thought of bringing him pleasure.

"This isn't about my past. This is about me wanting to feel you and taste you. You told me that you love how my body responds to you. I'm wondering how yours will respond to me."

With a growl, he crushed his mouth to mine. "You are making it really hard to say no."

I grinned and sunk to my knees. "Then say yes." I licked his cock from root to tip, swirled my tongue around the head, and licked off the drop of moisture that had formed.

His body jerked in response and he groaned a long, drawn out "Yessss."

I alternated between licking him up and down and drawing just the head of his erection into my mouth. Already large, he swelled with each touch of my mouth. Wanting more, I took more of his length into my mouth. Due to his size, I couldn't take all of him so I improvised by taking as much as I could and grasping the base with my hand. I sucked, nipped, and licked with pleasure as his hips started to thrust. I looked up at him, and he was watching me with blatant intensity. I gazed directly into his eyes and switched to all sucking as I used my hand to piston him in and out of my mouth.

"Oh, yeah, baby. It feels so good. You look so fucking sexy with your mouth wrapped around me."

I increased both the pressure and the pace, still not taking my gaze off of him. I had never seen a more arousing sight.

Moaning, he urged "Yes, sweetheart. Harder. Harder."

I complied and again increased the suction and the pace.

He threw his head back, the muscles in his neck straining. "Fuck, Paige. I'm gonna come."

I knew he was trying to warn me in case I wanted to release him before he shot into my mouth. Wanting to experience all of him, I keep my mouth and hand around him as he jerked and spilled himself down the back of my throat. Swallowing every drop, I used my tongue to clean him as the tremors ceased. I stood up and took the soap in my hand, washing him as he struggled to resume normal breathing. Seeing him experience such pleasure at the touch of my hands and mouth was incredibly arousing. My body was like a mass of nerve endings screaming for release.

When he brushed a kiss across my lips, my nipples scraped his hard chest and I whimpered.

"Getting me off turned you on?"

"That was the hottest thing I have ever seen. And to know that I can make you feel that way . . . let's just say that I am feeling the power of being a woman."

He grinned, running his hands across my breasts, tweaking my nipples.

I moaned in response.

"Just so you know, I don't think I have ever come that hard. Seeing you on your knees with your lips sucking my cock has been a long-standing fantasy."

"Did I live up to your expectations?"

"You crushed 'em, Paige. That sweet, sexy mouth of yours destroyed me."

"Good to know," I practically purred.

"And to know that it got you off is even sexier."

I rubbed against him, still sensitive. "I wouldn't exactly say I got off . . . yet."

His eyes darkened. "Let's see what we can do about that."

This time he was the one who got on his knees. Placing one of my legs over his shoulder, he looked at my center, wet with desire. "Damn, baby, you are practically dripping. You really did enjoy that, didn't you."

"It was incredible, Carter. The way you looked at me and the sounds you made." I shuddered.

"Glad you think so, sweetheart, since I'm all yours." With that he closed his mouth over my clit and sucked. Reaching up, he tugged on my nipples. Since I was already so close, a few minutes of the intense sensations sent me right over the edge. Again, I screamed his name as I came. He lowered my leg and wrapped his arm around my middle to help hold me up on my less than steady legs. His large hands quickly washed me again before turning off the water. He grabbed a couple of towels from the linen closet. Wrapping one around his waist, he gently dried me with the other and grabbed one of his T-shirts and slipped it over my head. After he put his sweatpants back on, we both did a quick brush of our teeth, and then he picked me up and carried me to the bed.

"You don't always have to carry me everywhere, you know."

"I love the feel of you in my arms, Paige. Any opportunity I get, they're going to be wrapped around you."

I sighed as my head touched the pillow. He pulled me close so he could spoon me. His hard chest and abdomen settled against my back. He wrapped his strong arms around me. I felt him semi-hard against my lower back and buttocks. Feeling warm and safe, I was asleep almost instantly.

CHAPTER TWENTY-SIX: CARTER

I woke up and glanced at the clock which read nine a.m. Normally, I awoke at around seven on weekends, but considering everything that had transpired last night and the fact that I was wrapped around Paige, it didn't surprise me that I'd slept in. During the night, we had switched positions so that I was on my back with one arm wrapped around her shoulder and the other on her hip. She had her head on my chest, one arm across my stomach, and one leg thrown over mine. Not being one to sleep over at a woman's house after sex, I marveled at how right this felt. But then again, this was Paige. I couldn't be in the same room with her and not want to touch her. I had come to the realization that she was the last voice I wanted to hear before I fell asleep. Now, I knew hers was also the first voice I wanted to hear in the morning.

She sighed and stroked my chest and abdomen in her sleep. Already hard, because it was morning and because Paige was wrapped around me, my cock swelled even more. Last night was incredible, but I was desperate to sink myself into her heat. I didn't know how she would be feeling about everything when she awoke, so I was determined not to ask for more than she was willing to give. I was certain that we would make love soon, but I wouldn't pressure her. Again, my dad's voice rang in my ears about letting the woman set the rules.

Paige had shocked me when she took off her clothes to show me her scars. I barely noticed them at first. I was too busy looking at her full breasts, trim waist, curvy hips, and toned legs. Her body had changed somewhat from ten years ago. Her breasts were fuller, her midsection a little longer and thinner, and her legs shapelier. Without a doubt, she was the most gorgeous woman I had ever seen. The scars were visible, but they didn't detract from her beauty. Nor did they dampen my desire for her.

She had also surprised me when she asked to suck me off in the shower. After hearing about what her attack consisted of, I had assumed that she would be averse to that particular act. I thought that maybe, over time, she might become okay with it. I had never expected her to take such enjoyment in it. I hadn't lied to her when I said I had never come that hard. Sure, other women had given me blow jobs, but it never felt that incredible. The way her sweet mouth sucked my cock while her hand stroked me blew me away, both figuratively and literally.

"Good morning," Paige said softly.

I smiled down at her. "Morning, angel. Did you sleep well?"

She smiled in return. "That is the best I have slept in a long time."

"Must be the company."

She grinned wider. "Must be." She squirmed against me a little. "Sorry, nature calls," she said and got up from the bed to walk into the bathroom. My shirt reached about mid-thigh on her and I enjoyed the sway of her shapely ass as she left the room. After a couple of minutes, she walked back towards the bed. "Stop," I commanded when she was about five feet from me.

"What?"

"You are so beautiful."

She blushed. "You're nuts. I have no make-up on and a little bit of bed head. And I'm dressed in a T-shirt."

"You are gorgeous with or without make-up. Your hair

looks like you spent the night in bed with a man and enjoyed it. And you're wearing my T-shirt, in which you look sexy as sin."

Her eyes darkened with desire and I saw her nipples pebble beneath the shirt. "The way you look at me makes me feel sexy."

"I'm glad I make you feel good, Paige, but you being sexy has nothing to do with me. It's all you."

She pulled the T-shirt over her head and stood naked before me. "And how about now? Do I still look sexy?"

She stunned me once again with her brazenness. I growled, "You look so fucking sexy I ache just looking at you."

She made her way over to the bed and climbed in beside me. "Let's see if we can ease that ache for you, Carter."

She licked the side of my neck and then sucked on a spot behind my ear. Softly pressing her lips to mine, she sucked my lower lip, drawing it into her mouth. I groaned, and she took the opportunity to insert her tongue into my mouth and tangle it with mine. Wanting to take control of the kiss and crush her underneath me, I held back, letting her set the pace. She licked a path from my chin to my shoulders.

Grasping my upper arms, she took a bite out of each one. "Have I told you that I have a thing for biceps? Yours are so big and strong." Her words and sexy voice were a huge turn-on. She sat up and took one of my hands in hers, inserting my index finger into her mouth and sucking. My cock jerked in response. "And your hands . . . they're so big, they make me feel small and delicate."

Sliding further down, she licked my pecs before murmuring, "Let's see if your nipples are as sensitive as mine." With that, she nipped at each one, then swirled her tongue to soothe the sting. My body jerked at the sensations.

She chuckled and worked her way down to my abdomen. Her hands caressed my stomach, followed by her tongue, which outlined my six-pack. "Do you know how sexy your stomach is, Carter? All that muscle definition. And the hair that covers both it and your chest. I like that you look like a man, not a boy."

Her hands toyed with the waistband of my sweatpants. She had me so worked up that I feared if she touched my cock I would come instantly. Slowly, she lowered my pants and took them off. "Even your feet are sexy, Carter," she insisted as she licked the bottom of one. Surprisingly, that sent a shockwave directly to my dick. She made her way up my legs, touching and massaging them. She gave me a little nip toward the top of my thigh. "And don't even get me started on your ass."

She started to slide back up my body without touching me where I wanted her to touch me the most, and I moaned in protest. Grinning wickedly, she looked up at me and placed her hand around my cock. "Am I forgetting something?"

I growled, "Paige . . ."

She licked her lips. "This is my favorite part of all, Carter. You know why?"

I couldn't form words to answer her, so I merely shook my head.

"This is the part that can't hide how much you want me. It's also the part that I know can fill me up like nothing else and no one else can."

Her words still impacting me, she lowered her head and closed her mouth around me. It took everything I had to stop myself from exploding as she sucked and licked me.

"Paige," I pleaded.

Eyes filled with desire, she crawled up my body and whispered in my ear. "You said I was so sexy that you ached. After touching you, I ache. I need you, Carter."

She straddled my hips and positioned her core over the head of my cock. Reason intervened through my passion and

I croaked "Condom. Gym bag."

She gave me a look and asked, "That much of a playboy, or that sure of me?"

"That desperate for you and hoping."

She grinned and grabbed a condom. After ripping the package open, she slowly rolled it over my erection, the act of which almost made me lose it. Repositioning herself, she inserted the head into her. "You're so big, and it's been so long," she panted.

I gritted my teeth as she took me inch by inch. I groaned from the sensation. "You feel incredible, baby. So fucking tight and so fucking wet."

She moaned in response. "I love how you fill me up, Carter. You feel so good."

Finally, I was all the way inside her. I looked up at her and instructed, "Ride me, baby."

"With pleasure," she breathed and started to move. She raised her hips until I almost came free of her and then slowly lowered herself back down. After a few minutes of this, my control finally broke. I sat up and took one of her nipples in her mouth, sucking furiously. At the same time, I grabbed her hips and thrust into her faster and faster.

She cried out, "Yes, Carter, yes!"

Knowing she was close, I reached down between us and rubbed her clit. Almost immediately, she came with a loud scream. Feeling her spasm around me, I thrust a few more times until my orgasm washed over me.

Spent and sweating, she collapsed on my chest. I wrapped my arms around her and rolled us both to our sides. Kissing her lips, I muttered, "You are amazing."

Her eyes closing in exhaustion, she answered, "You're not so bad yourself."

CHAPTER TWENTY-SEVEN: PAIGE

When I awoke two hours later, I was alone in bed. Disappointed, I glanced at the foot of the bed and saw Carter's gym bag still perched on the bench. Smiling, I stretched, feeling sore in places I hadn't used in quite a long time. I took a quick shower and dried my hair until it was barely damp. Putting on a minimum of make-up, I walked naked into my bedroom. I grabbed a peach colored satin and lace bra and matching boy shorts. In my closet, I slipped into black leggings and a peach tunic sweater.

As I headed downstairs, I smelled the delicious aroma of breakfast and coffee. Rounding the corner to the kitchen, I observed Carter at the stove. I took a moment to admire his muscular back and arms showcased in a dark gray T-shirt. Moving my focus downward, I practically drooled over his jean-clad tight butt and strong thighs. I could get used to the sight of him standing barefoot in my house, cooking me a meal.

"Good morning," I said softly. "Well, actually, it's probably good afternoon at this point."

He turned his head around from the stove to look at me. As he eyed me appreciatively, he greeted me with "Hello, angel."

His low, masculine voice warmed me all over. We'd just had sex a few hours ago and I was already aroused again. Would my attraction for him ever wane? I was starting to think I was making up for a two-year dry spell, but since I had never felt this way with anyone else, I knew it had nothing to do with abstinence and had everything to do with Carter. I walked over behind him and wrapped my arms around his chest.

"Everything smells delicious," I commented. Him included, I thought as I breathed in his scent. "I could get used to having my very own manservant," I teased.

He laughed. "Going to get me a little bell and everything?"

I chuckled and kissed the side of his neck. "I can think of better ways to get your attention."

His heartbeat quickened in response. Turning around so he could take me in his arms, he agreed. "I bet you could."

His gray eyes darkened as he captured my lips with his and proceeded to thoroughly kiss me. Breaking off the kiss, he put his forehead against mine. "Damn, I want you, Paige, but we're going to need food to refuel."

Mourning the loss of his lips, but knowing he was right, I grabbed the plates from the counter and served us both some scrambled eggs and home fries. "Then, let's eat." I brought our meals into the dining room, where Carter had already laid out the juice, coffee, and silverware. He followed me a few minutes later with a plate of toast.

"Everything looks great, Carter. Thank you. Do you cook often?"

"I am pretty good with breakfast and am a grilling specialist, but other than that not so much."

"I'm surprised Colleen didn't teach all of you guys to cook."

He smiled. "She enjoys it so much and we all moved out fairly soon after high school that there wasn't much an opportunity. Do you cook?"

"I can hold my own. I enjoy it, but sometimes there isn't a lot of time or I'm exhausted after a long day. Sometimes on Sundays, I make a few meals for the week and stick them in the freezer."

"Do you still make those incredible cupcakes?"

Flattered that he remembered, I nodded. "I've been known to break out the recipe for special occasions."

"Good to know."

We enjoyed our food in silence for a few moments.

"I called Jaxson this morning."

My stomach clenched as I thought about yesterday's events. "Oh?"

"I filled him in on Derrick and gave him a summary of what happened." He reached across the table and held my hand. "No details, but enough so he would know what we are dealing with."

"Thank you. Derrick's lawyers kept it quiet. I'm sure being that Jaxson is a cop, he has access to the reports. The girls know most of the details, but other than them — and you — no one else except the responding officers and the people at the hospital do." I looked out the window into my small back-yard.

"Paige?" I glanced at him. "You have nothing to be embarrassed about, sweetheart. That asshole assaulted you. He is the one who should be ashamed, not you."

I nodded slowly. "I know, but it is a rather . . . awkward conversation to have with someone. And the specifics are something I would rather not everyone know."

"I can understand that, but can you understand that the people who care about you would never judge you or look at you any differently because of what you have been through?"

With gratitude in my eyes, I squeezed his hand. "Thank you for saying that. Logically I know that, but that type of humiliation is tough to overcome."

"I think you're phenomenal. Some women might not have been able to deal with something like that."

"I don't know about phenomenal. I have come a long way, but I still have nightmares — as you know — and I still am wary about trusting new people. I also still have a problem being in the pitch dark."

"No one can expect you to not carry around some residual effects, sweetheart. In time, maybe some of those fears will fade."

"Maybe. I hope so. I think knowing that he is still out there somewhere and wondering if he is going to try to contact me again is a big obstacle in putting it all behind me. I know I can't live my life in fear, and I'm working to get stronger. I don't want to give him control over my life."

"He can only control your thoughts if you let him."

"I know. I'm working on it. Did Jax have any news?"

"He's having some officers contact people who attended the event to see if anyone saw anything. He got a copy of Derrick's driver's license photo from the Chicago P.D. to show around."

"I wish I could just chalk it up to an errant driver, but because there were four slashes just like the ones I have here," I gestured to my pelvis, "it seems too coincidental."

"The same thought occurred to me. Chances are it was just an accident, but I feel better having Jax check it out."

I nodded. "Me too, actually."

"Jarrod called this morning to let me know that your car will be ready tomorrow morning."

"That's great. I'm meeting Peyton for breakfast. She can pick me up and drive me there after we eat."

"I can drive you."

"Carter, I can't expect you to be with me every second of the day. You have a life of your own."

"You are a part of that life, Paige. Don't you think I want to take care of you and be happy to help you when you need it?"

"And I appreciate that, but I also know that part of my recovery is to be able to stand on my own two feet. I need to feel confident that I'm capable of handling things myself. I know that it's in your nature to look out for those close to you, and there are times when I will take you up on it, like yesterday afternoon. But I don't want to allow myself to rely on you too much and take it for granted."

He scowled slightly. "What is wrong with a man wanting to be there for the woman he is involved with?"

"There's nothing wrong with that, Carter, but there is also nothing wrong with that same woman being self-sufficient."

Grumbling, he countered "This situation is a little different. I'm concerned."

"If I am being honest, so am I," I admitted. "But I won't allow myself to shut down and hide. I live in a secure community with an excellent alarm system. My office is secure. When I'm out and about, I'll be extra careful and aware."

"Do you promise that you will let me know if anything out of the ordinary happens? Or if you just need some reassurance?"

"I promise."

We worked together and cleaned up the dishes from our meal. Not wanting to part ways just yet, I invited Carter to stay and watch the one o'clock game. I grabbed some waters and a bowl of fruit from the refrigerator to snack on. We settled down on the couch, side by side. Midway through the first quarter, I bit into a strawberry and felt his eyes on me. Looking right at him, I covered the remaining fruit with my mouth and sucked the juices gently before popping it into my mouth. After swallowing, I licked my lips. His eyes turned stormy.

"You're playing with fire, Paige."

I opened my eyes wide, batting my lashes. "Whatever do you mean?" I asked innocently.

Growling, he reached for me and covered my mouth with his. Plunging his tongue inside, he stroked both the inside of my mouth and my tongue. I moaned in response and thrust my fingers in his hair. Grabbing my butt, he lifted me so I was straddling his lap. Desperate to touch him, I slid my hands under his shirt and clutched at the muscles in his upper back. He reached for the bottom of my sweater and pulled it over my head.

As he cupped my breasts through my bra, he commented "You always wear the prettiest lingerie."

Dipping his head, he scraped my aching nipples with his teeth.

After unfastening my bra, he rumbled, "These are even more beautiful." Reaching behind me, he grabbed a strawberry from the bowl.

After taking a bite, he said "Not that these need to be any sweeter, but . . ." Then he lightly rubbed the juicy inside of the berry slowly on each of my nipples. My body jerked at the effect of the cool liquid.

Reaching up, he offered me the remaining half. I accepted the fruit, sucking on the tips of his fingers as he pulled them from my mouth. Groaning, he lowered his head and gently licked each bud. Lost in sensation, I threw my head back and moaned. After several minutes of liking and sucking, Carter stood me up and removed my leggings. He reached for another strawberry.

Taking a huge bite, he looked up at me and stated, "This definitely doesn't need to be any sweeter, but let's add some anyway."

With that, his eyes moved to look at my crotch which was level with his eyes. Parting the outer lips, he gently rubbed the juice first on my clit and then all the way down my center. I moaned in anticipation.

Taking the strawberry in his mouth, he closed his eyes and said, "Delicious." Putting his mouth on my core and holding on to my hips, he murmured, "but your pussy tastes so much better."

As he feasted, I could feel the beginnings of my orgasm. The sensations too much, I screamed, "Carter!" as wave after wave crashed over me.

Laying me down on the couch, he took off his clothes and rolled on a condom. "I need to be inside you, baby."

"Yes," I agreed.

Spreading my legs wide over his hips, he thrust into me. I moaned as I felt his large cock fill me. Slowly, he moved in and out. I dug my nails into his butt as he pumped, feeling the sensations start building all over again. From this angle, the friction was unreal.

"Harder, please, Carter. Harder."

"Fuck yes, baby," he groaned.

He slammed into me repeatedly. Harder and harder, increasing the pace. Crying out as I came for a second time, I felt him piston a few more times before throwing his head back and growling my name as he reached his own release. Withdrawing, he scooped me up and carried me upstairs to clean up. About an hour later, he reluctantly said goodbye.

I spent the rest of the afternoon cleaning the house, grocery shopping, and doing laundry. I called Peyton, Alyssa, Caitlin, and Sarah and assured them that I was feeling much better. I also told them about Jax's investigation, which they were happy to hear about. At nine o'clock, I settled into bed to watch the Sunday night game. When my phone buzzed, I knew who it was without even looking. Carter and I talked for a little while before saying goodnight. After only one night, my bed felt lonely without him in it.

Chapter Twenty-eight: Carter

Tuesday afternoon I met Jaxson for lunch. I wanted to see if he had any updates on the vandalism investigation. He had a meeting downtown at the capital with the governor, so we met up at an Italian place nearby. I was running a little bit late and he was already seated by the time I walked through the door. I placed an order for an eggplant sub and grabbed an ice tea from the cooler.

"Hey, man, what's up? Did the governor ask you to run for mayor again?"

Jaxson laughed. "Yep. And I turned him down. If anyone checked into my background, I'd never get elected."

I chuckled. "You weren't exactly a choir boy."

"Hey," he said acting affronted. "I *was* a choir boy, if you recall. I just used to be a little late for service sometimes because I was shooting dice in the lot behind the church."

Laughing, I asked, "Any news on who messed with Paige's car?"

He shook his head. "Nothing yet. So far no one we've talked to noticed anything unusual. And no one has remembered seeing Walters, either."

"Shit," I muttered. "I don't know whether to be relieved or worried."

"We're going to keep looking into it. I also contacted the investigating officers assigned to Paige's case in Chicago. They're sending me the file and their notes. And I called a buddy of mine in Boston, a P.I. who's going do some digging into Walters' past."

"Thanks, man. I feel better knowing you are on it."

"If that son of a bitch is behind this, we'll find out. Let's just hope he makes a mistake and we can put him away for something."

"As long as it doesn't involve him coming anywhere near Paige. Were you able to get patrolmen to drive by her house and office at regular intervals like we talked about?"

"Yep, all set. They started on Sunday afternoon."

"Great."

"How is Paige doing?"

"She's surprisingly okay. A little bit anxious, but determined not to let her fears rule her life."

"She's a strong woman to have survived everything she's been through. I was thinking that maybe she would be interested in speaking to other survivors."

"I don't know if she's ready for that yet. She's still fighting through feelings of shame."

"Shame over what? Nothing that happened to her was her fault. Sounds to me like Walters is one sadistic bastard who got off on causing her pain."

My jaw clenched. "If I could have just five minutes alone with him . . ."

"You and me, both. But you didn't hear that from me."

"The thought of him doing what he did . . . hitting her . . . cutting her . . . it makes me sick. How could that asshole still be walking around free? I wish he got locked up and somebody in jail did the same things to him, but worse."

Jax sighed. "Unfortunately, the justice system is far from perfect. Sometimes it makes me wish for the good old days when people were drawn and quartered."

"Even that would be too good for him," I complained.

"Agreed."

I stood up, gathering my trash and throwing it away. As I came back to the table, I noticed Jax checking me out.

"What the hell are you looking at?"

"Just trying to see if you're walking funny to compensate for the elephantitus."

I laughed. "Not so much of a problem anymore."

He raised an eyebrow. "Really?"

"Again, not that you need to know about my sex life, but since you're not getting any . . ."

"Fuck you."

I smiled. "She is incredible, Jax. I can't get enough of her."

He stood up and held out his hand to stop me from going any further. "On that note, I've going to go."

"Jealous much?"

"Again, fuck you. But kind of, yeah."

"You'll find the right one, Jaxson. And I can't wait to see you go through every tortuous, wonderful, all-consuming second of it.

This time, instead of him using the words, I was on the receiving end of a hand gesture.

Chapter Twenty-nine: Paige

Carter and I spoke every night before I went to sleep. Sometimes he would text me during the day, as well. He had also taken to sending me flowers every week — this week it was peonies. In his own sweet way, I think he was trying to replace my bad memories with good ones.

We hadn't seen each other since Sunday. Besides yearning for his touch, I missed seeing his smile and just being in his presence. Thursday night he gave me directions to the field where his baseball team would be playing the next night. Alyssa was joining me. She said she was interested in razzing Jaxson. Personally, I thought she was just interested in Jaxson. Carter asked me to bring an overnight bag to the game so I could spend the night at his place. Saturday, we were all heading over to Hunter's for a barbecue, and the two of us would drive over together.

I decided to take a half day on Friday. I was going to give myself a manicure and pedicure, enjoy a bubble bath, and wax any parts of me that needed a touch up. I had a little surprise for Carter as well. I asked Caitlin to meet me at noon at Underneath It All, a high-end lingerie store about fifteen minutes from my office. Being a wedding planner, Caitlin's schedule was a little more flexible during the week, though she sometimes had to work weekends if she needed to personally oversee a ceremony or reception.

I pulled up to the store at a little after noon and parked. I didn't see Caitlin outside, so I decided to go inside to wait. As I walked in the door, I spotted her sitting in one of the lavender chairs off to the side. I went over and gave her a hug.

"You look fabulous," she commented. "From the glow about you, I am assuming this shopping trip is not for a first time with Carter, but more of a wanting to make the next encounter even more exciting."

I blushed but didn't deny it. "If it was any more exciting, I would need to be hooked up to a ventilator."

Her eyes widened. "You lucky woman. Not surprising though, since the two of you needed to be separated with a fire extinguisher at the reunion."

I laughed. "Our chemistry is unbelievable, Cait. I have never experienced anything like this before. I mean, when we were younger, it was intense, but now . . ."

"Okay, stop talking or I may have to kill you in a jealous rage."

I chuckled. "He makes me feel so desirable. Even with the scars."

"If I know Carter, he doesn't think about the scars. He just notices *you*."

I nodded. "Exactly."

"One question . . . does the man look as good without clothes as he does with them?"

I visualized Carter's gorgeous, firm, muscular body. "Oh, yeah."

"You're drooling. And now I am officially an envious bitch who is outwardly ecstatic for you, but deep down so jealous that I want to go home and eat a gallon of ice cream and cry."

I put my arm around her and squeezed her shoulder. "Your time will come my friend, trust me."

"Yeah, yeah. But for now it's me and my battery-powered boyfriend. Did I tell you that I named him Steve? I figured I should scream out an actual name when I have an orgasm."

I laughed loudly. Caitlin never failed to make me smile.

As we walked further into the boutique, I commented, "I'm

bummed that you can't make it to Hunter's tomorrow."

"Yeah, me too, but duty calls. I will be glad when this one's over. I don't think I have ever had such a bridezilla for a client. Tonight, she wants me at the rehearsal dinner to make sure everything runs smoothly. She actually asked if I would personally count the number of shrimp in the appetizer to make sure everyone gets an equal portion."

"You're kidding?"

She rolled her eyes. "I wish I were. Tomorrow she'll probably want me to measure the space between the tables and chairs to make sure they are all equidistant."

I laughed. "Wow. I don't know how you have the patience."

"It is not always easy to bite my tongue, but overall the romantic in me loves my job. Where else do I get to vicariously get married a couple times a month? Plus, I also get to take notes on what I will want for my own wedding someday."

"Not to mention the opportunity to mingle with the hot male guests."

Her eyes sparkled, before she sighed. "Unfortunately, I'm usually too busy to stop and flirt with anyone, but there's always hope."

Wandering through the racks, I searched for something to catch my eye. Everything was so pretty. Admittedly, lingerie was my weakness.

"Just how slutty are we going for here?" Caitlin asked loudly.

I blushed slightly, but I was used to her lack of tact, especially in public.

"Nothing too over the top. Something that will make his eyes pop out of his head and cause some heavy breathing would be good."

She held up a mint bodysuit with lace inserts. The top consisted of a wire bra held up by satin straps. "This ought to make other things of Carter's pop out as well."

"It's perfect. I'm going to try it on in my size."

"While you do that, I'm going to look around for some things to add to my *when I have a man* stockpile."

In the dressing room, I slipped out of my clothes and stepped into the bodysuit. The bra covered all but the tops of my breasts, but the lace was so delicate and practically transparent my areolas and nipples were clearly visible. The sides were made of a firm satin in an angled cut that made my middle look trimmer. From my hip bones to my crotch was the same lace as the bra, so you could see my pubic hair. And, though, I didn't notice it earlier, there were no snap closures, as it was crotchless. My skin tingled against the material as I thought about Carter's reaction.

"Well, what's the verdict?" Caitlin asked from the other side of the dressing room door.

"It is gorgeous, though I am not going to show you. A little TMI, if you know what I mean."

She laughed. "Regrettably, you are not my type, so not necessary."

I got dressed and opened the door. Caitlin had some items in her hands. "I couldn't resist."

"And why should you? Fabulous lingerie is a perk of being female."

On our way to the register, I spotted a sky-blue bra and panty set that was covered with silk flowers. Instantly enamored, I found my size and added that to my purchases. We both paid and walked together to our cars.

With a hug, she said, "Bye, Paige. I would say have fun, but I know you are going to be having a hell of a lot more than that."

I sighed. "I sure hope so."

"Brat," she muttered jokingly. "While you are having sex with a hot man, I will be using an abacus for the shrimp."

Laughing, I waved goodbye and got into my car. I stopped at the grocery store to pick up the ingredients I needed for the cupcakes I was making to bring to Hunter's. As soon as I got home, I started baking. After I mixed the batter and put the two tins into the oven, I got to work on the icing. Being that it was mid-October, I was going with an autumnal theme. The cupcakes were an apple spice, so I chose cinnamon as the flavor for the frosting. While the cupcakes were cooling, I grabbed salad fixings and made myself lunch. I sat down at the dining room table and ate while I read the morning paper. About a half hour later, the cupcakes were cool enough to frost. Using a pastry bag, I squeezed the light brown buttercream icing in a swirl pattern on the top of each cupcake. Then I topped that off with a maple candy in the shape of a leaf. I put the finished treats in a long Tupperware container that had a handle for easy transport.

Looking at the clock, I realized it was already past three. I grabbed my purse and my purchases from the boutique and quickly ascended the stairs. After removing my current toe and fingernail polish, I painted my toes a subtle coral and my fingers a light taupe. When my fingers were dry, I headed into the bathroom. First I filled up the tub as I waxed my legs, underarms, and bikini area. Then, since I had washed my hair in the shower that morning, I put it on top of my head and got into the bubble bath. Taking special care to wash everything with a scented body wash, I then laid my head back and relaxed for a few minutes.

After the water cooled, I stepped out, dried myself off and put lotion on my body and face. Wrapping myself in a robe, I grabbed a small suitcase from my closet and packed for the next couple of days. After cutting the tags off my new bra and panty set, I added them to my bag. I then cut off the tag on the bodysuit and slipped it on. Putting on jeans and a soft, fuzzy cream-colored sweater, I slid into my slip-on sneakers.

Walking to my dresser, I brushed out my hair and left it long and loose. I put on some taupe eyeshadow, mascara, and a light coral lip tint. With one last look in the mirror, I headed downstairs just in time to get a text from Alyssa letting me know she was pulling in the driveway. I grabbed a short chocolate trench coat that I could put on to protect me from the chill in the air.

I placed my suitcase and the cupcakes in the trunk, then climbed into the passenger seat of Alyssa's white BMW convertible. She looked adorable in black jeans, a red sweater, and a varsity-style black and white jacket. Of course, being Alyssa, she had four-inch black wedges on. I had never seen her in flats. Even in high school. Her long chestnut hair was pulled back into a low ponytail.

"Thanks for picking me up, Lys."

"It's the least I can do to get you to your booty call," she winked. "Plus, how could I pass up the opportunity to watch Jaxson suck at baseball?"

"What makes you think he is going to suck? He was on the team in high school. He was their star pitcher remember?"

"Crap, I forgot. Well, I can still mess with him and break his concentration."

"What is with you two? You can't be within ten feet of each other without a war erupting."

She shook her head. "He's just so . . . infuriating. He doesn't take anything seriously, and I pretty much disagree with every word that comes out of his mouth."

I smiled. "He sure gets under your skin and seems to take great pleasure in doing so. You're not much better. You are forever needling him. How come you always rise to the bait?"

"Because he's so smug and someone needs to take him down a notch."

I looked at her. "Why don't you just sleep with him and get it over with?"

In response to my question, she almost hit the car next to her and had to swerve to get back in her own lane.

"What are you talking about? To even think about letting that man touch me is . . . well . . . it's . . ."

"Hot, right?" I smirked.

She made a gagging noise. "More like repulsive."

"Protest all you want, Lys, but the sexual tension between the two of you is off the charts."

She rolled her eyes. "I think all the sex you are having has fried your brain to even suggest something like that."

I laughed. "Oh, it's affected a lot of things, but my brain is not one of them."

"It's so good to see you happy, Paige. I'm so glad that you are being treated the way you deserve."

I grabbed her hand and squeezed. "I didn't know it could be like this, Lys. I mean, you know that I have dated since high school, but I have never felt like this. Carter makes me feel so special. And it's not just physical. I mean, I can't keep my hands off of him, but I really enjoy talking with him and spending time together."

"You're falling for him, aren't you?"

I thought for a moment before answering. "I think I was sunk the minute he asked me to dance at the reunion."

We pulled into the parking lot of the ball field. She turned to me and clapped her hands together. "Ooh, I knew it."

"Chill, Lys. Carter and I haven't really discussed anything long-term. I don't know how he feels about anything like that. I mean, I know he cares about me and I know that he desires me, but as for anything else . . . I just don't know."

"Women need the words and guys think that by showing physical attraction, we should know how they feel. Trust me, Paige, that man is in love with you."

We got out of the car and made our way to the bleachers. After climbing to the top row, we sat down just in time to see

Carter's team take the field for the third inning. As I predicted, Jaxson was pitching. Carter played second base, Hunter was in left field, Grayson was at first, and Jarrod was behind the plate as the catcher. As Carter took his position, I saw him look in our direction. Spotting me, he winked. I smiled back and gave him a little wave.

Alyssa looked between the two of us and nodded her head. "He's got it bad," she whispered in my ear.

I glanced back at Carter and saw him staring at me. My nipples tightened under his possessive, heated gaze.

"That's just lust," I whispered back.

She looked at Carter again. "Well, yes, there's that, but it's also a lot more."

Instead of being scared by the possibility, I felt an ache in my chest. In a little over a month, I already couldn't imagine being without him.

The first batter came up to the plate. Alyssa immediately stood up and started razzing Jax. He glanced in her direction and frowned. She stuck her tongue out at him. Looking on, I laughed out loud. Shaking his head, Jaxson threw his first pitch. The opposing player swung hard and connected. Everyone in the stands watched as the ball sailed over the back fence. Alyssa clapped her hands in delight and put her fingers in an L shape on her head. Jax narrowed his eyes at her and swore.

CHAPTER THIRTY: CARTER

"Shit!" Jaxson shouted.

Jarrod, Grayson and I approached the mound as the player rounded the bases.

Jarrod glanced up in the stands at Alyssa. "Having trouble focusing, Jax?"

"Fuck you," Jax responded.

"Somehow, I don't think Jarrod is the one you want to fuck," I teased.

"Screw you," he retorted.

"Again," I answered, "I don't think that I am the one you want to—"

"Knock it off!" he yelled.

I looked at Grayson and Jarrod, who were unsuccessfully trying to not look amused.

"Do we need to ask her to leave?" Grayson asked.

Looking murderous, Jaxson scowled. He held his glove out, and Jarrod put a new ball into it before Jaxson stalked back to the pitcher's mound. As we started back to our places, Grayson looked at me and muttered, "He's got it bad, huh?"

I grinned at him. "Oh yeah, he's screwed. He just doesn't know it."

I, on the other hand, was fully aware of how far gone I was over Paige. A part of me had never stopped loving her despite the years we were apart. Getting to know her again had deepened my feelings. Thinking back, I realized I knew I loved her and wanted to spend the rest of my life with her that night by the koi pond. It had been on the tip of my tongue to tell her ever since, but I didn't want to scare her off by coming on too strong, too soon. Yet every day it became increasingly hard to not let her know.

For the rest of the game, Jaxson pitched a no-hitter. In the seventh inning, he hit a home run. As he rounded third base, he took off his cap and tipped it in Alyssa's direction. I swear I saw steam coming out of her ears as he ran by. We won the game four to one. After shaking hands with our opponents, I entered the dugout and threw my glove and gear into my duffle bag. Grayson suggested going to grab a bite to eat. While I wanted to be alone with Paige, I hadn't had dinner and didn't know if she had either, so I agreed. Jaxson declined, saying he had some paperwork he had to finish up.

We all walked off the field towards the bleachers and the parking lot where Paige and Alyssa were waiting.

"Boy, that guy really smashed that home run, huh?" Alyssa commented.

"Lucky swing," Jaxson grumbled.

"Bad pitch," Alyssa countered.

Without another word, Jaxson headed off towards his car. Paige bit her lip to keep from laughing and said, "Lys, you are awful."

Alyssa shrugged her shoulders. "Evidently, he can dish it out, but can't take it. Shame."

I leaned down and gave Paige a kiss. Though brief, I savored the taste of her.

"Good game. Nice catch in the fifth."

I had caught a line drive and turned it into a double play. "Thanks."

"I suggested we all go out and get something to eat. I'm starving," Grayson offered.

"When aren't you starving, Grayson?" Alyssa asked. "I swear, you're a freak of nature. You've always eaten more than any human being I have ever known and yet you don't have an ounce of fat on you."

Looking sheepish, Grayson replied "What can I say? I've been blessed with a fast metabolism."

"I take it Jax is not joining us?" Alyssa asked looking off toward the direction he left.

I swear she looked both relieved and disappointed at the same time. "He said he had some paperwork to do," I responded.

I reached down and took Paige's hand in mine. As I stroked it with my thumb, I felt her shiver. "Cold?" I asked.

"No," she smiled. "Just . . .you."

I kissed her again. It never ceased to amaze me how responsive she was to my touch. Hell, she just had to look at me and I was ready, but it was satisfying to know that I had a similar effect on her. We walked over to Alyssa's car and I took Paige's suitcase from the trunk. As she took out another container, I inquired, "Those aren't?"

She smiled. "Yes, they are. Do I have to send them home with Alyssa to bring tomorrow, or can you be trusted not to devour them?"

I really had to think about that question. "I'll try to restrain myself. Maybe."

She narrowed her eyes at me and laughed. I threw my bag and Paige's suitcase in the back of my truck and then took the cupcakes and placed them on the back seat. Opening the front door, I helped Paige into the passenger seat, copping a bit of a feel as I did so. I climbed in the driver's side.

"Now for a proper hello," I said as I reached for her.

I kissed her like a man who hadn't seen her in the past five days. When we parted, her cheeks were flushed and her lips were moist and full.

"Well, hello to you too," she said, sounding breathy.

I caressed the side of her face, tucking some strands of her hair behind her ear. "What can I say? I missed you."

She put her hand on top of mine and leaned her face into it. "I missed you, too."

Buckling up, I reached for her hand and rested them both on her thigh.

"Where are we going?" she asked.

I wanted to say *home*. To my bed. But, forcing both my body and my dick to relax, I instead replied, "There's a great diner just down the road. We usually stop there after any games we play in this area."

"Oh, that sounds great. I love diners. My uncle Henry introduced me to the wonderful world of diners, insisting that they offered some of the best homemade food around. He was right. I love their soup and fresh baked bread."

"My favorite has always been the sandwiches. Everything tastes so fresh. Plus, you can't beat the pickles."

Her eyes sparkled. "So true."

We met Jarrod, Grayson, and Alyssa in the lobby and were seated almost immediately. The food came quickly, and as expected, was delicious. As we ate, we discussed the barbeque at Hunter's the next day, Grayson's bottomless pit of a stomach, and the upcoming Halloween party that Caitlin was helping organize for Yale New Haven hospital. After saying our goodbyes, I asked Paige if she wanted to take a walk down to Coldstone Creamery for an ice cream. She agreed. I ordered a hot fudge sundae and she got a small mint chocolate chip in a cone.

We sat down next to each other on one of the benches outside.

"Still your favorite, huh?" I asked, nodding to her cone.

"Yep. Can't beat a classic."

Fascinated, I watched her tongue lick the ice cream in long strokes. My cock hardened as I remembered how she licked me the same way. I finished my sundae in about two minutes.

"Wow, you were hungry," she commented.

Looking at her, I said softly, "I'm still hungry. And watching what your tongue is doing has me more and more famished every second."

She flushed. Then, very deliberately, she sucked the remaining ice cream into her mouth before she stood up and threw her cone away.

"Paige," I growled.

"Suddenly, I'm famished too."

I stood up and hauled her body against mine. Not caring who could see us, I devoured her mouth. I tasted the mint and chocolate as I thrust my tongue inside, using it to show her exactly what I wanted to do to her body. She whimpered and returned the kiss with equal fervor, wrapping her fingers in my hair. Reluctantly, I pulled away. My dick was like steel, and wearing a protective cup was getting uncomfortable. After walking back to the diner, I got Paige settled in the front seat and excused myself to use the restroom. After taking off the plastic cup, I felt better, though I was still painfully hard.

CHAPTER THIRTY-ONE: CARTER

As I pulled out of the parking lot, Paige put her hand on my thigh. My cock visibly twitched inside my baseball uniform.

Placing her hand on me, she asked, "Why, Carter. Is that your cup, or are you just happy to see me?"

Putting my hand over hers to stop her exploring fingers, I gritted, "No cup. I had to take that off back at the diner. My cock was going to burst through it."

She smiled and reached her hand underneath the waist-band of my pants then freed me through the front opening in my boxer briefs.

"Fuck, Paige!" I exclaimed as she stroked and squeezed me.

"Yes, you'll definitely get to do that later." She smiled. "But right now, like I told you, I'm famished."

She lowered her head to my lap and took my cock in her mouth. The sensation of her mouth cooled by the ice cream was unbelievable. I struggled to not run off the road. Spotting a school about a hundred yards up ahead, I managed to pull into the back parking lot and put the truck in park. Lifting her head slightly, she looked up at me with blue eyes darkened with desire.

"Problem, Carter?"

Panting, I swore. "Damn, sweetheart. You really expected me to keep driving with your mouth on me? I can barely see straight, much less drive."

"Poor baby. I didn't mean to distract you."

I emitted something between a chuckle and a groan.

She licked her lips and reached over me to put the seat back. "Now, where was I?"

Lowering her head back in my lap, she closed her lips over me again. Talking as much of me as she could, she pulled her mouth back, lightly scraping her teeth on the head as she retreated. My hips jerked in response.

"A little sensitive there, are you?"

She repeated the same thing several more times until I was sweating and on the verge. Sensing I was close, she put her mouth over the top half of my cock and sucked. My lower body thrust in and out of her, faster and faster as she applied more and more suction. Crying out her name, I came with a vengeance, shooting stream after stream into her mouth. As I struggled to regain normal breathing, she used her tongue to clean me off. After placing me back inside my underwear and pulling up the waistband of my pants, she gave me a huge smile and gently kissed my lips. I tasted myself on her.

Sitting back in her seat, she looked at me and said, "Thank you."

I adjusted my seat so that I was no longer laying back. "I believe I should be the one thanking *you*."

She laughed softly. "Thank you for letting me taste you. Thank you for being so incredibly sexy. And thank you for turning me on. Do you know how hot doing that to you makes me?"

My cock twitched, already coming back to life. I reached over and placed my hand over her mound. I could feel her heat through her jeans. Moaning, she took my hand and placed it in my lap.

"Uh-uh, Carter. When I come, it's going to be with you inside me."

At that, I started the car and got us to my house at warp speed. As we pulled in the driveway, she said, "It's beautiful."

I had bought a two-story craftsman a couple of years ago. My dad, Jarrod, Xander and I pretty much gutted it and rebuilt it, creating a modern open feel, but staying true to the style of the house and incorporating period details. After gathering our items from the backseat, I led Paige to the front door, unlocking it to show her inside.

"Oh my gosh, Carter. It's even more amazing inside."

The first floor consisted of a living room, dining room, office, half-bath, kitchen, and family room. There were moldings and built-ins throughout, staying true to the craftsman style. Setting our bags down in the living room by the stairs, I took her hand and walked her back to the kitchen. She put the cupcakes in the refrigerator. On our way back through the house, I watched her as she took everything in with her designer's eyes. She reached out and ran her hand along the various moldings. I picked up my duffle and her suitcase and led her up the stairs.

The second floor had four bedrooms and two bathrooms. Even though I was desperate to make love to her, seeing her appreciation for the house, I couldn't deny giving her a tour. Finally, we reached the master bedroom, which held my king bed, two nightstands and a large dresser with a mirror over it. There was a built-in window seat and a working fireplace with two large chairs in front of it. I placed her suitcase on the window seat. The large window faced the backyard, and I had no neighbors behind me, so I left the window without curtains. I liked the natural light. I threw my duffle in the walk-in closet and headed for the master bathroom.

"I'm just going to clean up a little," I said to her.

"Okay." She nodded. "I'll be here."

I entered the bathroom and closed the door behind me. Pulling off my uniform, I threw it in the hamper. I turned the shower on and stepped in, letting the spray from the dual shower heads wash over me. I soaped up my body and washed my hair, rinsing it off using the overhead rain shower. I towel-dried my hair, then brushed my teeth and pulled on a fresh pair of boxer-briefs.

Apparently, Paige had been busy during my time in the bathroom. A handful of candles bathed the room in a soft glow. As I walked further inside, I spotted Paige in the middle of my bed. I felt like the wind got knocked out of me as I saw her lying on her side facing me, her long hair spread out on the pillows. She was dressed in some kind of bodysuit that looked like it was made out of lace and silk. The top cupped the lower half of her breasts, but the plump tops spilled over. The mid-section hugged her torso, accentuating her trim waist and curvy hips. The very bottom was also lace, and I could see the shadow of her dark pubic hair.

"Do you like it? I bought it today. For you."

Forcing myself to breathe, I walked closer to the bed. "You are so damn beautiful."

She smiled. "Glad you like it."

"Like is not a strong enough word. It is almost as exquisite as you."

She sat up on her knees and ran her hands over my arms, chest and abs. My dick was so hard, it was standing straight out and up, the head poking out of the waistband of my underwear. She pulled my briefs off and I kicked out of them.

"You shouldn't have bothered getting dressed."

"I didn't want to be presumptuous."

Looking into my eyes and running her hands up and down my back, she said "Let me tell you something, Carter. With you, I am pretty much a sure thing."

I chuckled softly. "Thank gosh."

Tilting her head back by gently grabbing her hair, I licked the column of her throat before nipping behind her ear and then sucking on her earlobe. As she sighed, I moved my mouth to her lips where I outlined them with my tongue and then traced the seam. Gently, I sucked on first her top lip and then her bottom lip. When I released her mouth, she moaned in protest. I settled my mouth back over hers and used my tongue to stroke every inch of her mouth before moving on to do the same to her tongue.

We kissed for several minutes before she started whimpering. I sunk down to the floor and covered her breasts with my hands. Up close, I noticed that the lace covering them was so transparent I could see her nipples. Pushing her breasts together, I bit both tight buds and then licked them with my tongue. Her body jerked in response. I then sucked on each rosy, erect point.

Moaning, she breathed, "That feels so good, Carter."

I licked each one again through the lace. "Your nipples are so sensitive. Do you like it when I suck them, baby? Does it make you wet?"

She looked down at me, her eyes glazed with desire. "Everything you do me makes me wet, Carter."

I growled at her honesty. "Let's make you wetter."

"I don't think that's possible," she breathed.

Chuckling, I moved my eyes downward so they were level with the juncture of her thighs. Again, here the lace was practically transparent. I traced my tongue over her pubic hair, which made her whimper in response.

"Open for me, angel."

As soon as she spread her legs, I realized that the bodysuit was crotchless. I stared at her plump lips, glistening with her juices and almost came.

"Were you wearing this the whole night?" I asked her.

She looked down at me and smiled. "Yes."

"You mean to tell me that your pussy was naked the whole time?"

"Yes."

"Damn, Paige." I traced her with my fingers. "Can I put my fingers inside you, baby? Can I put them deep inside you and feel how hot and wet you are for me?"

She whimpered and begged, "Please, Carter."

"Please what, angel."

She panted. "Please, Carter. I want you to touch me so badly, I can't stand it."

"Lay back on the bed, sweetheart."

She settled down on her back. I lifted her legs over my shoulders which spread her wide open. Taking one finger, I touched her from top to bottom. Her hips lifted. Dipping one finger inside, I groaned at her warm, moist heat.

"You're always so wet for me."

She moaned and her hips moved towards me, begging for me to continue. I took my finger out and rubbed her juices on her clit. She cried out. Replacing my finger with my mouth, I drew the engorged bud into my mouth, sucking gently. Her soft moans filled the room as I inserted two fingers inside her while continuing to suck. I slowly pumped in and out of her, reaching up inside to find just the right spot. Her hips thrust up and down, searching for release. With a piercing cry, she came. I kept my fingers inside her to feel the spasms. Gently, I took her legs off my shoulders and withdrew my fingers. Looking into her face, I made sure she watched as I inserted them into my mouth and sucked off the juices.

"You have the sweetest tasting pussy. I could eat you all day."

I saw a tremor move through her at my words.

"I need you inside me, Carter."

"I need to be inside you too, Paige. I can't wait any longer."

As I got off the bed, she whimpered in protest, reaching for me.

"Don't worry. I'm not going anywhere, baby."

I picked her up in my arms and set her down in front of my

dresser. Placing her hands flat on the top of it, I bent her over and positioned myself behind her.

Taking the condom from my hand, I started to open it. Her eyes caught mine in the mirror. "I want to feel you inside me, Carter, all of you."

My breath caught. "Paige?"

"I'm on the pill. I haven't been with anyone in two years. I had a check-up just before I moved back, and I'm clean."

"It has been awhile for me too. I get tested every six months. And I always use protection."

"I always have too, but I don't want to with you. Please, Carter. I need to feel you."

Almost delirious with the thought that there would be no barrier between my cock and Paige's warm, wet heat, I held the head of my dick at her entrance. She was so wet that I slid right in, her body expanding to accommodate me. Every nerve ending was on fire as I felt her grip me. I forced myself to take a minute before things ended before we even got started.

Catching my eyes in the mirror in front of us, she pleaded. "Fuck me, Carter."

Undone by her words and the feel of her, I started to move. Slowly, I sank myself into her, retreated almost to the point of withdrawing completely, and then slid back in. Her eyes closed and she threw her head back, moving her hips in perfect sync with mine.

"Open your eyes, baby. Look at us."

Her eyes opened and she watched as I held her hips in my hands and fucked her from behind. The muscles in my arms, chest, and abdomen pulled tight with every move. I took one of my hands from her hips and reached around, cupped her breast, and tweaked her nipple. She cried out and her eyes started to flutter closed in response to the sensations.

I withdrew and her eyes sprung open. "Whatever you do,

Paige. Whatever I do to you, don't stop looking in that mirror."

She bit her lip, her arms tense as she leaned over the dresser. Taking both of her breasts in my hands, I pulled and pinched her erect nipples once more.

"I can't take much more, Carter."

Removing my hands from her breasts, I once again held onto her hips. "Look how sexy you are, baby. Your nipples are practically poking through the lace and your pussy is dripping. I'll make your ache go away, sweetheart."

"Oh, Carter, please. Fuck me. Fuck me hard. I need to come."

I pushed my cock back inside her. Over and over, I slammed in and out. Every move harder and faster.

"You're mine, Paige." I growled. "You'll always be mine."

"Yes, Carter, yes. Yours."

The sound of our bodies slapping against each other filled the room, along with her cries and my groans.

"I'm gonna come, baby. Let me feel you explode around me."

As the last of my words left my mouth, her orgasm hit. I watched her face as the sensations registered and she screamed my name in ecstasy. It was the hottest thing I had ever seen. Seconds later, I came with such force I practically saw stars. I yelled her name as she watched me in the mirror. Slowly, I withdrew. Noting her shaky legs, I picked her up and carried her to the shower.

Chapter Thirty-two: Paige

After the most intense sexual experience of my life, I was surprised I was able to stand up in the shower. As I leaned against Carter enjoying the feel of the warm water coming from the dual jets, he thoroughly washed both our bodies. Stepping out the shower, he turned off the water and wrapped me in a towel. After putting a towel around his waist, he left the bathroom, returning with my toiletry bag. We both finished drying ourselves off and brushed our teeth. Leading me by the hand, he walked over to the dresser and grabbed a pair of drawstring pajama pants and slipped them on. Taking a T-shirt from another drawer, he slipped it over my head. I went over to my suitcase and took out a pair of underwear and slid them up my legs. I heard him moving around the room, blowing out the candles. When I turned around, he was lying down in bed and pulled back the covers so I could slide in next to him. He pulled me close to him, his hard chest against my back and his arm around my waist. I glanced at the moonlight streaming through the window. The last thing I remember was Carter kissing me softly on the side of face and whispering goodnight.

I woke up to sunlight streaming through the window. Glancing at the clock, which read nine a.m., I slid out of bed trying not to wake Carter. Walking into the bathroom, I used the toilet. Last night I had been so out of it, I didn't fully appreciate the luxurious, spa-like space. The walls were painted a soft taupe. A large clawfoot tub sat beneath a picture window. There was a huge tiled shower with body sprays on either side and an overhead rain shower. Floating vanities held large glass bowls with faucets coming out from the wall behind them. The tiled floor below my feet was warm, which made me assume that radiant heat was installed.

I took my bodysuit from the hook behind the door where Carter must have hung it after undressing me prior to putting me in the shower. Glancing in the mirror, I grimaced at my reflection. My hair was wild, sticking up in different directions, and my eye makeup had smudged so that I looked decidedly raccoon-like. After running a brush through my hair, I washed my face and brushed my teeth. I put on a dab of mascara and some lip balm. Quietly, I crossed the room to put my bodysuit in my suitcase. Before I could stand up, I heard Carter's low voice behind me.

"Good morning, angel."

Standing up and turning around, I admired him from across the room. My gaze traveled from his thick, disheveled hair to his gray eyes to his square jaw covered with stubble. He was sitting up against the headboard, and the sheets had fallen down to his waist. My mouth watered as I looked at his strong arms and his broad, muscular chest and tightly muscled abdomen lightly covered with hair.

"If I didn't already have a hard on this morning, I certainly would now with the way you are looking at me."

I flushed at being caught but didn't deny it. "What can I say, you are one good-looking man."

"Glad you think so, sweetheart." He got up from the bed. As he was walking away, he said over his shoulder, "Feel free to admire me some more after I get back from the bathroom."

I grinned at his comment while admiring his muscular back and his tight rear end. I sat down on the window seat and looked out over the backyard. Carter must have inherited Colleen's green thumb, because his lawn was lush and green, bordered by bushes, flowering shrubs, and groundcover.

Hearing the bathroom door open, I turned to face him. Walking up to stand before me, he pulled me up against him and tipped my head up to brush his lips across mine. Leaning into him, I gladly deepened the kiss. Taking his lips from mine, he pulled me closer. I rested my head on his chest and breathed him in.

"Hungry?"

My stomached rumbled in response.

Laughing, he said "I guess that answers that question. Let's see what we can put together for breakfast."

I reached into my suitcase for a pair of leggings. He stopped me with "You don't need them. I like you in just my shirt. It's sexy as hell."

Smiling, I put the leggings back into my bag. Taking ahold of my hand, he led me down the stairs to the kitchen. Working together, we made spinach, tomato, ham, cheese and green pepper omelets. Orange juice and rye toast completed the meal. Bringing everything to the dining room, we sat down to eat.

Looking around, I commented, "Can I tell you again how much I love your house?"

"Thanks. I considered building new, but I saw this and like the potential. Dad, Jarrod, Xander and I gutted it and rebuilt it. I tried to pay homage to the craftsman style and era of the house itself."

"You did a fabulous job. The period details add so much character."

"Thanks, I think so too. I'm thinking of re-doing the front porch. Maybe you can take a look and give me some design ideas."

Warmed that he wanted my input, I teased, "It's going to cost you."

His eyes darkened with desire. "I can think of a lot of ways to pay you."

Heat flooded me. "I'm sure I can think of something."

"I look forward to it."

Just then Carter's cell phone rang.

"It's Jarrod."

I nodded. While he talked, I started cleaning up the dishes. I was just finishing washing the last pan, when he came up and wrapped his arms around me from behind.

"Did you and Jarrod have some kind of signal so that he would call and talk to you for exactly the amount of time it took me to clean everything up?"

I felt his rumble of laughter in his chest. "How did you know?"

"I've got your number, Carter."

"Damn right you do," he whispered in my ear. I shivered at both his words and his low, sexy tone.

Stepping out of his hold, I wandered over to the French doors leading out to the backyard. I looked to the left and noticed a hot tub surrounded by wood privacy screens.

"You have a hot tub."

"It's an awesome way to relax after a long day at work, especially if I've been hands-on at one of the sites."

My mind was filled with images of Carter's naked body sinking down into the hot, bubbly water.

"Want to check it out?" he asked.

"As tempting as that sounds, I didn't bring a suit."

"You won't need a suit," he commented suggestively.

"It's broad daylight, Carter."

"I believe I mentioned last night that I don't have any neighbors behind me. Plus, the privacy screens block what anyone might see."

Sensing I was still hesitant, he grasped my hand and led me onto the patio. Flipping a switch, he turned on the power and took off the hot tub cover. Somewhat turned on at the thought of being naked outside in the middle of the morning,

I twisted my hair into a loose bun and pulled off my under-wear. Carter's T-shirt covered me to mid-thigh so I wasn't re-vealing anything, but Carter's eyes darkened and I saw his erection tent his pajama pants. Standing on my tiptoes to kiss him, I brushed my lips against his. Groaning, he opened his mouth to let my tongue stroke against his. I put my hands down the back of his pants and squeezed his firm butt, rub-bing myself against him. When he tried to pull me closer, I retreated.

Pulling my T-shirt over my head, I stood naked in front of him for a minute before climbing into the hot tub and sinking down into the hot, rolling water. My nerve endings seemed super-sensitive. Rising out of the water slightly, I felt my nip-ples pebble as they were exposed to the cool, autumn air. Star-ing into his eyes, I cupped my full breasts in my hands before running my fingers around my areolas and then tugging on my hard, tight nipples. Breathing heavily, Carter pulled his pants down around his hips and took his large erection in his hand. As I touched myself, he started stroking himself in re-sponse. I watched as his cock swelled even more.

Excited by watching him masturbate right in front of me, I sat up further in the water, so that I was only submerged from mid-thigh down. Sliding my hands down my torso, I parted my core and ran my fingers over my lips before plunging a finger inside my wet heat. Withdrawing my finger, I brought it to my mouth and sucked on it, twirling my tongue around the tip. Carter groaned and increased the pace of his fist pumping up and down on his cock. Completely turned on, I slid my hand down again and started rubbing my clit vigor-ously. Locking eyes with Carter, I moaned in pleasure.

In two steps, he joined me in the hot tub. He sat down on the bench that went around the entire perimeter of the hot tub. He positioned me so that I my thighs straddled his hips. Plunging himself into me, he growled, "Do you have any idea how fucking sexy you looked? Your skin all flushed from the heat and your body wet? Touching yourself?"

I ground against him, begging him with my body to move. "Do you have any idea how hot you looked, stroking your huge cock with your hand, growing bigger and bigger as you watched me? All I was thinking when I was touching myself was how much I wanted you inside me."

Groaning, he dug his fingers into my hips and started thrusting into me. I arched my back and cupped my breasts in my hands. Growling, Carter alternately sucked on my nipples while he pumped in and out of me. The sensations were intense. My hips slammed up and down as I rode him, loving the feel of his cock filling me up. Placing my hands on his shoulders, I increased my pace.

"Oh yeah, baby. Faster. That's right, ride my cock."

I threw my head back and screamed his name, "Carter!" as I exploded around him. Seconds later, I heard him yell, "Paige!" and felt him spurt inside me, my core clenching in spasm as he emptied himself. As I collapsed against his chest, he captured my mouth, thrusting his tongue in my mouth mimicking how he had just thrust into my body. As he ended the kiss, I licked the side of his neck, tasting the salty sweat. He tightened his arms around me. Pulling his head back, he looked into my eyes.

"You are incredible. I can't get enough of you."

I kissed him softly. "It's never been like this for me before. The way that you look at me makes me feel so desired." I ran my hands over his arms, chest, and abs. "And when I look at you, I see the sexiest man I have ever seen."

Putting his hands on the side of my face, he stated, "I have never wanted anyone like I want you. Your body was made for me, Paige." He smiled. "And I am glad that you like what you see when you look at me. If I have anything to say about it, you're going to be looking at me—and only me—for quite a long time."

His possessive tone warmed me. "I like that idea, but only if it goes both ways. I don't share."

His gray eyes darkened. "There's no one else for me, angel. I've been yours since the first moment I saw you. No one else can compare."

I kissed him again, then laid my head on his shoulder. Wrapping his strong arms around my back, he held me close. Several minutes later, I reluctantly climbed off his lap. Climbing out the water, I slipped back into his T-shirt and my panties.

"I'm going inside to take a shower."

He made a move to stand up and follow me in, but I held up my hand to stop him.

"No, no. I am going alone. If you join me, we will never make it to the barbeque."

Smiling wickedly, he agreed. "You're probably right. I'll stay here and clean out the hot tub before taking my turn in the shower."

Taking one final look at his gorgeous torso and face, I headed inside to clean up.

CHAPTER THIRTY-THREE: CARTER

After cleaning out the hot tub and putting the cover back on, I headed inside. Trying not to think about Paige upstairs naked in my shower, I went into my office to do some work. After replying to some e-mails and reading over some contracts, I added this week's appointments to my calendar then leaned back in my chair.

When I had told Paige that she was it for me, I meant it. Sexually, I was insatiable for her, but it went much deeper than that. Every day, I looked forward to talking to her and hearing about her day. I was so proud of the things she had accomplished and shared in her excitement about her work. Being on the receiving end of her smile and seeing her face light up when she saw me made me feel like Superman. When she said that she wasn't going to share me, I had a hard time not laughing — as if there was anyone else I would even consider being with.

My cell phone rang. "Hey, Dad."

"Carter. How are you this fine day?"

Smiling, I answered, "I'm great."

"Good to hear. That wouldn't have anything to do with a certain beautiful woman would it?"

"She certainly has a lot to do with it, yes."

He chuckled. "Smart man. Paige is good for you. I have never seen you this happy."

"She is more than I deserve. I've never felt this way before."

"Don't let her go, son. When you were younger and she

went away, I know how hard that was, but now . . ."

"Don't worry, Dad. I have no intention of ever letting her go again."

"We Sullivan men fall hard and fast. It was just like that for me when I met your mother. I told her on our first date that I was going to marry her. Of course, she thought I was crazy."

Laughing, I responded, "I remember you telling us the story of how you met. And that you asked her to marry you every day for six months until she finally said yes."

"Damn stubborn woman. She kept saying it was too soon. Like there's a minimum time requirement. When you know, you know." He cleared his throat. "Hey, do you mind if I come by later this afternoon to take some measurements for the front porch remodel?"

"No, that's fine. Paige and I are headed over to Hunter's for a cookout, but we should be back about eight or so."

"I'll probably swing by around five-thirty. Would you mind if I put some proposals in your office, too? Jack Lawrence contacted me about the plans for his new house."

"No problem. You have a key."

"Great. Sorry to miss seeing you both. Why don't you bring Paige to dinner tomorrow night? I know your mom would love it."

"I'll ask her and let you know."

"Okay. Bye, son."

"Bye, Dad. I'll see you tomorrow."

Hearing how much my parents adored Paige made me feel good. And my dad was right, when you know you know.

Figuring I had given Paige enough time to shower and dress, I headed upstairs to clean myself up. When I walked into the bedroom, Paige was just slipping into her shoes. She looked gorgeous in dark jeans, a red V-neck top and matching sweater. The jeans outlined her curvy hips and ass and the top molded to her breasts. Her long hair was in a high ponytail and hoop earrings drew attention to her slim neck. Looking up, she saw me and smiled.

Admiring her, I stated, "You look beautiful."

"Thank you." I saw her eyes look over my chest hungrily. "You look yummy."

My body responded to her appreciative perusal. "If you want to make it to Hunter's on time, you need to stop looking at me like that."

Laughing, she picked up her small purse and scooted past me and down the stairs.

After showering, shaving, and putting on cologne, I put on jeans, a long-sleeved T-shirt and a lined flannel shirt. Grabbing my boots, I headed downstairs.

I found Paige in the family room watching ESPN. Her eyes were animated as she watched *NFL Weekly*. For as long as I had known her, football was her passion. She could talk about the sport with more knowledge than most men. Observing and listening to her as she sat forward on the couch and openly argued with the commentators made me smile.

The next words came out of my mouth naturally.

"I love you, Paige."

Whipping her head around to look at me, she stood up and asked, "What?"

"I said I love you," I repeated.

Looking stunned, she opened and closed her mouth. I could see her chest rise and fall as she struggled to breathe normally.

Unable to read her eyes, I continued, "I know you might be thinking it's too soon for me to say that. Or that it's just lust. You'd be wrong on both counts. I started loving you when I was twelve years old. When you left, you took a huge part of my heart with you. When you came back into my life at our reunion, you brought it back. Every day since then, what I feel for you has grown stronger every day. I know that I was in love with you when we were younger, but that pales in comparison to how I feel now. I've told you that your body was made for me—and it was—but, more importantly, *you* were made for me."

Her eyes were bright, and I saw a few tears slide down her cheeks. I walked over to stand in front of her. I reached out and wiped away the drops, noticing that my fingers were trembling slightly. Though I'd told her how I felt because *I* needed to, I was surprised at how much I wanted her to respond in kind.

She raised her hand and put her palm to my cheek. "I love you too, Carter."

CHAPTER THIRTY-FOUR: PAIGE

I was rewarded with a huge smile. Leaning forward, Carter wrapped me in his arms and kissed me slowly, sweetly, and thoroughly. When we parted, I brushed the hair back from his forehead and hugged him, running my hands up and down his back.

"I do love you, Carter," I said softly, my cheek against his chest.

He pulled back slightly and gave me another kiss. "Thank gosh," he breathed.

"Did you doubt it?"

He took a deep breath. "I wasn't sure if you had come to the realization yet. Every time you look at me or you touch me, I believed it to be true, but I still wanted to hear you say it."

"Last night you said I was yours. Since the first time I saw you, I've always belonged to you. Even when we were apart. No one even came close to making me feel the way I did when I was with you. When I saw you again, it just felt right. These past weeks, I have felt so special. I can't wait to talk to you at the end of the day. The way you look at me . . . it's like you're not afraid to show everyone how much I mean to you. And the way you accepted my past, looked at my physical scars and still made me feel desired means so much. You make me feel so beautiful."

"You are beautiful, sweetheart. Inside and out. You are the most beautiful woman I have ever seen. Do you know how lucky I feel to have you in my life? That I got a second chance?

Did you know that I was looking for you at our five-year reunion?"

I nodded. "Jax told me when we were dancing, but I don't know if I completely believed him."

"Well, it's true. I also told Jax on our way to the reunion that if you weren't there, I was going to find you."

My eyes grew wide at his admission. "Really?"

"Yes, really. I knew I didn't want to live without you. I needed you back. I missed you like crazy."

My heart full, I kissed him. "Oh, Carter, I missed you too. So much."

Picking me up in his arms, he sat down on the couch and put me in his lap. Turning my head to face him, I lifted my chin so he could kiss me again. My whole body warmed as he treated me to a slow, seductive onslaught of his mouth and tongue. I could've kissed him all day, enveloped in his embrace. Eventually, reluctantly, we parted. He grasped my hand and pulled me to my feet.

"If we don't stop now, we are not leaving this house for the rest of the day, never mind making it to Hunter's," he declared.

I chuckled and nodded. "You're right. Not that it isn't tempting . . ."

Groaning and reaching for me again, he said, "On second thought . . ."

I laughed and led him into the kitchen. We took the cupcakes out of the refrigerator and headed out. Bypassing his truck in the driveway, we headed for the detached two-car garage. He punched in a code and the right-hand bay opened to reveal a 1965 blue mustang convertible. I looked at it and then back at him.

"You finished it."

He nodded, pride in his eyes. "My dad and I worked on it for a few years together. Didn't she turn out great?"

Approaching the car, I admitted, "She's spectacular."

"Want to drive?"

I practically jumped up and down. "Uh, yes!"

He laughed and tossed me the keys. Setting the cupcakes in the back, we headed out. We stopped at a grocery store a few blocks from his house to pick up beer and the fixings for s'mores. Carter provided directions as I drove the half hour to Hunter's. The car drove like a dream. Carter kept his hand on my thigh the entire ride as we talked and enjoyed the feel of the breeze.

We pulled into the large, circular driveway, and I saw Hunter's spectacular house.

"Wow," I remarked, looking at the massive two-story structure.

"I know," Carter said. "As many times as I have been here, it always amazes me."

"The architecture is fabulous."

"Wait until you see the inside and the view of the lake."

We grabbed the things from the back seat and walked up the cobblestone path. Carter opened the massive stained wood door and led me inside. I briefly noticed the office to my left before my eyes were drawn to the view of the lake at the back of the house. Passing through the den, we made our way to the large kitchen—dining room—family room space. Floor to ceiling accordion-style glass doors had been pushed back so that you could walk directly out onto the massive deck.

Hunter met us at the kitchen island and took the cupcakes from my hands. After setting them down on the quartz countertop, he enveloped me in his arms.

"Paige. I'm so glad you could make it."

I heard a low growl come from Carter's throat. Amused at his possessiveness even with one of his closest friends, I looked in his direction. "Take it down a notch, honey."

Hunter laughed and Carter scowled slightly.

Walking over to him, I said, "You know I'm a hugger. You're going to have to get used to it, especially among our friends." Stretching on my tiptoes, I ran my tongue along his outer ear, then whispered, "You know there's no need to be jealous. You're the only man I want. If you behave, I might let you see what I have on under my clothes even before we make it back to your house."

Heat flared in his eyes and he grasped the back of my head and covered my mouth with his.

"Get a room," Alyssa commented walking into the kitchen.

"Really," Xander agreed. "If we're going to be subjected to that kind of behavior all day, I'm leaving."

"I think it's sweet," Peyton sighed.

Smiling, I greeted everyone with hugs and kisses. Carter picked up the beer from where he had set it down on the floor and carried it out to the huge cooler. On his way back, he said his hellos. In addition to Alyssa, Peyton, and Xander, Grayson had already arrived. Xander and Grayson brought dates. Hunter had also invited the other members of the baseball team and their significant others. After introductions were made, I grabbed a white wine and climbed down the stairs to sit in a group of Adirondack chairs with Peyton and Alyssa. Looking over the lake, I took a deep breath and sighed in appreciation.

"You are entirely too flippin' happy," Alyssa grumbled. "Stop making the rest of us envious of all the sex you are having with that delectable man."

I laughed and glanced back at Carter, who was standing on the deck talking to Hunter and Grayson by the massive grill.

"Sorry, not meaning to rub it in, but what can I say?" I asked. "I'm crazy about him and the way he makes me feel . . ."

"Fabulous," Alyssa stated. "Now, I'm not only jealous, but

unbelievably horny."

Peyton nodded. "I am seriously considering jumping into the lake fully clothed just to cool off."

Smiling, I turned to them. "Your time will come. Wait until *you* can't keep your hands off someone and turn into a raging nympho."

Alyssa raised an eyebrow. "Really? So that's how it is."

I sighed again, parts of me warming as I remembered the hot tub this morning. "I can't even put it into words. I mean, look at the man, for gosh sakes."

Peyton and Alyssa glanced at Carter and then back at me. "He is pretty hot," Peyton agreed.

Suddenly possessive, I stated, "And he is all mine."

Alyssa laughed out loud. "Retract your claws, Paige."

Smiling, I laughed with them.

"Speaking of hot men, where's Jaxson?" Peyton asked, winking at me.

Alyssa frowned. "Not here yet, thankfully. Maybe something came up and he won't be able to make it."

I turned to Peyton and said in a mock whisper, "You notice she didn't deny that he is hot."

Alyssa snapped, "Oh, shut up."

Raising an eyebrow, Peyton commented, "Touchy, touchy."

I laughed. From behind us, we heard a small commotion and turned to see Jaxson and Jarrod appear on the deck.

"And there goes my enjoyable afternoon," Alyssa complained.

I looked at Peyton and saw that she was suddenly quiet. "Are you okay?"

Glancing back at Jarrod, she said, "I'm fine."

"Is there something going on with you and Jarrod?"

Blushing, she responded quickly, "No. Why would you think that?"

Alyssa narrowed her eyes. "Because you are turning red and can't stop looking at the man."

Shaking her head, Peyton looked out over the water, not meeting Alyssa's gaze. "I'm not blushing."

"Oh, yes you are, sweetie. Unless you have suddenly come down with a bad sunburn."

"Spill, Peyton," I urged.

"This is so embarrassing," she began.

"Nothing is off-limits with your best friends. Sharing your humiliating experiences so we can laugh at you is part of the deal."

I kicked Alyssa in the shin.

"Ouch, Paige."

Looking at Peyton, I assured her. "What Alyssa means is that you know you can tell us anything." I shot Alyssa a dirty look.

"Nice try, Paige, but Alyssa meant what she said the first time," she rolled her eyes, smiling.

Alyssa crossed her arms and nodded in satisfaction. "So, fess up."

"You know that I went out with Travis a couple of weeks ago. And that it was not the best experience of my life."

"I always thought he was a jerk," Alyssa offered.

Smirking gratefully, Peyton continued, "Yeah, well, I guess I'm a slow learner. After suffering through dinner with him where all he did was talk about himself and how great he is, the only thing I could think about was getting out of there. Oreos and Netflix were looking really appealing."

"Why didn't you put one of us on emergency phone date interruptus?" I asked.

"I don't know. We talked at the reunion and he seemed attentive and interested, so I figured it would be okay."

"Important rule of dating: Never go on a first date without a backup plan," Alyssa stressed.

"I certainly won't forget that now," Peyton agreed. "Anyway, we finished dinner and he walked me out to my car. I lied and thanked him for a lovely evening. Totally clueless, he reached for me and tried to stick his tongue down my throat."

"Oh gross," I commented.

"Exactly," Peyton agreed. "As I was attempting to extricate myself from Travis' octopus hands, he was suddenly yanked away and unceremoniously pushed back several feet. Thankful, but startled, I looked up to see Jarrod standing there. Staring at Travis, he said *I don't think the lady is interested.* Travis started to come towards Jarrod, but then reconsidered. Jarrod has to be a good five inches taller and outweighs him by fifty pounds. Not giving up, Travis launched into an indignant tirade, boasting about his wealth and importance. Let's just say that Jarrod was not impressed. Again, he told Travis that he didn't care who he was, that if a woman is not interested, no means no."

"I think I am in love," Alyssa sighed. "Dangerously sexy, amazing body, and a gentleman . . . yikes."

Peyton looked at Alyssa and said sharply, "He's not your type. You need someone who can challenge you. Jarrod is too quiet."

I looked at Alyssa. "Now whose claws are out?" We grinned at each other.

"Anyway," Peyton continued, "Travis finally gave up and stalked off before peeling away in his Cadillac. I told Jarrod that while it was nice of him to step in, I was perfectly capable of defending myself. He looked at me, and . . ." Her voice trailed off and she looked away.

"And what?" Alyssa demanded.

I saw the flush come over her and her neck and face turned pink. "Well, he told me that any man could see when a woman was truly interested. That there were certain physical signs, like her eyes would darken, her breath would become shallower, and her lips would part slightly."

"Oooh, that man could write an erotic novel," Alyssa insisted.

"Definitely," I agreed.

Peyton cleared her throat. "Yeah, well. The crazy thing is as he was telling me all this, he had stepped closer to me and I found myself doing everything he had just mentioned."

"And?" I encouraged.

"He kissed me. I mean, really kissed me."

"Hot damn!" Alyssa declared.

"Exactly," Peyton nodded, fanning herself. "I have never been kissed like that before. I literally thought my clothes would fall off of their own accord."

"When a man really knows how to kiss and takes his time, not like he is rushing just to get to sex, like he actually enjoys it . . ." I shivered, thinking of Carter.

"Oh gosh, yes," Alyssa agreed. "It is a rare occurrence." She glanced at Jarrod. "You better hold onto that one, Peyton."

Looking incredulous, Peyton blustered. "There is nothing to hold on to."

Alyssa and I looked at Jarrod. Six foot three and muscled, dark hair cut short, and piercing dark blue eyes, the man was extremely attractive. "I beg to differ."

Peyton rolled her eyes. "You know what I mean. It's not like we have a relationship. It was a fluke thing. Some kind of weird chemical reaction."

"Like spontaneous combustion?" Alyssa teased.

Peyton stuck her tongue out. "Very funny."

"You had a crush on him in high school, Peyton. When we were freshman and he was a senior."

"That was just a silly schoolgirl thing. He didn't even know I was alive."

"Looks like he's aware you're alive now," I said nodding

in the direction of the deck.

Peyton and Alyssa followed my gaze to see Jarrod staring at us or, more specifically, at Peyton. She shivered and pulled her sweater to cover her chest.

I laughed. "Annoying how your body can respond, huh? Even from all the way over there."

"Shut up, Paige."

"Maybe this is going to be a fun day after all," Alyssa smirked.

Chapter Thirty-five: Carter

"Do you want all the corn, or just some of it?" I shouted to Hunter from the kitchen.

"Ten should be good. We'll cut them in half."

I grabbed the stalks and made quick work of shucking and cleaning them. Grayson passed by on his way to get the chicken and the burgers from the refrigerator. We were working to get all the food on the grill. Of course, Hunter's grill was like two normal-sized grills put together. Jarrod, Xander, Jaxson, and the rest of the guys were busy grabbing all the chip and side dishes to put out buffet style on the four large tables along the middle of the deck.

Paige, Peyton, Alyssa, and the wives and girlfriends concentrated on bringing all the plates, napkins, and utensils out to one end. Then they restocked the coolers with more wine, soda, beer, water, and juices. After handing Hunter the corn, I ducked into the kitchen for some platters on which to put the grilled items. Paige and Xander's date, Rachel, were at the island, slicing up tomatoes, lettuce, onions, green and red peppers, and pickles for the burgers. Peyton and Alyssa grabbed various salad dressings and mustard, mayo, and ketchup to set out as well.

Before I snatched the platters from the cabinet, I wrapped my arms around Paige from behind. Breathing in her citrusy scent, I planted a kiss on her cheek. She leaned back against my chest and sighed. After finishing up slicing the tomatoes, she laid the knife down and turned around in my arms, slipping her hands up my chest, and sliding them in my hair. She pulled my head down so that her lips met mine. Liking the way she initiated the contact, I took control of the kiss and happily devoured her mouth.

Swallowing her soft moan, I whispered in her ear, "Still thinking about what's underneath your clothes."

Smiling, she whispered back, "That's the idea, honey. When you're frustrated with wondering, just let me know . . ."

Before I could respond, Xander walked in. "Seriously, you guys. I'm sure Hunter can spare a room so you can satisfy your urges and give the rest of us a break."

I actually considered taking Paige's hand and dragging her upstairs, but controlled myself. Letting go of her, I retrieved the platters from the upper shelf and held them in front of my crotch as I walked back out on the deck. Laughing, Xander followed me outside. Trying to dampen my body's response to Paige, I busied myself holding the empty trays while Hunter placed the cooked meat and grilled vegetables on top. Once fully loaded, I brought everything over to the buffet tables. Hunter rang the dinner bell that hung from the corner of the deck, signaling that everything was ready.

Taking Paige's hand in mine, I walked up to the buffet and we waited our turn in line. Everything looked delicious and I had no problem filling up my plate. Paige, Hunter, Peyton, Alyssa, Jaxson, Jarrod, and I settled into the L-shaped built-in couch.

"I wish Caitlin was here enjoying this," Peyton commented.

"Where is she?" Jaxson asked.

"She had to personally oversee some big wedding tonight. The bride is a little, shall we say, particular," Paige offered.

"Ooh, bridezilla, huh?" Alyssa asked.

Paige nodded. "Pretty much."

"I don't know how she can put up with that," Alyssa

observed. "Why so many women get neurotic about all the details is beyond me. Eat, drink, dance, have a good time. What's the big deal?"

"How romantic, Lys," Peyton observed.

"So sue me, I'm not particularly girly. I could care less about the color of bridesmaid dresses or having pink toasted almonds instead of green as wedding favors."

"Said the woman who never met a high heel she didn't like." Jaxson smirked.

"High heels have nothing do with being girly," Alyssa shot back. "They're a power accessory. Like a man wearing a suit and tie. And, since when do you notice my shoes?"

"Since I can feel you silently impaling one up my ass every time you speak to me," Jax wryly responded.

The rest of us burst out laughing. Alyssa narrowed her eyes in Jaxson's direction.

"Speaking of weddings, where's your fiancé, Hunter?" Paige asked. "I was hoping to meet her today."

A shadow crossed his face. Pausing a moment, he replied, "We broke up."

Stifling a cheer, I asked, "What? When?"

He leaned back against the cushion. "Last night, actually."

Peyton laid her hand on Hunter's arm. "I'm sorry, Hunter."

Out of the corner of my eye, I saw Jarrod frown when Peyton touched Hunter. Odd. He almost looked proprietary. Of Peyton, not Hunter.

Hunter made a face and waved his hand like it wasn't a big deal. "It's been a long time coming. To be honest—and I know this sounds awful—but I don't think we were ever in love with each other. She liked the lifestyle I could give her and the clout my last name provided. And over the past few months, I realized that maybe I wanted something more and didn't want to settle."

He winked at Paige who smiled in return.

"What was the final straw?" Paige asked.

"Not to sound corny, but when I saw you and Carter at our game Friday. I had a *When Harry Met Sally* moment. And I thought *I want what they have.*"

I smiled at Paige and stroked her ponytail. "I told you it exists in everyone's world, Hunter. You just have to find it."

"Wasn't that during the fake orgasm scene in the diner?" Jaxson asked.

Alyssa looked at Jaxson incredulously. "*You* saw *When Harry Met Sally*? Aren't you more of a Sylvester Stallone kind of guy?"

Jax leaned forward and said, "Every guy who wants to get laid has seen *When Harry Met Sally*, counselor."

Hitting herself on the head with her hand, Alyssa replied, "Of course that would be your reason. Heaven forbid you actually have an intellectual interest in a woman."

"Women have brains?" Jaxon retorted

Alyssa jumped to her feet. "You are, without a doubt, the most—"

Laughing, Paige grabbed her by the arm. "Let's go get a refill on our wine, Lys."

As Paige practically dragged Alyssa away, we could all still hear her cussing Jax out as she retreated.

"Why do you insist on messing with her so much?" Hunter asked.

"A man's gotta have a hobby," he replied with a huge grin.

"Personally, I think it's foreplay," I added.

Jax choked on his beer and had a coughing fit. "You are fucking delusional."

The rest of us looked at each other and nodded in agreement. Gathering up his trash, Jax stomped off towards the kitchen. Our laughter followed him the entire way.

CHAPTER THIRTY-SIX: PAIGE

After calming Alyssa down enough that I felt confident she wouldn't go after Jaxson with a butcher knife, I went over and sat back down next to Carter. He wrapped his arm around me and pulled me into him. His scent enveloped me as he leaned down, his voice like a caress in my ear.

"I love you, angel," he whispered.

My heart full, I brushed my lips against his. Looking into his gorgeous gray eyes, I replied, "I love you, too." His eyes darkened and I felt his heart rate increase slightly. I liked how my words affected him. He always made me feel so special. I hoped I made him feel the same way.

Hunter leaned towards me. "Paige?"

I turned my head and looked at him. "Yes?"

"I will officially call Parker on Monday, but I wanted to let you know that I am awarding Perlman the bid."

I reached out and squeezed his hand. "Oh, Hunter, thank you! Though I hope us being friends didn't have any undue influence on your decision."

He shook his head. "You know how I feel about you, Doolittle, but business is business. Your firm had the best proposal and the experience to back it up."

"Parker is going to be so excited."

"Congratulations, baby," Carter said with a kiss.

"Thanks," I smiled at him. "I can't wait to get started."

We gathered up our plates and threw everything out in the large garbage can near the corner of the deck. Working together, the group put away anything perishable and left the rest out for grazing. Carter and I challenged Xander and Rachel to a ladder ball game. A few of the men and their wives or girlfriends played horseshoes. Hunter took Jarrod, Peyton, Alyssa, Jaxson, Grayson and his date out for a ride on his boat. Silently, I prayed that Alyssa wouldn't drown Jax. Luckily, everyone returned unscathed.

A few hours later, we cleaned up the remaining food and set out the desserts on the massive kitchen island. Jaxson picked up a cue stick and racked the balls on the pool table.

Turning to Alyssa, he challenged, "Game?"

"To kick your ass, always," she retorted.

He scoffed. "You think you can beat me?"

"Not even a challenge."

Jax raised an eyebrow. "Care to put your money where your mouth is?"

"Sure. How much?"

"Let's make it interesting. A piece of clothing for every game."

Lys snorted. "Why on earth would you think that I would like to see you naked?"

"I'm not the one who's going to be shedding clothes, sweetheart."

Clenching her jaw for a moment before smiling, she replied "We'll see about that."

Jaxson lined up for the break and sank two stripes. Looking slightly concerned, but hiding it well, Lys grabbed a cue and chalked the tip. Chuckling, I excused myself to use the facilities. When I exited the bathroom, Carter was waiting for me in the hall.

Eyes stormy, he leaned down so that only I could hear him. "I can't stand the suspense anymore, baby. I need to know what your hiding under there." His hand lifted the hem of my shirt and lightly stroked my belly.

My nipples tightened in response. "You need to know,

huh?"

"If I don't have you right now, I'm going to explode."

Smiling, I took his hand in mine. "Well, we can't have that can we?"

We crossed back through the main room on our way to out-side. Lys had obviously lost the first game, as she had taken off her shoes.

"Uh-oh," Carter commented. "Jaxson is pretty good. Not in my league, but pretty good."

I laughed softly. "Lys is just reeling him in, honey. She plays in a league on Wednesday nights with other lawyers. They won the championship this year."

Chuckling, he called out, "Looks like you got her on the ropes, Jax!"

He grinned devilishly and stared at Alyssa. "She better hope I'll let her count jewelry as clothing."

I caught Lys's eye and winked. Winking back, she pre-tended to be upset. "Just shut up and rack 'em, Barney Fife."

Laughing, Carter and I headed down the stairs and into the woods that surrounded Hunter's house. The sun was just starting to set, bathing the trees in amber light. After walking for about 10 minutes, I figured we were far enough away to be out of sight and sound from the others. We were sur-rounded by trees, and the ground underneath us was moss-covered.

I stopped and turned to face him. Very deliberately, I took off my cardigan and toed off my shoes. His eyes darkened considerably as he watched me. Reaching for the hem of my shirt, I pulled it up and over my head. Then I pulled my zip-per down an inch at a time before sliding my jeans over my hips and down my legs. He looked at me with such desire, I felt it in every part of my body.

"Damn, sweetheart," he croaked. "You are gorgeous."

After my shower, I'd put on a sheer red bodysuit. Lace

panels covered my nipples and my crotch, but everything else was completely transparent.

"Worth the wait?"

"Fuck yes," he breathed.

Loving the way his nostrils flared and watching the rapid rise and fall of his chest, I felt dampness flood my core. I unsnapped the fastenings at my crotch. "And you're still waiting because?"

In two strides, he was on me. Pulling down the cups, he freed my breasts. Taking both of them in his hands, he latched his mouth on first one nipple, then the other, sucking and scraping them with his teeth. Moaning with the intense sensations that shot straight through me, I tipped my head back and panted, "Don't stop. That feels so good."

He sucked and licked my breasts before pinching their tight peaks. Needing to touch him, I stripped both his flannel shirt and his T-shirt from his body, then slid my hands over his muscular torso while I sucked on his neck. Groaning, he captured my mouth, spearing his tongue inside. Whimpering, I reached down and cupped his huge erection in my hand.

Ripping his mouth from mine, he grabbed my wrist. "You know I love your hands on me, baby, but I am too fucking close."

Kneeling before me, he latched his mouth between my legs and inserted a finger inside me. Seconds later, I came with a scream. Pulling down his jeans, he grabbed my butt and lifted me. I wrapped my legs around his hips, and he backed me against a tree. Impaling me in one single thrust, his large cock stretched and filled me.

"I can't go slow, baby. I need you too much."

"I don't want slow, Carter. Fuck me hard and fast."

Something inside him unleashed. He pumped in and out, our bodies joining together with ferocity. I clawed at his shoulders while he plundered my mouth as he plundered my body.

"You're fucking mine, Paige. You'll always be mine."

"Yes, Carter, yes!"

Impossibly, he moved even harder and faster. With a scream, I exploded. Throwing his head back, he yelled "Paige!" and erupted inside of me. Still joined, he kissed my lips.

"That was nice," he joked breathlessly.

"What that was," I insisted, "was freakin' hot."

As I slipped my legs from around his waist, he growled, "I know I sound like a broken record, but you are the sexiest woman I have ever known."

I grinned as I refastened my bodysuit and pulled the cups back up to cover my breasts. "I'm glad you think so." I admired him standing there shirtless, with his jeans halfway zipped. "You are a walking X-rated dream."

Kissing me again, he said, "I like how much you want me."

I shook my head. "I don't just want you, Carter. I need you."

His eyes darkened. "Now you know how I feel."

I smiled. "You keep claiming me as yours. You do know that I think of you as mine."

Grinning down at me, he insisted, "You staked your claim a long time ago, Paige. And you have nothing to worry about. I can't even imagine being with anyone but you. I don't want anyone but you. I love you."

I responded, "I love you, too, Carter."

He brushed his lips against mine once more. Helping me on with my shirt, he remarked, "That tree did a number on your bodysuit, sweetheart." His fingers caressed my bare back through the rips.

"It was worth it," I assured him. "Guess that means I'll just have to get something to replace it."

His eyes lit up and he smiled. "I do love your lingerie.

Maybe I'll pick out the next one."

"That could be very . . . interesting."

After finishing dressing, we strolled hand and hand along the shore making our way back to Hunter's. The sun had set and the lights from houses around the lake sparkled over the water. Upon reaching the back lawn, it was evident that some of the guests had left for the evening. Peyton, Jarrod, Xander, Rachel, Hunter, Grayson, and his date, Cheryl, were seated around the fire pit making s'mores.

"Are you guys okay?" Xander asked, grinning. "We thought we heard some wild animals in the forest and were afraid they got you."

Even though I knew they couldn't have heard us, I also realized that I probably looked like a woman who had just been thoroughly made love to. I could feel myself flushing.

Carter took the teasing in stride, responding, "The only wild animal in the forest Paige encountered was me. And she handled that threat outstandingly."

Everyone laughed as I blushed more. Needing to clean ourselves up, Carter and I headed inside to use the bathroom. We entered the family room to see Alyssa still only missing her shoes. Jaxson, on the other hand, was missing his shoes, socks, watch, sweatshirt, and T-shirt. Carter and I laughed when we realized how many games he must have lost.

"Streak of bad luck, huh, Jax?" Carter asked.

Alyssa's eyes twinkled while Jaxson scowled. "She's a damn ringer."

Trying to swallow my laughter, I grabbed my purse and made my way to the powder room. I washed up, finger-combed my hair, and touched up my make-up. Carter was waiting as I exited. He leaned down and whispered, "You're beautiful, but I think I preferred how you looked before — thoroughly fucked."

I smiled. "An apt description. Maybe we can start a new

beauty line."

Grinning, he agreed. "Just think of all the research and development."

Kissing his cheek, I noticed that I had given him a hickey on the side of his neck.

"Well, now everyone will definitely know you're mine." I tilted my head towards the mirror.

Leaning around me, he looked and saw the quarter-sized dark mark. "As if it wasn't obvious before?" He grinned. "I like your mark on me. I believe I'm feeling branded from your nails on my back, as well."

I smiled unapologetically. "What can I say? You tend to make me a bit wild."

His eyes darkened. "I like it.

Giving me a brief kiss, he smiled and entered the bathroom. I walked back to the kitchen and grabbed a water and a peanut butter cookie from the island. Minutes later, Carter joined me. He reached for one of my cupcakes and took a big bite.

Groaning in appreciation, he said, "These are even better than I remembered."

I used my finger to wipe a bit of frosting from the corner of his mouth, then licked it off the tip. His eyes darkened.

"I think my cupcakes are the real reason you missed me," I joked.

"As fantastic as these may be, they're not even in the top ten reasons."

"Shit!" Jaxson exclaimed.

I looked over just in time to see Alyssa sink the eight ball. Lys's face registered satisfaction and she grinned broadly. Jax laid his cue on the pool table and reached for the snap on his jeans.

"Never let it be said that I welch on a bet," he grinned. "Just so you know, sweetheart, I usually go commando."

I watched Alyssa's face as it went from shock and then briefly to desire. Flushing and breathing faster, she held her hand up and turned away. "Okay, match over. I won."

Grinning wickedly, Jax slid his zipper down an inch. Carter covered my eyes.

"But don't you want to enjoy your victory?" I heard Jax coyly ask.

Before Alyssa had the chance to answer, Carter's phone rang. Taking his hand from my eyes, he accepted the call. "Mom, what's up?" His face went ashen. "When?" he asked. He paused for a minute, listening, then asked, "Where did they take him?" Another brief pause. "We'll be right there."

Concerned, I asked "What's going on?"

"My dad went over to my house to measure the front porch and drop off some paperwork. When he was inside, someone hit him over the head from behind. When he woke up, the garage and part of the porch were on fire. Luckily, one of my neighbors called 911. They got there pretty quickly, but he experienced some smoke inhalation and they think he has a concussion. My mom is on her way to the hospital."

Jaxson had been putting his clothes on as Carter explained. Jarrod and Xander burst in from outside.

"What the hell?" Xander asked.

Obviously, Colleen had called them too.

"Mom didn't know too many details. Let's just get to the hospital," Carter instructed.

"I'm going to head over to your house and see what I can find out," Jaxson offered.

Alyssa looked at Jax, insisting, "I'm coming with you."

Nodding, Carter said, "Thanks."

"I'll meet you all at the hospital later. Hartford, right?"

"Yeah."

Grayson offered to stay and help Hunter clean up, then drive Cheryl and Rachel home. Hurrying to their cars, Jarrod and Xander took off. Peyton followed behind them.

As we exited the driveway, Carter swore. "Shit! Who could've done this? And why?"

CHAPTER THIRTY-SEVEN: CARTER

Driving fast, I racked my brain to think of anyone who could do something like this. It had occurred to me that Dad wasn't the target. Maybe I was. After all, Dad was in my house when he was hit. Our hair color was similar, though his had started to gray. He was about my height, and he had kept himself in shape through the years. And, if they were after my dad, why attack him at my house?

I squeezed Paige's hand as we pulled into the hospital parking garage. I had been quiet for practically the entire ride, immersed in my thoughts. I appreciated that she understood my silence and didn't feel the need to press. I was grateful to have her sitting next to me with her hand in mine.

Meeting Jarrod, Xander, and Peyton by the entrance, we headed inside. We found Mom sitting in the Emergency Room waiting area. When she spotted us, she hugged each person individually. Xander sat down next to her, with Jarrod and Peyton across from her. I sat on her other side, with Paige next to me.

Looking at me and my brothers, Mom asked, "Why would anyone want to hurt your father?"

Jarrod and Xander shook their heads. I answered, "I'm not sure it was Dad they were after."

Everyone looked at me. "Think about it. He was attacked in my house. My house was set on fire. If someone wanted to hurt Dad, why would they wait to do it in my house? How would they even know he was going to be there? We just talked about it this morning."

"Who would want to hurt you?" Xander questioned. "Did you piss somebody off?"

I shook my head. "I've been racking my brain on the way over here and can't think of anyone."

Jarrod looked at me. "Vesper."

I sighed. "I didn't put that together."

Xander looked at Jarrod. "What about Vesper?"

Jarrod described about the vandalism on the Vesper project site.

"We've had small incidents like that happen before. Tools or materials stolen," I clarified. "It wasn't that big of a deal and no one got hurt. I had no reason to think that it was against me personally."

Xander looked at me. "Well, evidently, someone does have it out for you, whether professionally or personally."

I felt Paige's arm slip around my back as she leaned her head against my shoulder. I lifted my arm and wrapped it around her and squeezed.

"Tomorrow morning, let's meet at the office and go through the files to see if we can find anything that is a red flag," I instructed Jarrod and Xander. "Our offices have twenty-four-hour security monitoring and guards. I'll call Axel and have a camera system installed at my house. In addition, I'll ask them to put 24-hour security at the job sites."

"I'll swing by your house before we meet at the office and we'll take a look at the damage," Jarrod offered.

"I'll stay at Mom and Dad's tonight, and indefinitely until Dad is back on his feet," Xander stated.

"I still can't believe anyone could be so horrible. There's no excuse for harming your father or trying to burn down your house," Mom stated.

"We'll get to the bottom of it, Mom," I assured her. "Jaxson's over there now finding out exactly what happened."

"Thank goodness," Mom exclaimed. "I feel better knowing he's looking into it. What's taking so long here though? I wish someone would come out and tell us something,"

I held her hand, and Xander put his arm around her shoulder. Looking across, I noticed that Peyton had slipped her hand into Jarrod's.

A half hour later, a doctor approached.

"Mrs. Sullivan?" He stuck out his hand in greeting. "I'm Dr. Samuels."

We all stood up and took turns shaking his hand.

"Yes," Mom answered. "How is he? Can I see him?"

The doctor smiled. "Your husband is doing well. We cleared his lungs of the smoke and he is breathing fine. He does have a concussion and will need to be looked after for the next few days."

Mom sagged against Xander in relief. "Oh, thank you, Dr. Samuels. Thank you so much."

"Give us another few minutes, and you can go back and see him. He should be able to go home with you in a little while."

I gave my mom a kiss on the top of her head. Then I enveloped Paige in my arms and held her. Having her body close to mine and breathing her in calmed me. Out of the corner of my eye, I saw Jarrod pull Peyton into an embrace as well. In spite of the circumstances, I was curious if there was something going on between them.

"From all the hugging and smiles, am I correct in assuming that Patrick is okay?" Jaxson asked upon entering the waiting area.

I noticed he was carrying a piece of paper. I glanced at Alyssa, who looked shaken and concerned. She also kept darting glances at Paige.

Mom walked into Jax's hug and then gave Alyssa a peck

on her cheek.

"Yes, he is doing okay. He has a concussion, but he can come home tonight. I always said the man had a hard head."

We all chuckled.

Taking Alyssa's hands in hers, Mom commented, "And look at you, Alyssa. I haven't seen you in so long. You are gorgeous."

"Oh, Mrs. Sullivan," Alyssa smiled. "It is so good to see you again. I wish it were under better circumstances, though."

"Colleen, please," Mom insisted. "Well, regardless of why, I feel like the boys are back in school again. It brings back memories of everyone over at our house. I always loved having you kids around."

"Well, I can't lie, Mrs. Sullivan—I mean, Colleen," Alyssa said. "I have missed your delicious food."

Mom beamed. "Once Patrick is back up on his feet, we'll have everyone over and catch up."

Leave it to my mom to plan a party while in the Emergency Room lounge. The woman was a force of nature.

Jaxson cleared his throat. "After visiting your house, there is some good news."

"What's that?"

"While the fire did burn a good portion of the garage, the damage to the house itself is not horrible. The front porch suffered the most, and there was a little damage to the left side. Luckily, you have alert neighbors who called 911 pretty quickly."

"That's good to hear. Do the police know what happened?"

"It looks as though the perp entered the house after your father was inside. Patrick probably left the front door open. He used the fire poker as a weapon to hit your dad. The police found it lying on the floor in your office. No prints, though. He probably wore gloves."

"Shit," I muttered.

"The fire chief confirmed arson. Started with gas. Poured all over the garage and around the front of the house. Left the gas cans right in the driveway. Again, no prints."

"Did anyone see the asshole walking around Carter's place?" Jarrod asked.

Jaxson shook his head. "This happened about six, so it was dark by then. Someone thought they saw a dark blue or black SUV parked down the block a little bit earlier though."

"Great," I replied, sarcastically. "That'll help narrow down the suspect pool."

Glancing at Alyssa and then at Paige, Jaxson continued. "We, uh, actually have a pretty good lead on who did this."

"Who?" Xander demanded.

Unfolding the piece of paper in his hand, he said, "This is a copy of a note that was left on the windshield of your truck."

Taking it from him, I read aloud, "By now you've seen my mark and know she's mine. Keep your hands off my property. This was just a warning. Next time I won't be so nice."

I heard Paige gasp, and when I turned to her, all the color had drained from her face. Rushing from the room, she dashed into the ladies' bathroom. Peyton and Alyssa followed her.

"What the hell?" Xander asked.

"What is going on, Carter?" Mom demanded. "Why is Paige so upset?"

I asked everyone to sit down. Summarizing, I told them what Paige had been through and filled them in on Derrick Walters. Their faces reflected horror, sadness, and anger.

Mom put her hand on my shoulder. "Oh, Carter. How awful. How could anyone hurt Paige, of all people?"

"How is that animal still walking the streets?" Xander raged.

"Our fine justice system at work," Jaxson lamented.

"If this asshole thinks he is going to scare me off, he's dead wrong," I declared. "There's no way in hell he's getting anywhere near her."

"Damn right," Xander agreed.

"Even though her house is in a gated community, I'll get the local cops to post a car at the front," Jaxson stated. "I assume she has a security system?"

I nodded. "Yes, but it could stand to be beefed up a bit."

"Let's add that to Axel's list," Jarrod noted.

"Her office has a security guard in the lobby," I told Jax. "I don't know about back entrances or anything, though."

"I'll check it out. We'll give the guard Walters' picture and have him keep an eye out. I can also see if we can get one of the Greenwich patrolmen stationed in the parking lot."

"Find this fucker, Jax," I demanded. "Soon. If he touches her ever again, I'm going to kill him with my bare hands."

"And I'll help," Jarrod chimed in.

"Count me in," Xander added.

"Well, fuck," Jax sighed. "Lieutenant or not, I'm in too."

Mom smiled at all of us. Turning to me, she said, "You really love her, don't you sweetie?"

I nodded, my chest tight. "I can't live without her, Mom."

Chapter Thirty-eight: Paige

Peyton held my ponytail while I dabbed my face and neck with a wet paper towel. Knowing my mouth would taste horrible after throwing up in the toilet, Alyssa reached in her purse for a travel-sized mouthwash. Thanking her, I looked in the mirror. Some of the color had come back to my face, but my hands were still shaking.

I couldn't believe Derrick had found me. Even more horrifying was the fact that he had gone after Carter and wounded Patrick in the process. I'd been so blinded by my feelings, it hadn't even occurred to me that Derrick would be a threat to Carter. How could I have been so selfish and stupid? By simply being around me, Carter could have been hurt—or worse. Guilt ate me alive. Resolute, I knew what I had to do.

Taking a deep breath and putting on a blank face, I walked back out to the waiting area. Carter made a move towards me and I held up my hand to ward him off.

Turning to his mom, I said, "Colleen, I don't even know what to say to you. Patrick is back there, hurt, because of me. Words cannot express how sorry I am. I hope you can forgive me."

Colleen looked at me concerned. "There's nothing to forgive, Paige. This was not your fault."

Knowing she was just being kind, I continued, "Yes, it was. I exposed your son and your husband to someone who is pure evil. I should've known better."

I had a hard time looking Carter in the eyes as I spoke, but I forced myself to. "Carter, I can't apologize enough for what happened. Being in a relationship with me has put you and your family in danger. Your house has been vandalized and your father has been attacked. Your business has been affected. I don't know if I can ever forgive myself for wanting to be with you so badly that I overlooked putting you at risk. I am so, so sorry."

Grasping my hand, he searched my face. "Paige, none of this was your fault. Do you honestly think that I regret one single moment we've had? How can you think I could ever blame you for what that sick bastard has done?"

Biting my lip so not to cry, I answered, "Even if you don't blame me, I blame myself. If anything ever happened to you . . ." I looked away, unable to finish the thought. "We can't be together, Carter. I don't want you or your family subjected to the danger. If we aren't involved, Derrick won't see you as a threat. You'll be safe."

"The hell with that, Paige!" he yelled. "I love you. I want to spend the rest of my life with you. Do you think I'm just going to let you go?"

"You don't have a choice, Carter," I said softly. "I love you too much to put you in harm's way."

With that, I turned around and walked out of the hospital. Behind me, I heard Carter start to follow and Alyssa tell him that she and Peyton would stay with me. I barely made it to Peyton's car before breaking down and sobbing. I cried the entire drive to my house and was still crying as I walked up the stairs to my bedroom. I grabbed some pajamas from my dresser and walked into the bathroom. I took off my torn bodysuit and threw it in the garbage.

After showering, I walked back out to my room and crawled in bed. Being there brought back memories of Carter. In such a short time, our lives had become intertwined. I already missed him terribly. The hurt was unbearable.

Peyton and Alyssa each cleaned up and borrowed T-shirts

and leggings. Sensing I didn't want to talk yet, they sat on either side of me and put on a silly comedy movie. I tried to pay attention but couldn't. All I could think about was Carter's face as I walked away. I knew I did the right thing, but it was killing me. If Derrick thought I was no longer interested in Carter, he would leave him alone. He'd obviously seen us together. If he didn't continue to see us as a couple, he likely wouldn't continue to focus on Carter.

I didn't know if Jaxson would be able to find Derrick and stop him from hurting me again. Part of me wanted to believe it, but I just wasn't sure. With Derrick's money and connections, he seemed to be able to weasel out of everything. I contemplated picking up and moving again before dismissing the thought. I was so tired of being scared. I wanted to fully claim my life back. I just wasn't sure how to go about it. All I knew was that right now, I would do anything to keep Carter safe, even if it meant being without him.

Two hours later, the doorbell rang. Alyssa got up and started down the stairs.

"I don't want to see anyone, Lys."

Nodding in understanding, she headed down the stairs. I could hear a male voice. My heart started beating rapidly thinking it might be Carter. Despite my resolve, I desperately wanted to see him. A few minutes later, Alyssa came back up the stairs with my suitcase in her hand.

"That was Jarrod," she explained. "Carter thought you would want your things, so he had Jarrod bring them by."

And, just like that, the finality of not seeing him again hit me full force and I burst into tears.

"Oh, sweetie, do you really think you're doing the right thing?" Peyton asked me.

Gulping for air, I answered, "How could I live with myself if anything happened to Carter? Being with me puts him in danger. If Derrick thinks we are broken up, then he will leave him alone."

Alyssa softly said, "Maybe, but Carter can take care of himself. He's smart and very capable."

Peyton nodded. "And you heard him, Xander, and Jarrod at the hospital. They already have a plan to up security measures. Plus, do you think Derrick would be so stupid to try something again when he knows the police are aware who he is?"

"I think that Derrick is so unhinged that he could do just about anything. I won't continue to put Carter in the middle of this."

"That man loves you, Paige," Alyssa insisted. "I mean, really loves you. He said he wanted to spend the rest of his life with you."

"And if I keep seeing him, the rest of his life may not be very long." I shuddered. "As much as I love him, as much as I want to be with him, I can't bear the thought of that. I would rather not see him and know he is alive and well, than be the reason he is physically hurt — or worse."

"I saw that man's face when you walked out of the Emergency Room, Paige," Alyssa stressed. "There is no way he is giving up on you."

Selfishly, hope sprang in my chest. "Then I'll just have to make sure I'm strong and logical enough for the both of us."

Peyton and Alyssa fell asleep about midnight, but I couldn't sleep. I slipped out of bed and sat on the chaise. Torturing myself, I glanced at the photos on my cell phone. Smiling through tears, I scrolled through the pictures from the past several weeks. A rush of anger filled me knowing that I had found the love of my life only to not be able to be with him. Staring out the window, I prayed for a solution. I also prayed for God to keep Carter safe.

When my phone buzzed with an incoming text, I jumped.
I miss you, Paige.
Crying, I stared at the message from Carter and forced

myself not to respond.

I know you are feeling guilty and responsible, but you shouldn't and you aren't.

I knew that if I answered him back, I would be back in his arms in the blink of an eye.

I watched you walk out of my life once before. It's never happening again.

Oh, Carter, I thought. Can't you see that being around me is dangerous? That I am trying to protect you? That I couldn't stand it if anything happened to you?

I love you, angel. You're mine and I'm yours. Always.

Unable to keep quiet any longer, I replied, *Carter, you have to let me go. It's not safe. I have to live with this, but you don't.*

You actually think being with you is a choice for me? I need you more than I need to breathe.

My heart felt like it was going to burst out of my chest. I loved him so much.

Carter, please . . .

Please, what, baby? Please stop loving you? Please stop wanting you? Please stop needing you? Not an option.

Both thrilled and angry with his persistence, I typed. *Stop being so damn stubborn and think of your safety. Derrick warned that he was going to do worse if we stay together.*

Do you really think I am scared of him?

You should be.

I'm not stupid, Paige. I know he's dangerous. But now that I know he is out there, I can be prepared. Jax and I are not just going to sit around and wait to see what Walters does. He will not get anywhere near you. Or me.

Wanting to believe what he was saying, but knowing that there was no guarantee, I responded with *You don't know that. And I will not risk you getting hurt. And by being with me, there is a good chance of that happening.*

Not being with you hurts more.

At least you'll be alive.

I'm not alive without you.

Seriously sobbing, I could barely see the keys.

Don't do this baby. Don't shut me out.

It's tearing me apart, but I know it's the right thing to do. I love you too much to see anything happen to you. Especially if I know there is something I can do to prevent it. Good-bye, Carter.

I quickly turned off my phone so that I wouldn't see his response. Laying down on the chaise, I wrapped my shivering body in a throw and cried myself to sleep.

Chapter Thirty-nine: Carter

When I tried to call Paige in response to her last text, every attempt went directly to voicemail. Miserable, I gave up calling at around three in the morning and spent the rest of the night tossing and turning. While I understood why she decided it would be safer for me to not be seen with her at least until Walters was behind bars, I wasn't happy about it. I knew she thought she was protecting me, but why couldn't she see that I wanted to protect her? We had spent ten years apart. I didn't want to spend another day without her, regardless of the circumstances. She may have thought she could keep me away, but like I told her, that wasn't happening.

Sunday morning at seven, I dragged myself out of bed and took a shower. I grabbed a quick breakfast and a cup of coffee and walked outside. Jaxson was correct in his assessment of the damage. Luckily, the garage was detached, so even though the fire did the most damage there, it didn't spread to the house itself. Unfortunately, I would have to tear down the entire thing and rebuild it, as nothing could be salvaged. The existing front porch had some burned areas, but since I was planning to redo it anyway, having to tear that down wasn't a big deal. The siding near the foundation on the left side of the house had been slightly scorched and warped. Thankfully, only about 10 boards needed to be replaced. The smell of smoke was evident, but not so much in the house, and there was no water damage inside, either.

Last night, I had called some of the guys from my crew and arranged for them to come to the house to help with the cleanup. Xander, Grayson, Hunter, and Jaxson were arriving at nine to lend a hand as well. Jarrod was joining us later, after he went over to Paige's and oversaw the upgrade of her alarm system. I grabbed some tools from the lockbox in my truck and started removing the siding. After that, I began tearing down the charred wood perimeter of the front porch. At eight-thirty, the dumpster was delivered. Taking a break from the demolition, I hauled the debris into the dumpster.

Xander was the first to pull up.

"How's Dad?" I asked him.

Grabbing tools out of his truck, he replied, "He has a headache, but overall doing pretty good. Mom's fussing over him, which is driving him crazy. And Lucky won't leave his side."

I chuckled. "It's like Kodak all over again."

"Yeah, pretty much. Dad pretends he's annoyed, but you know he secretly loves it."

We waved as Hunter and Grayson pulled up, followed by Jaxson.

"I have some news," Jax stated.

"Did you catch the bastard?" Grayson asked.

"Not yet," Jax responded. "I did hear from the P.I. though."

"And?" I inquired.

"Turns out Walters has a history of stalking and attacking women."

"What the fuck?" I exclaimed.

"Yeah," Jax continued. "Since his twenties, he has been accused of stalking and attacking four different women, besides Paige. Two of them filed charges, two didn't. With the two that did report it, there wasn't enough evidence to convict. Walters' rich daddy got to all of them, too. Threatened the two who told into silence and paid off the two that didn't go to the police."

"This piece of shit should've been behind bars a long time ago." I snapped.

"He's a slimy bastard. He makes sure there are no witnesses, so it's his word against theirs. And with Daddy footing the bill for the best defense money can buy, he's been able to get away with it," Jax explained.

"That all fucking ends here," I insisted.

Jax nodded. "Well, now he's in for more than just stalking. He's going to be on the hook for the attempted murder of your dad and arson. Those two things shouldn't be easy to weasel his way out of."

"How's Paige?" Hunter asked.

I filled Hunter and Grayson in on what happened at the hospital and Paige's insistence that I stay away from her.

"Damn, Carter," Hunter exclaimed. "Paige has always been very headstrong, but doesn't she realize that if you love her, you want to be with her no matter what? Especially if she is in danger?"

I threw my hands up in the air. "Exactly! Why do you get it and she doesn't?"

"So, what are you going to do?" Grayson asked.

"I don't know. Yet. But you can be damn sure that I'm not walking away."

Over the next six hours, we all worked together to clean up all evidence of the fire. The crew had brought a backhoe so we could tear down the entire garage and lift everything into the dumpster. We built temporary steps to the front door. Axel came by after finishing at Paige's and installed a security camera system on my property. At three o'clock, all the guys left except Jaxson. After thanking them and paying the dumpster workers for picking up the massive bin filled with trash, I grabbed two beers from the refrigerator and joined Jax on the back patio. Trying not to concentrate on the hot tub and visions of Paige, I sat down in a chair.

"You have to catch this fucker, Jax."

"I know, man. We've got a bunch of guys on it. We've

verified his movements for the past month and a half. He's made several trips to Connecticut. The first of which was the day of our reunion."

Incredulous, I turned to him. "You've got to be kidding me."

"Nope. I don't know how he found out about it, but it looks like he was definitely there. I don't remember seeing him, but there were so many people. And, he might not have actually ventured inside. He may have just been watching from the parking lot."

"So, he could've followed Paige home that night, which means he knew what kind of car she drives. It would've been easy to wait outside her complex and wait for her in the morning to follow her to work."

Jaxson nodded. "Seems logical. And if he followed her . . ."

"Then he knew about me and most likely followed me too." I finished. "Fuck!"

"Hey, man. Who knew this psycho was still stalking her? From the reports I read, the last time they saw each other was the night of Paige's attack. The civil suit settled out of court."

"Did he continue to terrorize the other women after he had attacked them?"

"No. He moved on to the next."

"Then why is he still after Paige? Why is she different?"

Jaxson sighed and looked at me. "She's the only one who had never been in a relationship with him. She also the only one he never actually . . ."

"Actually, what, Jax?"

"Paige is the only one he never raped, Carter. I think he wants to finish what he sees as being interrupted."

I stood up and roared, "The hell he will!" I was so incensed, I was shaking.

"I'd tell you to calm down, but I can only imagine how I would feel if some maniac was after the woman I loved."

Stalking into the yard, I tried to force myself to calm down. Taking a deep breath, I sat down again.

"What's the plan?"

"In the morning, I am going over to Paige's office and talk to the security guard. Starting tomorrow, a Greenwich officer will be stationed in the parking lot. In addition, another Greenwich patrolman will be stationed at the back doors. They are normally locked, but just in case. Starting this morning, I have a cop stationed outside Paige's house. I'm going to go over to Paige's in a little while and try to convince her to let me put an officer in her house with her at night as well."

He noticed my face as I reacted possessively to the thought of another man being in Paige's house.

"Ease up, Godzilla. I'll get a female detective, if that will make you feel better."

I blew out a breath and shrugged my shoulders. "Crap. I know I should just be grateful someone is there to protect her, but the idea of another man in her house . . ."

"Yeah, I get it. Female it is. I am also going to talk to the security guard at the entrance gate to Paige's complex and provide him with a picture of Walters. As you know, Paige has to put all visitors on a list in order to gain entry, but I don't want to take any chances. I'm providing him with pictures of all of her close friends so he can compare names to faces if Walters tries using any of our names to make it past the guard."

"All of that sounds good. What are you doing to find Walters?"

"Like I said earlier, we're methodically tracking him. He's wised up somewhat, though, and is using cash, which makes it tougher. We're canvasing motels and rental houses within ten miles of Paige's house, but that's a lot of ground to cover. The P.I. is still in Chicago, talking to Walters' friends in attempt to get any information he can. I should have Walters' cell phone records and his financials within the next couple of days as well."

"Thanks, Jax. I can't tell you how glad I am that you are coordinating this."

"Hey, it's my job. Plus, it's Paige. My boss has given me some leeway on this one."

"Just get the asshole."

He nodded. "You be careful, okay? I have a feeling that not seeing Paige is a very temporary thing."

Smiling slightly, I confirmed. "Damn straight. I love her so much, Jax. Nothing or no one is keeping me away."

"I thought so," he said, grinning.

CHAPTER FORTY: PAIGE

Feeling guilty that they had spent the whole night, I shooed Alyssa and Peyton out the door by nine, though Lys grumbled at being awakened so early. After taking a shower and dressing in leggings and a green tunic sweater, I spent the next hour cleaning every room in the house. I stripped all the linens in my bedroom and bathroom and began washing three big loads of colors, whites, and delicates. I gathered my dry cleaning into a bag to drop off the next morning. Finally turning my phone back on, I saw the numerous missed calls from Carter. My fingers itched to call him back, but I forced myself to abstain. At ten-thirty, my doorbell rang. My heart galloped in anticipation, both dreading and hoping it was Carter. I looked through the peephole to see Jarrod standing there.

Opening the door, I greeted him. "Hi, Jarrod. What are you doing here?"

"I brought Axel with me," he gestured to the man next to him. "He's going to upgrade your security system."

My first reaction was to decline, but, given the circumstances, I figured it wouldn't be a bad idea to have some added assurance.

"Okay, thank you. Come on in."

Axel shook my hand and then proceeded about his work. I invited Jarrod into the living room.

"Can I get you anything?"

He looked at me, searching my face. "How are you?"

"I'm fine."

"Paige, don't lie to me. I've known you since you were twelve. For almost four years before I left for the army, I saw you almost every day. You were like my little sister. Regardless of the fact that I haven't seen you for years, I know you. Some maniac is making your life a living hell. You are *not* fine."

I looked at him while fighting back tears. "Okay, you're right. I'm not fine. I'm pissed. I'm scared. And I miss Carter so much. This whole situation is like a nightmare, except I can't wake up."

He took my hands in his as we sat down on the couch. "I'm not going to bullshit you. Walters sounds like a sadistic asshole and you should be concerned. But he's becoming more and more unhinged, which means he's apt to make mistakes. Jaxson is damn good at his job, and I'm confident that he will keep you safe. I'm also certain he will find Walters and put him where he belongs."

Appreciating his candor, I sighed. "I trust Jax. And I really want to believe that he can locate Derrick and put a stop to all of this, but I've seen Derrick go unpunished before. I don't want to get my hopes up."

"Understood. Promise me you'll be careful and follow what Jax instructs you to do."

I nodded. "I'm not going to take any chances, Jarrod. Right now, Derrick doesn't need any more reason to escalate his behavior. Seeing me with another man obviously angered him. And I can't stand the thought of him hurting Carter. That's why I'm not going to be with Carter anymore. At least until Derrick is behind bars. If Carter still wants me when — if — that happens, remains to be seen."

He chuckled softly, surprising me.

"Oh, Paige. You really have no clue, do you? I watched Carter fall for you as a teenager. I wasn't around a lot after you left, but when I was home, the light was gone from his eyes. Since I came back to town, he and I have talked about how much he missed you. I don't think he has ever forgiven himself for not chasing after you.

"For the past several weeks, I've watched him fall hard for you. You've made him happier than I have ever seen him. I don't know if I am that much of a believer in fate, but the two of you were clearly meant for each other. He's miserable without you. It's killing him that you're pushing him away instead of letting him protect you through this whole ordeal. He doesn't understand why you're not facing this together."

Dumbfounded at Jarrod's words, I couldn't speak.

"One more thing, Paige," he began. "While I understand you feeling responsible for what happened to my dad and to Carter's house, that's bullshit, too. The only person to blame for that is Walters. Period. No one in our family holds you accountable. You're family, Paige. We're angry and saddened for you. We worry about you and want to make sure you're safe. Most of all, we want to see you with Carter like you should be."

At that moment, Axel came into the room and asked to show me the new system. After pointing out the outside cameras, the monitors, how to use the phone app, and instructing me on how to disable and enable the alarm, he left. Following him out, Jarrod walked to the door. Turning around, he planted a kiss on my forehead.

"Think about what I said, Paige."

I went back to sit on the couch. For the next hour, I mulled Jarrod's words over. I struggled to reconcile my fears with my feelings. I didn't know if I could stay away from Carter until this was all over. I wanted nothing more than to have his arms around me to make me feel safe and loved, to replace fear with passion and security. Yet I didn't know how I could live with knowing he might be hurt just because we were together. Would I ever be able to forgive myself if Derrick went after him again? And, despite the wonderful sentiment Jarrod expressed, would the Sullivans truly not blame me if something catastrophic did happen?

Unable to come up with a decision, I continued with the laundry and then cooked several meals for the week ahead. Keeping busy helped calm me down. In the middle of cleaning up the kitchen, Caitlin called me. Alyssa had phoned her and filled her in on the events from the night before. After assuring her that I was okay, she not so politely let me know exactly what she thought of my decision to stop seeing Carter. To put it mildly, she thought I was out of my mind. After enduring a twenty-minute lecture, I was finally able to get off the phone with a promise to text her later. Almost immediately after I hung up with Caitlin, Sarah called. She essentially gave me the same lecture as Caitlin, though with a softer touch. After telling her how much I missed her, I disconnected the call.

Not really hungry, I forced myself to have some soup and crackers around five-thirty. As I was putting the bowl and spoon in the dishwasher, there was a knock at the door. Walking into the hallway, I looked at the small monitor on the wall to see Jaxson standing outside.

Opening the door, I motioned him inside. I walked into the living room and took a seat on the chair. He sat down on the couch facing me.

"I stopped by to see how you were doing."

"I'm fine."

He raised an eyebrow in disbelief.

"Why can't anybody believe that I am fine?"

"Because you would have to be inhuman to not be affected by what is happening in your life right now, Paige. Plus, you look like you haven't slept all night."

"Great, thank you," I said sarcastically. At this point, my nerves were shot. "Other than coming here to comment on my appearance, what brings you by?"

"Hey," he cajoled softly. "I'm not the bad guy here."

I looked away and sighed. "I know, Jax. I'm sorry to be a bitch. It's just . . . I'm so frustrated. And angry. And scared."

He took my hand in his. "I know. I would give anything to not have this be happening to you. I'm going to do everything in my power to make sure that you are safe and that Walters is behind bars where he can never threaten you again."

I squeezed his hand in appreciation. "Thanks, Jax. It does make me feel better to know you're in charge of the investigation. Even when we were kids, no matter how wild you were, I could always count on you to have my back."

"Yeah," he agreed, smiling.

Returning his grin, I asked, "Do you remember that time Eddie Burns took my bike and wouldn't give it back? You punched him smack in the nose and told him if he ever bothered me again, you'd tell everyone he wet the bed."

Jaxon laughed. "And then Alyssa marched down to his house and told his mother that her son was going to wind up in juvenile hall if she didn't enforce good manners."

I laughed out loud. "She was a real goody-two-shoes, wasn't she?"

"What do you mean *was*?"

I narrowed my eyes at him and shook my head.

"I wish it were that easy this time, Paige, but we both know it's not. There are things I want you to do to help ensure your safety. I want you to be very aware of your surroundings at all times. Stick to public places. If you get the sense that something is wrong, trust your instincts and leave or tell someone. Don't dismiss it as just your imagination."

He went on to describe all the security measures he had put in place at my house and my office. When he mentioned that he wanted a detective to stay with me overnight, every night, I declined. I didn't think it was necessary. Knowing that there was a police car right outside and a brand-new security system in place, I felt that was enough. He argued with me, but I stood firm.

"Of course, you could always have someone else spend nights with you. Say, Carter for instance?"

I shot him a look. "Don't you start, too, Jax."

"You mean others have suggested that perhaps you should rethink breaking it off with him?" he asked feigning ignorance.

"Only Peyton, Alyssa, Caitlin, and Sarah," I listed. "Oh yeah, and Jarrod."

"Wise people," he commented.

"Watch it, Jax," I warned. "Or I'm going to tell Lys you think she's smart."

He grinned. "You wouldn't."

"Try me."

"Seriously, Paige. I know you have your mind made up, but I think you're wrong. You need Carter with you now. And I damn well am sure that he needs to be with you. If the woman I loved was in any kind of danger, nothing could stop me from being with her. It's destroying him to not be able to see for himself that you are okay. It ate him up being away from you for ten years. Once he found you again, he swore that he would never let you go. You keep saying that you couldn't bear it if something happened to him, Paige. What if something does happen to him? Will you be kicking yourself for pushing him away instead of taking the opportunity to be together?"

Pulling me up, he put his arm around me as he walked to the front door. He gave me a hug and told me to lock up behind him.

After Jax left, I finished the laundry and remade my bed. I did some work in my office and added to my calendar for the week. At eight o'clock I went upstairs and took a bubble bath.

When I finally climbed into bed at nine, I sat staring at the wall, not even reaching for the remote. I couldn't recall the last Sunday during football season that I didn't watch any games all day. Clicking on the app on my phone, I saw the police car parked by my curb via the camera over my front door. Changing views, I looked at my small backyard courtesy of the camera over the French doors in my dining room. Marveling at the security system's technology, I closed the app and put my phone under my pillow. I was emotionally and physically exhausted, but my brain wouldn't stop thinking.

What Jaxson said right before he left had stuck with me the rest of the day. Shouldn't I be spending every moment I could with Carter? If, God forbid, something horrible did happen, would I regret not being with him when I had the chance?

And what about what Jarrod said? Shouldn't we be facing this trouble together? When you loved someone, you were a team. I recognized the irony in the fact that I had been so angry with Carter for deciding that we should break up when I went to college, and yet here I was deciding we should not see each other because of Derrick. He didn't give me a choice then and I wasn't giving him a choice now. But this was a life and death situation, so it was different, wasn't it?

Seriously considering drinking an entire bottle of wine just so I could pass out and get some sleep, I was turned on the Sunday night game in hopes of distracting myself. Five minutes in and I wasn't having any luck, but the Cowboys were playing so I decided to give it a little more effort. My phone buzzed from underneath my pillow.

The Cowboys are looking pretty sorry tonight.

I smiled at the dig. Carter was a die-hard Giants fan.

I wish I was there to tuck you in.

Heat rushed through me as I remembered all the times he had said the same thing.

I miss you, Paige.

Oh, how I missed him. My chest tightened and I felt like I couldn't breathe.

I wish I was there holding you.

Closing my eyes, I could actually feel Carter's arms around me.

I love you, sweetheart. So much.

"I love you, too," I whispered.

Goodnight, angel.

When I woke up the next morning, I was still clutching my phone.

Chapter Forty-one: Paige

As I got ready for work on Monday morning, I was looking forward to the busy week ahead. With the number of projects I was involved in, I was hoping that focusing on my tasks would keep my mind off how much I missed Carter and the knowledge that Derrick was nearby. I chose a black pencil skirt, blush-pink blouse and black strappy heals. As I put on my make-up, I noted the dark circles under my eyes. My lack of sleep was taking a toll. I grabbed my purse and briefcase and headed to the garage, setting the alarm on my way out. I nodded to the patrolman sitting outside as I pulled out of the driveway. Jaxson had told me that someone would be here around the clock, even while I was at work, in case Derrick decided to pay a visit.

On my hour and a half drive to Perlman, I again thought back to my conversations with Caitlin, Sarah, Jarrod, and Jax yesterday. I hadn't reached a decision regarding seeing Carter. My heart and my body said yes, but my mind was still holding on to the need to protect him, which meant that he should be as far away from me as possible.

Jaxson must have provided the Greenwich police with a description of my car and my license plate number, because an officer met me as soon as I pulled into the parking lot. He escorted me inside the building and then went back to his post outside.

I stopped at the security desk to say hello to Al.

"Good morning, Miss Paige."

I smiled at him. "Good morning, Al."

Looking serious, he said, "I just want to let you know that the police have filled me in on what is going on. I am going to be extra aware of every person who walks through that door."

"Thanks," I acknowledged. "I'm sorry about all this."

"Why should you be sorry? It's not your fault."

"Still . . ."

"Your safety is what's important. I'll do my part to make sure you're being looked after."

Nodding and smiling my thanks, I headed to my office. Greeting several staff members, I set down my things and got to work. At ten o'clock, Parker poked his head in the doorway.

"Got a minute?"

"For you, always."

He closed the door and sat down in one of the chairs in front of my desk.

"I received a call from Hunter Carlson this morning. We got awarded the bid."

Smiling, I nodded. "I know. He told me Saturday when we were at a cookout together. I was so excited, but he wanted to tell you himself."

"I want you to head up design. They want everything complete by March thirty-first, so it's going to be a tight deadline."

"Thanks, Parker. We'll get it done. Who's on the team?"

"Steve, David, and Melissa are going to work with me on the space planning. I am thinking Ann as the on-site supervisor and Meryl and Tim assisting you with design."

I nodded. "Sounds good. Do we know the name of the contractor?"

He smiled at me. "Sullivan & Sons."

My heart skipped a beat knowing that I would be working with Carter's firm. I frowned.

"I thought you would be happy working with your boyfriend," Parker commented confused.

I sighed and filled Parker in on the events of the last few days.

"Detective Mancini came in this morning to talk to Uncle Mike and me about the added security, so I knew most of what you just told me. What I didn't know — and what I don't understand — is why you decided to stop seeing Carter."

"Not you, too," I lamented.

"You mean I'm not the only one who doesn't agree?"

"Hardly," I informed him. "Parker, how can I continue to be with him if by doing so, I am making him a target for Derrick?"

"You can't take responsibility for what that sicko is thinking. Why should you let him dictate what you do and who you are with?"

I shook my head. "I don't know what to do anymore."

"In my opinion, it really isn't a hard decision. I have known you for ten years, Paige. I was there when you were miserable after saying goodbye to Carter. And since you've reunited, I can see how in love you are. When you find the right one, you should hold on with everything you have."

Leaving me with my thoughts, he quietly exited my office. Forcing my mind on my work, I spent the next couple of hours calling suppliers and vendors and scheduling on-site visits. At noon, I headed to the cafeteria to grab a bite to eat. When I returned to my office, there was a small, wrapped package on my desk. Trying not to panic, I walked out to Gail's desk.

"Did you put this on my desk?"

"Yes. Al called me out to the front to let me know it had been delivered for you."

Still concerned, I thanked her and walked back to my office. I assumed that all deliveries were being vetted by both the police officer out front and Al, but my heart was racing as I unwrapped the gift. I took off the bow and pretty paper to reveal the Foreigner "4" CD. Closing my eyes and smiling, I inserted the disc into my computer and selected track thirteen. The opening music of our song began to play. Halfway through the song, my phone buzzed with a text message.

A tear ran down my cheek as I read Carter's text containing lines from the song.

I've been waiting for you to come back into my life, Paige. Knowing you're so close, yet I can't see you or touch you is torture. I am trying to respect your wishes, but I can't stay away from you for much longer. I need to be with you. I love you.

My heart broke. I loved him fiercely and missed him so much, I physically ached. But the thought of him hurt, or worse, stopped me from responding. Determined, I put my phone down and got back to work. But I played the song repeatedly for the rest of the day.

Friday was Halloween. The past three days during our morning workouts, Peyton, Alyssa, and Caitlin had pleaded with me to attend the Yale New Haven Hospital event. I wasn't in a party mood, but I had finally acquiesced and agreed to go. I knew that Carter had been invited and I didn't know if I could handle seeing him. Every night he texted me to say goodnight, just as he had done on Sunday. Every day there was a new delivery. Tuesday, I received the Dr. Doolittle DVD, which I had watched in bed every night since. Wednesday morning, a bouquet of gerbera daisies — my favorite flower — was awaiting me at the security desk when I arrived at work. Thursday, Gail brought me another small wrapped package that held a glass slipper. Carter had planned to be Prince Charming to my Cinderella at the gala.

As sweet as the gifts were, the voicemail messages Carter left for me every day were even better. The sound of his deep, masculine voice sent tingles down my spine.

Tuesday: "I wish we could watch this together, you wrapped up in my arms. I miss the feel of your body against me. I miss hearing you laugh and remember how you cry at movies even when you watch comedies. I love you, Paige."

Wednesday: "Remember when I gave you daisies for the first time? I think we were thirteen. The smile you gave me in return took my breath away. I want to make you smile like that for the rest of your life. I miss you. I love you, baby."

Thursday: "I hardly think of myself as a prince, but you are definitely the woman of my dreams. Just like Charming, I knew you were the one the first moment I saw you. I am praying you'll be there tomorrow. I miss the way you kiss me, touch me, and make love to me. Please say you've changed your mind. I need you. I love you."

Today: "I'm so proud of the woman you've become. I am in awe of your strength. Thank you for trusting me with your past. Please continue to trust me with your heart. I love you."

With every message, my will cracked. I questioned my decision continuously. I loved him so much. I missed seeing him, talking to him, just being with him. I yearned for the security he offered and I ached for his touch.

After showering and putting on my lingerie, I curled my hair. Pulled back with a few tendrils around my face, the tight waves cascaded down my back. To keep with the costume, I brushed tan eyeshadow on my eyelids and lined black near my upper lashes. I used a heavier coat of mascara than usual, blush on my cheeks, and a light pink lipstick. After putting on the white petticoat, I stepped into the blue dress and pulled on the long white gloves. I finished the outfit with crystal high-heeled pumps. Hearing Peyton honk her horn, I slipped on my white and crystal mask, grabbed a small clutch and headed outside to meet her.

Chapter Forty-two: Carter

As I drove with Jarrod to the Halloween party, my heart pounded in my chest. All I thought about the entire day was the possibility of seeing Paige. If she wasn't there, I was getting back in my truck and heading over to her house. I had held out for as long as I could. If I had to sleep on her front steps until she opened the front door, I would see her face to face and convince her that we belonged together.

The gala was being held at Saint Clements Castle in Portland. We pulled up to the entrance and I handed my keys to the valet. We approached the moss-covered doorway outfitted with white lights and got in line to present our invitations. I was happy to see that there were security guards at the front door. Jaxson had informed me that he requested some undercover officers to attend as well, and no one could get in without an invitation. As one of the party planners, Caitlin had checked to make sure that none of Derrick's family had been invited.

Caitlin greeted us as we handed our invitations to the folks at check-in.

"Oh my gosh, you guys. Look at you!" she exclaimed. "Carter, you make a handsome Prince Charming, and Jarrod, even though it's cheating a little because it's not really a costume, you make a dashing army captain."

Jarrod smiled at her. "How did you know it was us, Caitlin? Even with the masks on?"

She grinned. "I would recognize you guys anywhere. The Sullivan eyes give you away."

Looking her up and down, Jarrod asked, "And may I say that you look exceptionally beautiful tonight, Caitlin?"

Batting her eyelashes and doing a turn to show off her Glinda the Good Witch costume, she curtsied. "Why thank you, kind sir."

Giving her a kiss on the cheek, I asked, "Paige?"

She frowned and shook her head. "Not yet."

Disappointed, I told her I'd see her later and headed inside the ballroom. The entrance opened to a huge room with tables lining the sides and a large dance floor in the middle. Three huge glass chandeliers hung from the ceiling. Servers milled about offering hors d'ouevres, but my stomach clenched at the thought of eating anything. At the far end of the room was a bar. I turned to Jarrod and signaled I was going to get a drink. He nodded. I made my way through the crowd and chatted with a few people I recognized.

After grabbing two beers, I headed to the table that Jarrod had claimed. Hunter, Jaxson, and Grayson and his date, Cheryl, had joined him. I shook hands with everyone before sitting down. Jaxson was dressed as Batman and Grayson and Cheryl came as Bonnie and Clyde. I looked at Hunter, who was outfitted in a three-piece suit, a tie, and wore glasses over his mask.

"Did you just come from the office?" I inquired, puzzled. "What the hell are you supposed to be?"

Grinning, he loosened his tie and unbuttoned a few buttons on his shirt to reveal a T-shirt with Superman logo.

I laughed. "Clark Kent. Of course."

"And now the party can officially begin!" Xander exclaimed walking towards us.

Grayson took one look at Xander and his date dressed as The Beast and Belle and started laughing.

"How appropriate," I commented.

"If you are referring to my strong animal physique, thank

you," Xander said.

I rolled my eyes. "Yes, that is exactly what I was referring to. Your build. Not your personality."

He held up his middle finger. "Very funny."

In the middle of taking a sip of his beer, Jax suddenly choked and started coughing.

"Are you okay?" Hunter asked.

Unable to speak, Jax simply stared towards the door, eyes huge.

Everyone at the table turned to see what he was looking at. A woman dressed as Catwoman was walking our way. Her skintight costume hugged a tall, curvy figure. Long, black hair hung halfway down her back. Her eyes were lined kohl black, and her mouth was painted deep red. Cat ears and thigh high five-inch spiked heel boots completed the look. Though I was madly in love with Paige, even I could admit the woman was hot.

"Hello, everyone," Alyssa purred.

"Wow," Xander breathed.

Jaxson continued to stare, his mouth open.

"Cat got your tongue, Barney?" Lys asked him.

Clearing his throat, Jax rebounded. "Hardly, counselor. Just thinking how appropriate your costume is. Claws and all."

Eyes narrowing, she scoffed. "Sure. I bet that's exactly what you were thinking. I'm surprised your brain can still function, given all the blood in your body is now located in your crotch."

And with that parting shot, she strolled away towards the bar. Jax's eyes were on her ass as she walked off.

I struggled to stifle a laugh. Grayson, Hunter, and Xander weren't so successful.

"Why don't you two just fuck and get it over with?" Xander asked.

Looking thunderous, Jax stormed off in the opposite direction.

I scanned the room, my heart skipping a beat when I saw a few other Cinderellas in the crowd before realizing they weren't Paige. Taking a big drink from my bottle of beer, I looked at my watch. If she didn't arrive soon, I would head to her place. Sitting next to me, I heard Jarrod gasp. Following his eyes, I saw Peyton at the entrance. Dressed in a harem girl outfit that showed off her toned midsection and long legs, she looked gorgeous. Glancing to her right, I saw Paige slightly behind her. Taking in her beautiful face and long neck, my gaze traveled down to the tops of her full breasts revealed by the neckline of her gown and her small cinched-in waist.

Not taking his focus off Peyton, Jarrod whispered, "Go get your girl."

I walked over towards Paige and saw the panic in her eyes the moment she recognized me. I leaned down and gave Peyton a kiss on the cheek in greeting. She hugged me and whispered, "Don't let her go," in my ear.

I responded, "Count on it."

Bowing at the waist, I looked at Paige. "May I?"

My heart galloped as I waited for her response. I watched her struggle, seemingly torn between throwing herself at me or running in the opposite direction.

"Please?" I practically begged.

Releasing a breath as she put her hand in mine, I led her out to the dance floor. Gathering her in my arms, I pulled her tight against me. The erection that began the moment I saw her, swelled further. Lightly stroking her back, I nuzzled her cheek and inhaled her scent. Her body trembled in reaction.

"I've missed having you in my arms," I whispered in her ear.

She stayed silent, but her trembling increased.

I continued to caress her back. "I've missed the feel of your skin."

"Carter, don't," she shakily pleaded.

I pulled back so I could look at her face. Her eyes were shiny and she bit her lip.

"Don't what, Paige? Don't want you? Don't love you?" I demanded.

Wrestling herself from my hold, she fled from the dance floor towards the hallway. Naturally, I followed. She dashed into the ladies' room. Parking myself outside the door, I leaned against the wall and waited. Fifteen minutes later, she finally emerged looking as though she had been crying. Spotting me, she attempted to go around me. I grabbed her hand and pulled her further down the hallway to a small alcove. Placing my body between her and any escape route, I let go of her hand. She wouldn't quite meet my gaze. I noticed the shadows underneath her eyes.

"Cater, please let me go."

"You mean right now or in general?" I asked. "It doesn't matter. I'm not doing either."

"Why can't you just leave me alone? At least until Derrick is caught. When or if that happens, you can decide if you still want to be with me."

I forced myself to count to ten before responding. I was so damn frustrated and didn't want to speak harshly.

"I will always want to be with you, sweetheart. There will never be a day that goes by when I won't need to see you. Being away from you for these past five days ripped me apart, baby. Not hearing your voice, seeing you smile, kissing your lips, making love to you—I missed you so damn much. I miss talking to you about your day and sharing mine with you. I want to say goodnight to you every night and good morning to you every day. I love you."

She closed her eyes and took a deep breath. When she reopened them, I could tell she was fighting back tears.

"I wish I could lie to you and tell you that I don't miss all of those things too. It would be so much easier, but I can't." Looking up and sighing, she continued, "What I can do, though, is try to keep you out of Derrick's sights. If he doesn't see us together, if he thinks we broke up, he won't see you as a threat."

"You don't know what that asshole is going to do, Paige. I understand you feeling the need to try to protect me, because God knows I would do anything to keep you safe. But here's where our thinking differs. When adversity strikes, I want to challenge it head on. Separating doesn't accomplish anything except to make us both miserable. A very wise woman recently told me — and rather angrily, I might add — that, when faced with a tough circumstance, we should work it out. Together."

Smiling wryly, clearly recalling her own words, she stated, "True, I did say that, but that was not a life or death situation. This is."

"That's just semantics, Paige."

Touching the side of my face, she lamented, "I couldn't live with myself if something happened to you."

I took her hand and placed a kiss on her palm. "I'm not going anywhere, sweetheart. I have too much to live for."

Choking up, she whispered, "You can't know that for sure, Carter. What if —"

I cut her off. "We can ask *what if* all we want. I spent ten years kicking myself for letting you go. The second I saw you again, I knew that you were back for good. The bottom line is I can't be without you. I won't. We're going to see each other through this and anything else that comes along."

Not wanting to give her a chance to argue further, I took her face in my hands and kissed her. I could feel the tension in her body release, and she melted against me. I groaned as she wrapped her arms around my neck and ran her fingers through my hair. Releasing her face, I slid my hands over her shoulders, down the sides of her breasts, and then rested them at her waist, pulling her tight against me. She whimpered and squirmed against me in response.

"Let me taste you, angel. It's been too long."

Moaning, she opened her mouth. I explored her lips and mouth with my tongue. Slowly, I stroked her tongue with mine. She tasted so sweet and the sounds she made drove me crazy. I feasted on her mouth like a starving man. Not content to be just a recipient of my onslaught, she sucked my bottom lip into her mouth and gently bit down. I growled as the sensation went straight to my cock. After several minutes, I pulled my mouth from hers. She whimpered in protest. I looked at her lips, plump and wet from my kisses. Her breasts moved up and down as she tried to control her breathing and her nipples were pebbled against her gown.

"I need to be inside you, Paige.

"Yes, Carter, please. I need that too."

Chapter Forty-three: Carter

K nowing that the pants of my costume would not hide the raging erection I was sporting, I slipped my arm around Paige's waist and walked slightly behind her, using the full skirt of her gown as cover. Spotting Jarrod exiting the men's room, I let him know that we were leaving and asked if he could hitch a ride with someone. Smiling, he said it wouldn't be a problem. As soon as we got into my truck, Paige texted Peyton and let her know we had left together. My house was closer, so I headed there.

As we drove up, Paige reacted to the newly framed garage and lack of a front porch.

"Oh, Carter. I'm so sorry."

I lifted our joined hands and placed a kiss on the back of hers. "I hated that front porch anyway, remember? You're going to help me design the new one."

She smiled slightly. "Where's the mustang?"

"At my parents' house. They have plenty of room in their garage. Plus, I told my dad he could drive it if he wanted to."

"Ah, you bribed him, huh?"

I grinned. "Let's just say I knew how to make him an offer he couldn't refuse."

We headed in the front door. After disabling and then resetting the alarm system, I turned to face her.

"Hungry?"

Her blue eyes darkened. "Just for you."

Scooping her up in my arms, I carried her up the stairs. As we entered the bedroom, we both caught a glimpse of ourselves in the mirror. Staring at our reflection, we burst into laughter.

"Oh, this is hysterical," she sputtered. "I knew someday my prince would come and sweep me off my feet."

Laughing, I set her down on her feet. She took her hair down and ran her fingers through it. It was wild and wavy. I stroked some of the strands.

Looking at her costume, I commented, "I don't even know where to begin to figure out how to get that off of you."

Smiling, she insisted, "You first."

I unbuttoned my jacket and took off my shoes and socks. Next, I removed my T-shirt. She watched my every move with interest. I loved how her breath quickened and her eyes darkened as she appraised my chest and torso.

"I love how strong and masculine your body is."

Grinning, I answered, "I like how you look at me, sweetheart. I never tire of knowing that I turn you on."

"Like no one else," she admitted.

"Again, nice to know. Especially since I am the only man you're going to be seeing naked."

"Lucky me," she confessed.

My erection grew as she looked at me, eyes blazing. As I lowered my zipper, she licked her lips and I almost came on the spot. Pulling off my pants and underwear in one motion, I stood before her completely naked, my cock pointing straight out.

"Now you," I instructed.

Bending down, she grasped underneath her skirt and pulled out a huge, full-length slip covered in ruffles.

Amazed at the size of it, I joked, "How did that fit under there?"

She chuckled before sliding each of her long gloves down her arms. She reached behind her back, and I heard her unzip the top of her gown. She removed one arm out of a short sleeve and then the other, the entire time holding the top close to her chest, not revealing anything underneath. My breathing increased in anticipation. Slowly, she slid the costume down her body. With every inch she uncovered, my dick twitched. When she stepped out of the dress, I took a long look at her and moaned.

Her breasts were barely contained in a blue lace corset. I could see her nipples poking against the fabric. A few inches of her stomach were on display before the top of her lace garter belt wrapped around her waist. Blue lace bikini panties tied at the sides and showcased her curvy hips. The garter belt was fastened to white sheer stockings, leading down to four-inch sparkly heels. My cock was now so swollen, it was almost pointing straight up against my belly.

"I was going to ask you if you liked my outfit," she teasingly said before looking at my erection, "but it's pretty evident what you think."

"You are the sexiest fucking woman I have ever seen."

"And just think, I'm all yours."

"Damn right you are," I claimed.

Needing to touch her, I walked over and ran my hands over her breasts and ass. I squeezed her breasts and bent my head to suck each lace-covered point in my mouth. Moaning, she threw her head back and grabbed my biceps.

"Turn around," I instructed.

She did as I asked, and I drew in a deep breath at the sight of the crisscrossed ribbon that fastened her corset. I untied the bow and removed it from her, running my tongue up her spine. She shivered at my touch. Turning her back around to face me, I gazed at her full breasts tipped with dark rosy nipples.

"You have the most beautiful breasts," I murmured before squeezing the full flesh and tweaking her nipples. She cried out. "You like that don't you, baby? Your nipples are so sensitive."

Bending down again, I traced around each nipple before gently biting them.

"Oh, Carter, that feels so good," she breathed.

Continuing, I licked a path down her torso. After dipping my tongue into her belly button, I put my face between her legs and inhaled her scent.

"You smell so sweet, baby. I can't wait to taste you."

She whimpered in response. I reached up and untied her panties, slipping off the scrap of lace. I nuzzled her pubic hair and parted her lips with my thumbs.

"You're always so wet for me," I marveled.

I fastened my lips over her clit and sucked. Moaning, she thrust her lower body toward me. Relentlessly, I licked, sucked, and nipped at the engorged bud while I held her hips as she thrust back and forth.

"Don't stop, please, Carter. Don't stop. Oh, oh, yes!"

Even though her legs were shaking, I kept my mouth on her, enjoying the taste of her juices as she rode out the spasms. Spent, she practically collapsed in my arms before I carried her to the bed. Laying her on her back, I placed a hand on either side of her shoulders. I leaned down and kissed her, letting her taste herself on my lips. Her mouth opened underneath mine and she sucked on my tongue. I made love to her mouth for several minutes until I could feel her getting restless beneath me. Reaching down, she made a move to unclasp the clips of her garter belt. I grabbed her hand to stop her.

"No," I told her. "That, your stockings, and your shoes are staying on. I want to feel the silk against me and your heels digging into me as I slide my cock in and out of you."

Her eyes clouded with desire. Kissing me again, she ran her hands over my chest, shoulders, and stomach. My muscles were taut, straining for release. I pulled her legs wide and kneeling, I positioned myself at her entrance. I slid into her inch by inch, savoring the feel of her walls gripping me.

Once all the way inside, I commanded, "Wrap your legs around me."

She complied, and I felt her heels dig into my ass. Lifting her arms above her head, I took each nipple in my mouth and sucked. She whimpered and rubbed against me, urging me to move. I captured her mouth with mine and started to move. I slid my cock in and out of her slowly, the sensations building. Kissing her again, I looked into her eyes.

"I love you, baby."

"I love you, too, Carter."

Pumping slightly faster and harder, I implored, "Don't ever leave me again, Paige."

Looking up at me, her eyes filled with a combination of love and lust, she promised, "Never."

With that, my control broke and I fucked her harder and faster, loving the feel of her heels digging into me and her hips meeting mine with each thrust. Knowing I was close, I reached between her legs and rubbed her clit.

"Come for me, baby."

Almost immediately, she exploded, crying out, "Carter!"

As I felt her spasm around me and watched the pleasure on her face, I slammed my cock into her, faster and harder. Seconds later, my orgasm hit with a fierceness as I spilled myself inside her. Removing my hands from her wrists, I pulled out of her and laid on the bed, fitting her against my side. Once I had my breath back, I led her to the bathroom where I took off the rest of her clothes and gently washed both her and myself. After drying us both, I handed her a spare toothbrush and left the bathroom so she could have some privacy. A few minutes later, she walked out of the bathroom, and I slipped one of my T-shirts over her head. Pulling back the covers, I settled her into my bed. By the time I used the bathroom, turned off the lights, and got in next to her, she was already asleep.

"Goodnight, sweetheart," I whispered before kissing her gently on the forehead.

CHAPTER FORTY-FOUR: PAIGE

Saturday morning, I awoke to the light streaming through Carter's bedroom window. Slipping out from underneath his muscular arm wrapped around my waist, I tiptoed to the bathroom. After using the toilet, I washed my face, brushed my teeth, and ran a comb through my hair. I decided to make breakfast, but noting the chill in the air, I went into the closet and grabbed one of Carter's flannel shirts to put on over his T-shirt. After rolling up the sleeves several times, I located a pair of sweatpants. Folding the waist down to take up some of the length, I let them rest at my hips and hoped they wouldn't fall down while I was cooking.

Quietly, I descended the stairs and walked into the kitchen. I took a look in the refrigerator and the pantry, deciding that I had the ingredients to make eggs and pancakes. I added the coffee grounds, a filter, and water to the coffeemaker and turned on the power. Humming, I set to work mixing the pancake batter and whisking together the milk and eggs. While the pans were heating up, I grabbed the orange juice, hot sauce, butter, and syrup and put them on the dining room table. I also set out napkins, forks, and knives as well. Satisfied the griddle pan was hot enough, I poured several circles of batter. After a few minutes, I flipped the pancakes over to brown the other side.

"Brilliant, gorgeous, and a great cook. The ideal woman," I heard Carter's deep voice say from behind me.

Smiling, I turned to face him. He wore only drawstring pajama pants, and I openly admired his muscular arms and torso.

"Keep looking at me like that and your yummy breakfast is going to burn."

I licked my lips. "What if I want you for breakfast first?"

Eyes darkening, he strode across the kitchen in three steps. Pulling me tight against him, he ravaged my mouth. Lifting me up and sitting me on the island, he pulled back my hair and licked the side of my neck. The whiskers on his jaw lightly scraped me as he crushed his lips to mine once more. Dazed, it took me a minute to realize someone was knocking on the front door.

"Someone's at the front door."

"Shit!" Carter swore, breathing heavy.

"Who is it?"

"I completely forgot that I had invited the guys over to work on the garage this morning. I'll get rid of them."

Secretly wanting him to do just that, I shook my head. "No, it's okay. We can continue this later."

Looking frustrated, he swore again.

Laughing, I climbed down from the counter and gestured towards the very obvious erection tenting his pants. "You may want to take care of that, though."

Turning away from me, he muttered, "I'd rather have you take care of it."

Laughing louder, I continued cooking. I heard him yell, "Hold on a minute!" and then run up the stairs. Five minutes later, dressed in jeans and a sweatshirt, he led Xander, Jarrod, Hunter, Jackson, and Grayson into the kitchen. Acutely aware that I had neither a bra nor underwear on, I hastily buttoned up a few buttons of Carter's flannel shirt.

"Well, surprise, surprise, guys. It's Paige," Xander announced with a grin. "Imagine seeing you here."

"Nice outfit," Jackson noted.

"No need to get dressed up on our account," Grayson

joked with a smile.

"Keep it up and I'm only making breakfast for Carter," I warned.

Smiling, but instantly mute, they all gathered plates, glasses, napkins, and silverware and set their places in the dining room. I added more eggs to the frying pan as the guys took care of toast and grabbing some fruit from the refrigerator.

Laughing as he came and put his arms around me, Carter said, "You're all just jealous. I've got a gorgeous woman, looking sexy as hell wearing nothing but my clothes, cooking breakfast after an incredible night. How many of you woke up to that this morning?"

As every single man in the room looked at me, I felt myself turning red. Turning to Carter with eyes narrowed, I muttered through clenched teeth, "A little TMI, honey."

Jackson laughed. "Like we didn't know what was going on, Paige? Really?"

Still embarrassed, I took the eggs and first batch of pancakes from the stove and wiped my hands on a dish towel.

"On that note, I am going to call Peyton to see if she can give me a ride home."

I made it as far as the living room before I felt Carter's grab me around the waist.

"Don't rush off, sweetheart. I didn't mean to embarrass you."

"I'm okay. Really," I assured him. "I'm going to go home, clean up, and do some chores while you all work on the garage."

"Am I going to see you later on?" he asked. His brow furrowed. I could sense he was a little worried I would distance myself again.

"Definitely."

He let out the breath he had been holding and treated me

to a huge grin. "Can I pick you up at six? We'll go to dinner."

"Sounds great."

As I headed up the stairs, he called after me. "Paige?"

I turned to face him. "Yes?"

"Pack a bag, would you? I want you to stay the weekend."

"Try to keep me away."

Smiling, he sprinted up the stairs and kissed me senseless.

After texting Peyton to secure a ride, I answered a few e-mails then gathered up my underwear, shoes, and costume. I walked through the downstairs, noting the dining room table was empty and the kitchen was spotless. Sitting on the counter was a plate of eggs and toast, along with a freshly picked bouquet of wildflowers. Carter never ceased to surprise me with his thoughtfulness. His romantic gestures were a constant reminder of how much I meant to him. I sat down at the island and enjoyed my breakfast. After putting my dishes in the dishwasher, I found a small pitcher in the cabinet and arranged my bouquet, leaving it in the center of the island.

Figuring Peyton would be arriving shortly, I let myself out the back door. Sitting down in the bed of Carter's truck, I watched the men put the new roof on the garage. They worked well together, and I enjoyed the view of their muscles flexing with their efforts. My eyes were mainly drawn to Carter as I admired his tall, strong body. The man was gorgeous. Over the past few months, I still had a difficult time believing he was mine.

Peyton pulled her jeep into the driveway and waved. I shouted goodbyes to everyone. Carter winked at me and mouthed, "I love you," to which I responded in kind. I shoved my things in Peyton's back seat and bucked myself in front.

Glancing at me, she commented, "Walk of shame this morning, huh? Barefoot and everything."

I smiled broadly, not even bothering to pretend to feel guilty. "What can I say?"

Smiling back, she said, "I am just so happy that you changed your mind and are seeing him again."

"Me too," I admitted. "I'm still scared, but I guess I would rather be with him than without him."

"There is something to be said for having a strong man by your side."

"Not to mention hot," I added, raising my eyebrows.

She laughed. "Well, yes, that is a plus."

"Speaking of hot men, what is going on with you and Jarrod?"

She clutched the steering wheel until her knuckles turned white and I saw a flush spread across her cheeks.

"I don't know what you are talking about."

I smirked. "Peyton, don't lie to me. I have seen the way that he looks at you. I have also seen the way he touches you whenever he can."

"Oh, Paige, I am so confused. Have you taken a good look at him? The man is sex on a stick."

I chuckled. "He is a fine-looking man."

"I know, right?" she continued. "I mean, I had a little crush on him back in high school, but now . . . It's like every time I see him all I want to do is . . ." she broke off, a bit embarrassed.

"Strip him naked and devour him like your favorite dessert?"

Eyes wide, she nodded. "Exactly!"

"Welcome to my world," I confided. "If I even think about Carter, I suddenly need to fan myself."

She laughed. "Yeah, but you and Carter have an actual relationship. With Jarrod, it's just this unbelievable attraction."

"Chemistry is a powerful thing."

"You're telling me. I have never, ever felt this way before. Do you know the kiss he gave me in the parking lot that night got me hotter than any kind of sexual contact I have had to date? I know I'm not that experienced, but what the hell?"

"Just imagine if you were to actually sleep with him?"

She shuddered. "I don't think I would survive it."

I laughed. "Are you going to find out?"

She bit her lip. "I can't believe I am saying this, but God, I hope so."

CHAPTER FORTY-FIVE: PAIGE

Carter texted me that we weren't going anywhere too fancy for dinner, but still I wanted to impress. I settled on a charcoal boatneck cashmere sweater with three-quarter length sleeves, an A-line crepe black skirt that fell to mid-calf, and black four-inch sandals with ankle straps. I put my hair up in loose bun and kept my make-up simple with taupe eye-shadow, mascara, and mauve lipstick. After inserting small diamond hoops in my ears and putting on a silver watch, I grabbed my suitcase and headed downstairs. I grabbed a black trench coat from the hall closet and, because it was a nice fall evening, I locked up and went outside to sit on the porch to wait for Carter. I waved to the officer parked at my curb and sat down on one of the rocking chairs.

At five forty-five, Carter's truck pulled into the driveway. He got out and walked up the front steps. He looked gorgeous in a pair of black dress pants, a deep blue V-neck sweater, and a dark brown leather jacket. I smelled his familiar, spicy sent as he hugged me and kissed me hello.

"You look gorgeous," he complimented.

"Right back at you," I returned.

Grinning, he took my hand and picked up my suitcase with the other. After opening my door and helping me inside, he walked around and put my bag in the back before joining me in the front seat. Taking ahold of my hand, he brought it to his lips and kissed it.

"Have I ever told you how much I love your cologne?"

"I think you may have mentioned it once or twice."

"You've worn Eternity since we were in high school. There's something about the scent, combined with you, that is just so . . . delicious."

Grinning, he squeezed my hand.

"What have you been up to since I saw you this morning?"

"I did my usual weekly house cleaning, took a bike ride, and jotted down some notes for a couple of work projects. I also got the chance to catch up with Sarah which was nice. I miss her."

"She's still in London, right? When is she due back?"

"If all goes well, she's hoping to return the week after Christmas. I can't wait to see her."

"I haven't seen her since the last reunion. Does she still live in New York City?"

"Yes, she's been there ever since college."

"It's great that the five of you have stayed close."

"I don't know what I would do without them. You have the same kind of bond with Hunter, Grayson, and Jackson too. Plus Xander and Jarrod."

"Yeah, true. Though Jarrod was away for all those years, having him back for the past couple has been great."

"Speaking of Jarrod, I had an interesting conversation with Peyton today."

"What is going on between the two of them lately? When he saw her at the Halloween party, I thought he was going to swallow his tongue."

I chuckled. "Really? I missed seeing that."

"They never had anything between them when we were younger did they?"

Not wanting to reveal Peyton's crush, I simply said, "As far as I know they were just friendly. Being three years older than us, he was usually off with his group of friends, and then he enlisted right after our freshman year."

"Jarrod is not very revealing, but even so, he never

mentioned anything going on back then to me."

"Have you seen the way he looks at her?"

He nodded, grinning. "Yep. My brother is definitely interested."

We pulled into the restaurant parking lot. Benini's was one of our old favorites from date nights in high school. The food was great, and the atmosphere was romantic and intimate. We walked hand and hand to the entrance. Once inside, he helped me off with my coat before hanging both of ours of the rack just inside. As our hostess was seating us, I noticed the grin on his face.

Once seated side by side at our table, I asked, "What are you thinking about that's putting that smile on your face?"

"The coat you are wearing tonight reminded me of another time you had on a similar one."

Knowing exactly what he was referring to, I smiled. "I was so nervous that night."

Raising an eyebrow, he replied, "Really? Could have fooled me. You were like a woman on a mission."

"I was scared to death on the inside. I was so afraid you were going to turn me down."

"Are you kidding me? I had wanted you forever. For all my trying to be strong, as soon as you walked through the door of the tree house, I was a goner."

"Do you know that I shopped for a month before I bought that outfit? I knew you were attracted to me, but I was so self-conscious because I was heavier. At that age, I didn't have the best self-esteem about my body. Though you always made me feel beautiful."

"You have no idea how much you turned me on back then. You were the sexiest thing I had ever seen. You still are."

I brought his hand to my lips and then rested it against my cheek. "I am so glad it was you, Carter. The way I felt about you made it so special."

"Even after I acted like an asshole?"

I chuckled. "Even then. I have never regretted my choice to have you be my first."

"You gave me a something so precious. I had always wanted to be your first."

"You did?"

"Oh yeah," he admitted gazing into my eyes. "Honestly, I wanted to be your first and your only. Now, I want to be your last."

I leaned in and kissed him gently. "I love you, Carter."

"I love you too, angel."

Breaking the spell, our waiter came over and asked for our orders. Carter decided on the NY sirloin and I chose the grilled salmon. We also requested a bottle of white wine to share.

"Jaxson updated me on the investigation this afternoon."

Tensing a bit, but knowing we needed to talk about it, I asked, "Any news?"

"They tracked Walters to a rental house in Simsbury, but when they got there, he was gone."

I sighed. "Damn."

"They'll catch him. He's getting a little more careless in covering his tracks."

"I just hope that doesn't mean he's also getting more desperate."

He put his arm around me and squeezed. "Have faith, sweetheart. Between me and the police, you have twenty-four-hour protection."

"And what about you?" I asked a bit anxiously.

"Let's just say Jax is looking out for both of us."

I let out a huge breath. "That's good to hear."

"Some more good news," he began. "They found two witnesses who saw a man keying your car at the adoption event. They couldn't pick him out of a photo array, though.

Hopefully, they'll be able to add more charges."

"If they catch him."

"When they catch him."

I looked out the window and then back at him. "When they catch him."

When the food arrived, we moved on to more pleasant subjects. Carter updated me on his current work projects and I did the same. We spent a long time discussing our ideas about Hunter's riverfront offices. I appreciated Carter's ideas and his knowledge. It was exciting to share that commonality with him. I grabbed a pen from my purse and we sketched out some ideas. I imagined Parker's face when he saw the napkins with our notes.

Dinner long finished, Carter turned to me. "I don't want you to think that I have a one-track mind, but ever since I picked you up tonight, I have been wondering what you have on under your clothes."

Laughing, I stated, "You are such a man."

He grinned. "Hey, you are the one who always wears the sexy lingerie. It's your fault I wonder. You've set quite the precedent."

I threw my head back and laughed. "I guess that is true."

"So?" He looked at me expectantly.

I leaned close, put my hand on his upper thigh and whispered, "What if I told you that I am not wearing anything?"

His cock jumped at my admission.

"What?" he practically croaked.

I leaned back in my chair and offered, "Check for yourself."

Carter's eyes darkened as he reached under the tablecloth and slid his hand under my skirt and up my thigh until he reached between my legs. Detecting no barrier, he stroked my pubic hair before inserting his finger inside me to feel my wetness. My hand still on his thigh, I felt his erection swell.

His gray eyes turning stormy before closing and then

reopening them, he breathed, "You mean to tell me that I have been sitting next to you all night and there was nothing between me and your sweet pussy?"

I reveled in his look of desire. Grabbing his wrist and removing it from beneath my skirt, I brought his wet finger to my mouth and sucked off my own juices. "True," I admitted.

Growling, he reached into his wallet and threw down more than enough money to pay for our meal. Practically running, he grasped my hand and led me to the front door, barely remembering to take our coats of the rack on the way out. As soon as we got in the car, he crushed his mouth to mine. Gasping at the intensity of his need, I opened my lips beneath him and moaned as his tongue plunged in and out of my mouth. Tearing his mouth from mine, he started the truck.

"Underwear or no underwear, I can't win." I joked.

Grinning, he answered, "Oh, we're both going to win. But, you first."

With that he pulled up my skirt so that it was covering only the tops of my thighs. Not taking his eyes off the road, he inserted one, then two, then three fingers inside me. I gasped at the sensation as I stretched to accommodate the invasion. He thrusted in and out, burying his hand so deep I felt his knuckles on my clit. Using the back of his hand to apply direct pressure to the engorged bud, his fingers continued sliding inside me at increasing pace. My orgasm hit me full force and I screamed in release. Showing no mercy, he stayed inside me, stroking as I spasmed around him. When I stopped trembling, he slowly removed his hand and then brought his fingers to his mouth, cleaning each one with his tongue.

As we pulled into his driveway, I put my head back against the seat and sighed. "Yeah, I'd say I won that one."

Smiling, his face taught with desire, he stated. "Now, my turn."

Chapter Forty-Six: Carter

My heart was still galloping after the sight, feel, and sounds of bringing Paige to orgasm. Seeing her ecstasy got me so damn hard. I had never met a more sensual woman. She made no apologies for wanting me and enjoying the pleasure we brought to each other. And she never ceased to surprise me with her boldness. I hope she never stopped.

I took her suitcase from the backseat and followed her to the front door. After unlocking it, disabling the alarm and then locking back up, I motioned towards the stairs. I was mesmerized by the sway of her curvy ass and hips as I walked behind her. I set her suitcase on the window seat. By the time I turned around, she was walking to the bathroom, taking off her clothes and discarding them on the way. Like a dog on a leash, I followed, ripping off my clothes in record time. As I got to the door, she was closing it behind her. Over her shoulder, she said, "Give me a minute."

My dick was so hard, I could've used it to knock the door down, but I waited patiently while I heard the sound of running water and then the toilet flush. A few minutes later, Paige opened the door completely naked. I don't think I would ever look at her and not be astounding by her body. She looked like a woman should look. She felt soft and smooth against me and I wanted to sink into her. Walking towards the middle of the bathroom, she treated me to the incredible view of her back and ass.

"Ever since the first time you brought me here, I have been dying to try out this tub," she confessed. "With you."

The thought of her body, warm and wet entangled with mine in the large soaker tub caused my dick to twitch. She climbed over the side and sunk into the water up to her shoulders. I climbed in on the opposite side. Before I could sit down, she raised up on her knees so that her face was just about eye level with my straining erection.

Looking up at my face, she licked her lips and said, "I've been wanting to do this all night."

She licked my cock from base to tip, humming with pleasure. Never taking her eyes off mine, she opened her mouth and took as much of me as she could until the head touched the back of her throat. Slowing withdrawing, she repeated the same motion several times, adding more suction each time. The sight of her, naked and wet, on her knees sucking my cock like it was the best thing she ever tasted was the stuff of fantasies. I put one hand on the wall and fisted one hand in her hair as my hips thrust towards her. Already on the edge, I knew I wasn't going to last long. When she increased her speed and put a hand around the base of my cock, I exploded into her mouth, her name on my lips.

When I opened my eyes, Paige looked up at me and smiled. "Now, we're tied."

Still regaining my breath, I lowered myself into the tub to sit opposite her. She took a washcloth from the towel bar and lathered some soap onto it. Starting with my feet, she gently began washing my body. She slid the soft cloth over my calves and thighs with long, smooth strokes. From there, she thoroughly washed my now semi-erect cock. Leaning towards me, she ran the washcloth over my shoulder and biceps, moaning appreciatively as she felt their size and strength. Putting the washcloth on the side of the tub, she soaped up her hands and used them to clean my chest. Her nails circled and scraped my nipples before trailing downwards to stroke my abdomen, running her fingertips over every muscle. By this point, I had completely recovered, and my dick was fully erect, pointing straight up, the head just breaking the surface of the water.

As I reached for the washcloth to repay her in kind, she quickly took it in her hand. Lathering more soap onto it, she ran her eyes over my body. With eyes darkened by desire, she declared, "Since you still seem to be recuperating, I'll just take care of myself."

With that, she sat up in the tub and started washing. After cleaning the long, slim column of her neck, she wiped the fabric over her collarbone and lathed her breasts, paying extra attention to her pebbled nipples. Moaning, she slid the cloth over her torso and down her stomach. I was practically panting as she washed herself, leaving a trail of bubbles wherever she touched. As she reached between her legs and rubbed the washcloth over her pubic hair, she threw her head back and moaned louder. I was so fucking turned on, I couldn't stop my hand from wrapping around my dick and stroking the steel flesh.

Starting the tub faucet, Paige held the washcloth underneath before squeezing it out so that the fresh water ran over her body, rinsing away the soap. As the water ran over her lush curves, I stroked myself harder and faster. Smiling, she grabbed my wrist and removed my hand from my dick. Turning around to face away from me, she spread her legs wide so that they were outside my thighs. Holding my cock in her hand, she inserted the head in her opening and sunk all the way down so that I filled her. Looking over her shoulder, she asked, "Can you get my back?"

I picked up the washcloth and ran it over her smooth back. Holding onto her hips, I pulled out of her. Whimpering, she protested.

"You wanted me to wash your back? That's exactly what I am going to do."

With that I took the cloth and ran it over her round ass. Sliding the fabric in between her cheeks, I stroked her from the bottom of her back to the start of her pussy. She squirmed and started to moan. Lightly soaping my hands, I rubbed and washed her ass before inserting my index finger into warm channel. As I gently plunged in and out of her, she moaned with pleasure.

"Oh my gosh, Carter. I can't stand it."

Continuing to finger her, I growled, "You thought it was fun to tease me, huh, sweetheart? Let's see if you can take it."

Inserting another finger into her, I pumped in a slow, steady rhythm. After a few minutes, her gasps became cries.

"Please, Carter. Please."

Not stopping, I asked in a low voice, "Please what, baby? Tell me what you want."

Panting, she begged. "You. I want you."

Relentless, I asked. "You have me, Paige. Tell me what you really want."

"Fuck me, Carter. Please. I need you inside me so bad."

Moaning, I removed my fingers and slammed my dick into her with one huge thrust. Grabbing her hips, I fucked her deep and hard.

"Is this what you wanted, baby? My cock deep inside you, filling you up?"

Throwing her head back, she moaned riding me faster and faster. "Yes, Carter, yes!"

Removing my hands from her hips, I reached up and covered her breasts, pinching and tugging on her hard nipples.

"You got me so hot, baby. Come for me."

Bouncing up and down frantically, she reached her orgasm with a wild scream. Feeling her spasm around me, I burst, shooting stream after stream into her quaking channel. As she slumped back against my chest, I drained the tub and quickly washed us both with fresh soap and water. After brushing our teeth, we crawled into bed. Placing her on her side, I spooned her body from behind, one arm beneath her head and one arm around her waist.

"Goodnight, Carter. I love you."

Smiling, I whispered, "Goodnight, Paige. I love you, too."

Chapter Forty-seven: Paige

I slowly awakened wrapped in Carter's arms, his muscular chest against my back and his strong legs intertwined with mine. Last night had been incredible. From our conversation to working together to dinner and finally the explosive way we made love, everything had been pretty perfect.

When we had first reconnected, our chemistry was off the charts. That, combined with our history, was a strong pull. In the past few months, we had gotten to know each other as adults. The connection that had begun when we were kids had deepened. I was in love with Carter, the man, who had become a great friend, a valiant protector, and the kind of lover I didn't think actually existed in real life. I admired all that he had accomplished, was insanely attracted to him, adored his family and friends, and couldn't imagine a future without him.

He had indicated a future for the two of us, but we hadn't actually talked about anything concrete. Of course, the situation with Derrick certainly hindered any prospective plans. Could I really expect Carter to start talking about promises with all the danger that surrounded me?

"It's too early in the morning for your brain to be working that hard," Carter stated in a low, sleepy voice.

"I didn't know you were awake," I commented.

Pulling me closer to him, his erection was warm and hard against my lower back. "Really?" he asked. "Nothing gave it away, huh?"

I grinned as my body reacted to his. "Okay, maybe there

was a little clue."

Growling in my ear, he said, "Little, huh?"

"Sorry, poor choice of words," I admitted. "Definitely nothing little about that. But how was I to know that meant you were awake? That particular sign could have just been your normal morning state."

"Physiologically, that could be true," he acknowledged. "However, I do believe it also has to do with the fact that the woman I love is pressed up against me, deliciously and wonderfully naked."

I sighed and felt a whole bunch of my naked parts react. "Well, in that case, it would be a shame to waste the opportunity."

Kissing the back of my neck, he breathed, "Excellent idea."

He hooked an arm under my knee, lifting my leg slightly before slowly entering me from behind. In this intimate position, I felt every ridge of him as he filled me inch by inch.

"Damn, baby. I'm in so deep. You feel so fucking good."

Where last night had been frantic, this was deliberate and sensual. He kept the rhythm unhurried, as if he wanted to savor every stroke. He reached his hands around and lightly traced my nipples with his fingers. We had made love several times before, but this felt different, like our souls were connecting along with our bodies. In and out, over and over, we moved together. I felt my orgasm build, but I wanted to hold it at bay so I could continue to feel the closeness. After several minutes, my body wouldn't be denied any longer. With a long moan, I came, riding wave after wave of pleasure. As he felt me spasm, he groaned my name and spilled himself inside me. When he withdrew, I whimpered at the loss and realized that tears were running down my cheeks. Turning me to face him, Carter wiped them with his thumbs and kissed me gently.

Looking into my eyes, he declared, "As many times and as

many ways as we have made love before, that was on a whole other level. I love you, Paige."

I kissed him back. "I can't even put it into words except to say that I love you, too, Carter. So much."

Gathering me into his arms, he held me tight to his chest. I listed to the solid beat of his heart and then the steady sound of his breathing as he fell back to sleep. Waiting a few minutes, I quietly got out of bed. Grabbing my toiletries and clothes, I went into the bathroom to shower and get dressed. As I walked out into the bedroom in jeans and a navy shell and long cardigan, Carter was just getting out from under the covers. Seeing his naked body, I was tempted to throw off my clothes and climb back in. I really was turning into a nympho-maniac around this man.

Walking over to me, he kissed me before inhaling deeply. "You look and smell delicious."

"Thank you," I accepted. "Right back at you."

Grinning, he chuckled. "I didn't like waking up without you, though."

"Sorry, but I just figured if I didn't get up we stood the chance of not leaving the bed all day."

Eyes darkening, he asked, "And that would be bad be-cause?"

Smiling, I replied. "As tempting as that is, last night at din-ner you mentioned you had a surprise planned today."

He grinned. "Oh, right, that I did. Well, I'll forgive you this time. Should I be hurt that you are choosing your surprise over me?"

I shrugged my shoulder and threw up my hands. "What can I say?"

Laughing, Carter headed off to the bathroom. While he was in the shower, I located fresh sheets and stripped and remade his bed. I brought the soiled linens down the hall to his sec-ond-floor laundry room. I had just finished putting on my watch and earrings and was slipping into my sneakers when he joined me. He looked yummy in faded jeans, boots, and a V-neck burgundy sweater with black vertical stripes on either side of his wide chest.

"Grab your coat, sweetheart. We're going out to eat before the surprise."

I put on my dark brown thigh-length car coat and we headed down the stairs. He grabbed his leather jacket from the hall closet and we headed to his truck. It was a gorgeous fall day, sunny and about sixty degrees. The leaves were at peak color-changing and we admired the view as we drove. A half hour later, we arrived at a diner, where we enjoyed a brunch of omelets, waffles, and coffee. Bellies full, Carter put his arm around me on the way out of the restaurant. After we got into his truck, he turned to look at me.

"Did you ever wonder why I didn't send you anything on Friday?"

"What?" I asked him, confused.

"Last week, when I was missing you like crazy, I delivered something to you every day. But not Friday."

I had thanked him for all the sweet gifts. I had assumed that there was nothing from him on Friday because he had been hoping he would see me at the Halloween party where he wanted to convince me to start seeing him again. Since that is exactly what happened, I didn't give the absence of another gift a second thought.

Grinning, I said, "You gave me plenty on Friday, if you re-call."

His eyes turned stormy at my reminder. "I was the one who received the gift that night, sweetheart. You came back to me."

I kissed him, savoring the feel of his lips against mine. "I was a fool to have stayed away as long as I did."

He kissed me again, longer this time. When we broke apart,

he said, "I was going to give this to you Friday night, but as soon as I saw you, all I could think about was making sure you changed your mind."

With that, he pulled a small box from his jacket pocket and placed it in my hand.

"Carter, I don't need anything else. I have you."

Leaning down to kiss me gently, he nodded. "Yes, you do. I am completely yours, but this is something I got especially for you. Open it."

I carefully unwrapped the gift, revealing a small jewelry box. Lifting the top, I gazed at a platinum charm in the shape of an angel, encrusted with small diamonds, and attached to a delicate chain. My eyes, shining with tears, met his.

"Oh, Carter. It's exquisite."

"You always have been and always will be my angel, Paige."

I removed the necklace from the box and fastened it around my neck. Leaning across the seat, I wrapped my arms around his neck, threaded my hands in his hair, and put my lips to his, sliding my tongue across the seam of his mouth. He opened, and I slipped inside to stroke his mouth. Groaning, he took control of the kiss, and devoured my mouth. As we parted, I grasped the angel.

"You make me feel so special. Thank you for this. I love it. I love you."

Pushing my hair behind my ear, he gazed down at me. "I love you, too, baby."

CHAPTER FORTY-EIGHT: CARTER

After another fifteen-minute drive, we arrived at our destination. We got out of the truck and I took her hand in mine.

Recognizing our surroundings, Paige asked, "What are we doing at Grayson's clinic?"

Smiling, I answered, "You'll see."

We walked up to the front door and rang the bell to gain entry. A minute later Grayson opened the door. I shook his hand and he gave Paige a kiss on the cheek.

"Are you guys ready?" he asked.

Paige looked back and forth between the two of us. "Ready for what?"

I looked at Grayson and nodded. Leading us down a long hallway, he opened a side door. The three of us stepped outside to a large, fenced in area. Approximately fifteen dogs of various ages and sizes romped about. Toys, tennis balls, frisbees, and various agility course items scattered the yard.

"Have fun," Grayson instructed before shutting the door behind him.

Paige looked at me, her blue eyes sparkling with excitement. "Do we get to play with them?"

I smiled down at her. "For as long as we want."

I whistled, and all the pups came running over to greet us. Paige laughed as we were bombarded with paws, wet noses, and licks. Taking time to hug every one, she beamed at me, saying, "Thank you!" I kissed her, no easy feat as she was surrounded by wiggly, jumping bodies.

For the next few hours, Paige and I had a blast frolicking with the dogs. I enjoyed watching the delight on her face and hearing the constant sound of her laughter. It was exactly what I had hoped for when I set this up with Grayson. Knowing how concerned Paige was with the whole Derrick situation, I had wanted to take her mind off things for a while. From the flush of her cheeks and the sparkle in her eyes, I could see that I accomplished my mission.

At two o'clock, we reluctantly left the clinic and thanked Grayson. I slipped my arm around Paige's shoulders on our walk back to my truck. After I opened her door and got her settled, I walked around the front, climbed in the cab, grasped her hand and put it on my thigh.

As we pulled out of the parking lot, Paige kissed me on the cheek and said, "That was so much fun. Thank you for arranging that."

I stroked my thumb across the back of her hand. "You're welcome, sweetheart. I'm glad you enjoyed it."

She nodded. "Without question. I'm just lucky that the Shepherd pup wasn't still there. I don't think I would have been able to resist taking him home. And until the whole Derrick situation is resolved, I don't want to take any chances."

I brought her hand to my lips. "You'll have a puppy before you know it."

Looking at me, concerned, she said softly, "I hope so."

The rest of the drive was spent listening to a mix of classic rock and heavy metal while admiring the fall foliage. When we pulled into my driveway, it was after three. We planned to clean up and then head over to my parents' house for dinner. Unfortunately, I had an early meeting in Boston the next day so I would drive Paige back to her townhouse after dinner.

When we got to my bedroom, Paige walked over to her suitcase and grabbed a sketchbook from her suitcase.

"You have been surprising me so much over the past week, I thought I would return the favor."

Sitting down on the edge of the bed, she patted the spot beside her. Curious, I sat down.

"I've been working on this over the past week. Even though we were apart, I hoped I would be able to show you this before the construction began."

Paige turned to a page in her book and placed it in my lap. I looked down to see a detailed drawing of my front porch. She had sketched a ten-foot-wide decking that ran the full length of the house. Four white vertical pillars were placed equidistant from the corners, leaving a wide expanse for large steps leading to the front door. Flanking the four-riser cement staircase were two large potted plants. Barn-style sconces bordered each side of the front door and a large hanging lantern hung above it. The tall, wood paneled ceiling sported two large ceiling fans. The left end of the porch held a large porch swing. The right side contained three Adirondack chairs with side tables in between. Keeping in line with the deep gray siding, white trim, and forest green front door, the overall color scheme was gray, dark green, and deep orange.

"This is incredible," I commented.

Smiling, she asked, "Really?"

I nodded in appreciation. "It's exactly what I had in mind. You captured the craftsman touches perfectly."

She clapped her hands together in delight. "I'm so glad you like it. I wanted to stay true to the era of the house."

Leaning over, I kissed her. "You do fantastic work. I love it. Thank you."

She tore out the drawing and handed it to me. I took it from her and walked over to put it on my dresser. I approached her as she sat on the bed and offered her my hand to help her up.

"Let's go get washed up."

Her eyes darkened with desire at my invitation. She took

off her sweater, top and jeans to stand before me in a navy satin bra and panties. My dick responded immediately to the sight of her. Looking at her admiringly, I quickly divested myself of my clothes. Watching her appreciate my body and seeing the quickening of her breathing turned me on further. I would never tire of how she openly wanted me. Reaching out, I gently removed her bra and panties before scooping her up in my arms.

I carried Paige to the master bathroom and slid her body down mine, keeping her tightly against me as I turned on the shower. She reached up and pulled her hair in a messy bun on top of her head. We stepped in the shower where we washed each other slowly and thoroughly. Looking at and caressing her naked body was exciting enough, but her touch on my skin inflamed me. After rinsing, I sat down on the large bench on one end of the shower. She climbed over me, kneeling, with her thighs on either side of mine. She sank down onto my rigid cock, engulfing me in her moist heat. She threw her head back as she rode me, moving up and down with long, fast strokes. Watching her pleasure, I took her full breasts in my hands and squeezed the firm flesh. Unable to resist her hard nipples that begged for my mouth, I sucked the sensitive points. Moaning at my touch, she moved faster as I reached one hand down to cup her ass, pulling her tighter against me so that I could provide pressure where she needed it most.

Moaning deeper, she told me, "You feel so good, Carter. I love how you fill me up."

Her sexy words never failed to turn me on. "That's right, baby. I was meant for you."

"Yes," she groaned, close to reaching her peak.

Sensing she was on the edge and knowing that I was too, I grabbed her ass with both hands, increased the force of my thrusts, and ground against her.

"Come for me, sweetheart. Let me feel you grip my cock and scream my name."

A few seconds later, we both exploded. I stayed inside her, still pumping while we rode out our orgasms. Breathing heavy, she licked the side of my neck before fusing her mouth to mine. I fucked her mouth like I had just fucked her pussy, groaning with the taste of her. Reluctantly, I stood and unwrapped her legs from my hips. Quickly, we washed and exited the shower. After wrapping herself in a towel, she watched me dry myself.

"I wonder if my need for you will ever lessen, even slightly."

I grinned. "I sure hope not."

She smiled in return. "Even after we have just made love, I want you again. It's like I can't get enough of you."

Grinning wider, I responded. "It's never been like this for me before either, sweetheart. I'm hoping we feel like this about each other for at least the next fifty years."

Her eyes widened. "Oh my gosh. If we keep this up, I'll die of exhaustion by the time I'm forty."

I laughed. "Yeah, but as they say, what a way to go."

She rolled her eyes as I walked past her to go get dressed. After I threw on some jeans and a sweater, I went back into the bathroom to brush my teeth and hair. She was just finishing brushing out her hair and was about to put it up in a ponytail.

"Can you leave it down?" I requested. "I like the way it feels between my fingers."

Smiling, she nodded and raised up on her tiptoes to give me a kiss. Walking towards the door, she took the towel off and threw it to me before leaving the bathroom. And just like that, I was hard again. I could hear her giggling as she went to get dressed.

CHAPTER FORTY-NINE: PAIGE

Dinner at the Sullivans' that night was emotional. Patrick had almost fully recovered, thank goodness. When I attempted to apologize to him, he stopped me short saying, "Paige, darlin', you are family. You are in no way responsible for what that horrible excuse for a man did. Colleen told me how you wanted to protect Carter and the rest of us. While the sentiment is appreciated, if I had been in the room when you said it, I would have not let you get past the first sentence. When there is trouble, we stand together. My son is head over heels for you, and I sense you feel the same. Let someone just try to hurt you or him and they're going to have to answer to me."

After his speech, I had a lump in my throat so big all I could do was hug him. Xander and Jarrod threw in their two cents as well, threatening severe bodily harm to anyone who even looked at me wrong.

It was Colleen who had me crying, though, when she pulled me aside after dinner. "I need to tell you something that I have never shared with anyone, even Patrick. One afternoon, right before you left for college, Carter came home extremely distressed. I had never seen him that devastated. I took one look at his face and gathered him in my arms because, as a mother, all I wanted to do was take away his pain. He never said what happened, but I understood. My heart broke for him because I knew his heart was breaking saying goodbye to you."

As she went on with her story, I realized she was referring

to the afternoon in the park. Through all his excuses, I hadn't known until recently that, in his mind, he loved me enough to let me go. When Colleen admitted how upset he was, the depth of his feelings astounded me.

She took my hands in hers and continued, "I know that the two of you were young, but that doesn't diminish the connection you had. Nor does it lessen the love. I can't tell you how glad I was to learn you were back. Sure, Carter had dated other women since you left, but he never brought any of them to meet Patrick and me. That told me something. Now that you are here, I have never seen him so happy. I knew you were the one for him all those years ago. I believe he knew that too. He looks at you like his father looks at me. When Sullivan men love, they love with all their hearts. Thank you for loving him the way you do."

Touched beyond measure, I replied, "I am the lucky one, Colleen. Carter is the most wonderful man I have ever met. Even when we were kids, he always treated me like I was the most special person in his life. Leaving for college not being together demolished me. I have compared every man I dated in the past ten years to him and not one made me feel a fraction of the way I felt when I was with him. Since reconnecting, the feelings I had for him have deepened. I'm sure you know this, but your son is extraordinary. I have never known love like this."

Smiling through a few tears of her own, she repeated, "Like I said, the Sullivan men love with everything they've got. Enjoy being on the receiving end. There's nothing like it."

I hugged her tightly. "I won't take it for granted, I promise. Every day I thank God to have Carter in my life."

She nodded. "Now we just have to worry about Jarrod and Xander."

I laughed but kept mum on the whole Jarrod and Peyton situation. I thought it wise to not open that can of worms.

Xander was a different story entirely. I didn't have any idea what kind of woman could keep up with him.

When Carter dropped me off at my house, we spent several minutes making out at the front door like teenagers. Wanting him with a fierce need, I almost begged him to come inside but I knew that he had to be up by five in the morning to get on the road to Boston. With one last brush of his lips, he told me he loved me and would call me after work the next day. After unpacking my suitcase and brushing my teeth and washing my face, I crawled into bed already missing him.

Monday morning dawned rainy and cold. I dressed for work in a pair of chocolate brown slacks, a pink blouse, a chocolate blazer, and silver sandals. Adding a silver watch and diamond studs to compliment my angel necklace, I grabbed my purse, briefcase, and raincoat and headed off to work.

I pulled into the parking lot and was greeted by the Greenwich officer on duty, who held my umbrella over us as we walked into the lobby. Thanking him, I greeted Al and made the trek to my office.

I met with Gail regarding scheduling some vendor visits. At eleven, I had a meeting with my team to start preliminary discussions regarding the Carlson job. Grabbing some lunch from the cafeteria, I ate at my desk while answering e-mails. Carter texted me at four o'clock to let me know that he was just getting on the road back to Connecticut. We made plans to meet up at his baseball game Wednesday evening. At five, Parker poked his head in my doorway to let me know a new client would be in about six-thirty and he wanted me to join the meeting. I spent the next hour finishing up some plans and recording notes in my mini-tape recorder that either I or Gail would transcribe later in the week. As the staff left, I wish them a good night and had just turned off my tape recorder and put it in the top desk drawer when Parker entered my office along with a heavy-set blonde-haired gentleman.

"Paige Turner," Parker introduced, "Please meet Bill Darrod. His company just bought some office space in Greenwich and would like to talk to us about designing the space."

I stood up and offered my hand in greeting. Mr. Darrod shook it, holding on a bit too long and tightly. Removing my hand from his, I sat back down at my desk.

"Parker, do you mind getting those project samples we were discussing?" Mr. Darrod inquired.

"Sure, let me just run to my office."

As Parker left, I offered, "Won't you have a seat?" I waved my hand towards the two chairs opposite my desk.

Stepping closer, but not sitting down, he stated in a low voice, "You look good, Paige."

A bit startled, I looked at him closely. Taking in his short blonde hair, full mustache and beard, dark blue eyes, and a bit of a paunch, I tried to place him.

"I told you we weren't done yet."

My heart galloped in my chest as I recognized the voice. I felt my blood run cold with fear.

Grinning, he stated, "I knew you couldn't forget me."

"Derrick," I whispered in shock.

"That's right, Paige. Your one and only."

I made a move towards the door. He stopped me by pulling out a long knife from a compartment in his briefcase.

"Uh-uh," he scolded. "You're staying right here with me. And, if you want your boss to stay alive, get rid of him."

Thinking frantically, I agreed. "Please don't hurt him. He has nothing to do with this."

"You're right, this is between you and me. However, I won't hesitate to kill him, so make it good. If I think you are tipping him off in any way, he'll be laying on your office floor."

Trying to control my breathing, I nodded and sat back

down. Derrick took a seat on the loveseat near my door and slid the knife into his pants pocket.

"Here you go, Bill," Parker began as he walked into my office and handed Derrick some samples of our recent work.

"Thanks, Parker," Derrick acknowledged, never taking his eyes off me. "Paige and I were just talking and realized it would make sense for she and I to discuss things ourselves. I'd like to get her perspective on the space."

Parker turned to me and I nodded ,hoping I didn't look as frightened as I felt. "Yes, I think it would be a good idea for, uh, Bill and I to start planning what he is looking for. Plus, don't you have that dinner party you wanted to attend tonight?"

Looking a little perplexed, Parker looked between the two of us before agreeing. "Okay, if you're sure . . ."

I smiled at him, hoping he would leave and be safe. "Sure. I'll fill you in tomorrow."

Parker turned to shake hands with Derrick. As he did, I discreetly turned my tape recorder back on and left the top drawer slightly ajar.

"Nice to meet you, Bill."

"Same to you, Parker. Paige and I will work everything out."

Looking at me, Parker said, "I'm sure you will. Goodnight, Paige."

"Goodnight, Parker," I called as Parker strode towards the hallway. "And thank Jax for me, will you? For finally getting my bio up on the website. So prospective clients, like Mr. Darrod, can feel confident in my abilities."

Parker looked taken aback for a second, but quickly recovered. I prayed Derrick didn't notice. I also hoped he didn't realize that I had just sent Parker a message. I held my breath until I heard Parker's office door shut and the sound of his retreating footsteps.

Derrick stood up and approached me. "Very good, Paige. Your boss will live another day."

I stood up, trying to back up slightly. "Thank you, Derrick. There was no—"

Before I could finish my sentence, Derrick punched me across the side of my face. "You fucking slut!"

I fell to my knees and struggled to stay alert. Grabbing me by the hair, he dragged me over to the loveseat and threw me down on it.

"Did you think I wouldn't find you? You can never hide from me. I own you."

Struggling to get away, I scratched at his face. To stop my efforts, he drew back and punched me again in my left eye. Tears clouded my vision and I cried out in pain.

Grinning, he stated, "That's right. You like it rough, don't you?"

He grabbed at my breasts and ripped my shirt open. As I tried to hold the sides together to cover myself, he took the knife from his pocket. "Let's see how you look with my brand on you. Every day since I last saw you, I have been imagining how good it looks."

As he started to slit my bra strap, I tried to stall him by appealing to his ego. "How did you find me?"

Proud of himself, he preened a bit. "That was easy. I had a private detective look into your background. Your parents' phone number is the same as it was when you were growing up. He called them pretending to be from *Design Today*. Your mom was only too happy to let him know where you were working."

Of course, my mom would have no issue telling a reporter all about me if she thought I would get publicity and make the family look good. Since I had never revealed anything about the attack to my parents, they would have no reason to be suspicious.

"So, you have been following me the whole time I have been in Connecticut?"

Smiling again, he answered, "Not every day, but plenty of times. I had to fly back and forth to Chicago and keep up appearances. I couldn't let the probation office wonder where I was now, could I?"

Eyes narrowing, he slapped me several times on the right side of my face before grabbing my upper arms. "I had to clean up the side of the highway, picking up fucking trash for days because of you. Do you know how humiliating that was? I'm a Walters, for fuck sake!"

Trying to keep him talking to buy time as I hoped Parker had informed the officer outside who had gotten in touch with Jaxson, I prodded, "And did you disguise yourself like you are now so no one would recognize you?"

Eyes wild, he nodded. "Stupid cops were showing my picture around. No one was looking for a blonde fat guy with a beard and blue eyes."

Knowing that the tape was rolling, I hoped it could pick up our voices. I didn't know if anything he said could be used against him, but I was going to get him to admit to what he did anyway. Plus, if he was talking, he wasn't hitting me.

"So, you wore the disguise when you scratched my car?"

Grinning devilishly, he admitted, "Yep. I figured I would make your car match you. I knew you would recognize my signature."

Feeling physically ill, I prodded, "And you were disguised when you broke into Carter's house, attacked his father, and set everything on fire?"

He frowned. "So that's who the guy was? I was hoping it was Sullivan himself. The bastard. He should be dead for touching my property."

Wrapping his hands around my throat he squeezed tightly. "And you, you bitch. You let another man touch you? You let that bastard fuck you!"

His hands squeezed tighter and tighter, and I struggled to breathe. Everything started to fade before he suddenly removed his fingers from around my throat.

"No, you don't get off that easy. We're going to finish what we started. I think I may record it all and send your boyfriend a nice memento. That way he will know whose property you are once and for all. I'll make sure he watches it over and over. Then I'll kill him for touching you."

My fear intensified at the thought of Derrick doing anything to Carter. Convinced I was going to die, I wanted to protect Carter any way I could. Struggling to speak loud enough so my voice could be recorded, I ignored the pain in my throat.

"That would be a waste of time," I lied. "Carter broke up with me last night. He said he couldn't stand to be with a woman who was disfigured."

He smacked my cheek again, hard. "Don't lie to me, Paige."

Reeling from the pain, I forced myself to continue. "I'm not, Derrick. He said he tried to pretend it didn't bother him, but he was disgusted by the sight of the scars."

The smile that spread across his face made my skin crawl. "I told you no other man would want you. Because I own you. I can't wait to see my mark on you, Paige."

He crushed his mouth to mine. I kept my lips closed tightly and attempted to move my head to the side. I felt the bile rise in my burning throat as his erection pressed against my belly. Taking the point of the knife, he traced around my right nipple. I winced at the pain. Grabbing me again by my hair, he yanked me to my feet.

"We're going to get out of here so we can be alone. I've got a nice place all set up for us. Fix your shirt. We're going to walk right out the back door. If you make any move to signal the cop, I will slit your pretty little throat."

I struggled to stand and adjust my blouse so that the rips were not as noticeable. Recalling from my self-defense classes that you should never let your attacker take you to another location, I tried to think of anything I could to stall. I was still hoping that Jaxson was on his way. Eying my purse containing the pepper spray on my credenza, I angled my body towards it. Realizing my intent, Derrick grabbed my upper arm and held the knife along the side of my face.

"Where do you think you are going? Try anything like that again, I will cut you deep and drag you out of here if I have to."

We were steps from the doorway when Jaxson and two uniformed police officers burst through with their guns drawn. I almost sobbed in relief.

"Drop the knife, Walters!" Jax commanded.

Clutching my arm harder and using me as a shield, he responded "Not a fucking chance. Throw down your guns or I slice her."

He held the long knife against my abdomen. I felt a prick as the tip penetrated my skin.

"Calm down," Jax appeased. "Let's talk about this."

"There's nothing to talk about. We're leaving, and you're going to get the fuck out of our way."

Wanting to be free of this nightmare, I summoned all my courage. Using skills I had learned from the instructor, I stamped down hard on Derrick's instep before snapping my head back, smashing into his face. I barely registered the pain to my skull as he loosened his hold. I heard shots ring out and then I felt like someone hit the side of my head with a baseball bat. As I lost consciousness, I thought I saw Jax leaning over me.

"Top drawer," I whispered. "Tell Carter I love him. I love him so much."

Then everything went black.

CHAPTER FIFTY: CARTER

I was just about to take the exit off the interstate when I got the call from Jarrod.

"Hey, man. What's up?"

"Where are you?"

"I just got off of 84. I'm headed to the office to drop off some paperwork."

"Pull over."

A horrible fear gripped me. As quickly and safely as I could, I cut across two lanes and parked on the shoulder.

"What's going on, Jarrod? Is it Dad?"

"Dad is fine. Jaxson just called me. Apparently, Parker just ran outside and told the cop in front of Paige's building that Walters has Paige inside her office."

Fury flooded through me. "How the hell did he get inside?"

"Parker said he was wearing some kind of disguise, passing himself off as a new client. Neither the cop nor Al recognized him when Parker met him in the lobby."

"How did Parker know it was him?"

"Paige, smart woman, gave him some kind of signal as he was leaving. He went immediately to the patrolman who called Jaxson."

"What's going on now? Have they arrested the bastard?"

"I don't know anything more than what I told you."

"Fuck!!" I screamed in frustration.

"Carter, I'm not going to tell you to calm down because I know you can't," he said. "But try to get to her in one piece."

Disconnecting the call, I drove straight to Paige's office. A drive that would normally take about an hour took me forty minutes. When I arrived, the parking lot was filled with police cars and a couple of ambulances. Rushing towards the entrance, I was stopped by several officers.

"You can't go in there, sir."

"The hell I can't! My girlfriend is in there with some psychopath. I have to get to her."

Physically restraining me, they tried to calm me down.

"Carter?"

I turned to see Al standing in front of me.

"I'm so sorry. I didn't know it was him."

Still furious and frantic, I forced myself to not take out my anger on him.

"It's okay, Al. It's not your fault."

"Carter?"

Turning to my other side, I saw a tall man with light brown hair.

"Yes?"

"I'm Parker. Paige's boss."

I held out my hand in greeting. "Parker. Thank you so much for recognizing she was in danger."

He hung his head a bit. "I wish I could've done more. All I could think to do was get to the police so they could contact Jaxson."

"You did what you thought was best. Walters is a dangerous man. He very well could have hurt you if he thought you were trying to come between him and Paige."

Nodding in thanks, he stood next to me as we watched the entrance for any sign of movement. It was driving me insane to not be able to see Paige. I needed to know that she was okay. I couldn't even entertain the possibility that she had been harmed. Suddenly, Walters appeared in the doorway, handcuffed and flanked on each side by police officers. He had a bandage on his shoulder, blood all over his nose, and was limping slightly. Jaxson followed closely behind them.

"Jax!" I shouted.

Walking towards me, he motioned for the officers to let me through. I practically ran to him.

"Where's Paige?"

"The EMTs are with her. They should be bringing her out to the ambulance any minute."

A chill went down my spine. "Is she okay? Did that asshole hurt her?"

He looked at me, concerned. "He roughed her up pretty badly. And she hit her head on the side of her desk in the struggle. She's still unconscious."

"Shit!" I swore.

Spotting Walters about ten feet from me, I ran over as they were about to put him in the car. In a blaze of anger, I punched him in his already broken nose. I continued to pound on him until Jaxson and another officer pulled me off of him.

As Walters was helped up, he yelled, "I'm going to have your ass for assault!"

I stepped towards him again, wanting to kill him. Jaxon stepped in between us and put his hands on my chest to stop me.

"What assault?" Jax asked. "I didn't see any assault. Did you guys?"

Every officer in the vicinity shook their heads.

"Get him the hell out of here," Jax commanded.

Walters was loaded into the back of the cruiser and driven away.

"You should've let me kill him," I grumbled to Jaxson, the rage inside me burning.

"Assault, I can look the other way," he stated. "But murder is a whole other deal."

Still seething, I realized he was right to stop me, but that didn't mean I was glad he had. The idea that he had put his hands on Paige was excruciating. She just had to be okay. She had to.

"Here she comes," Jaxson said, nodding his head in the direction of the front door.

Rushing over, I planted myself at the side of the stretcher. The top of Paige's head was wrapped in gauze, her left eye was swollen, and there were marks on either side of her throat. I could also see the imprint of Walters' hand on her right cheek. Acid churned in my stomach as I saw the damage he had inflicted. I stayed glued to her side until they reached the back of the ambulance. There, I leaned down and kissed her gently on the forehead and told her I loved her. After letting the EMT's know I would be right behind them, I turned to Jaxson.

"They're taking her to Yale," he informed me. "It's not the closest, but it's the best. I'm headed to the station to question Walters. I'll be at the hospital as soon as I can."

Nodding, I headed to my truck. As I drove, I called Jarrod and filled him in. I put him in charge of calling our parents and Paige's friends. The whole drive I prayed to God to let Paige be all right. I couldn't lose her again. I wouldn't even consider the thought of her not surviving.

CHAPTER FIFTY-ONE: CARTER

When I got to the hospital, I parked and followed the EMTs into the Emergency Room. As they were admitting her, I turned to see my parents, Xander, Jarrod, Hunter, Grayson, Peyton, Alyssa and Caitlin in the waiting room. I walked over to them and they hugged me one by one.

"How is she?" Dad asked.

"I don't know the extent of her injuries. All I know is that she is unconscious."

"Fucking bastard!" Xander exclaimed. "Too bad they didn't kill him when they had the chance."

"Jaxson told me you came pretty close," Jarrod said.

"If Jax hadn't stopped me, I would have," I admitted.

My mom grabbed my hand and squeezed.

"I called her parents, but I just got their answering machine," Alyssa informed us.

"She's just got to be okay," Peyton sobbed.

Jarrod wrapped his arm around her, and she laid her head against his chest.

"Paige is going to be fine," Caitlin insisted, as if trying to convince herself. "She's strong."

Alyssa chimed in. "Remember that time she fell off the balance beam in gym class and got right back on it to finish her routine even though she had sprained her ankle?"

The women all nodded.

"And remember that time we were at the quarry and she slipped off the zip line right onto her back?" Hunter recalled. "She smacked into the water so hard that she had a huge red mark on her back, but she came up laughing."

We all smiled slightly, lost in memories. What seemed like hours later, the doctor entered the waiting room. Going up to my parents, he inquired "Mr. and Mrs. Turner?"

Not bothering to correct him, they stood.

"Paige has suffered a severe concussion, a crushed windpipe, a black eye, a stab wound to the lower abdomen that required stitches, and various other contusions. Due to the blow to the side of her head, she has yet to regain consciousness. There is no skull fracture, but there is some brain swelling in the area. We'll be monitoring her closely for the next forty-eight to seventy-two hours. We've given her pain medication so she's resting comfortably."

Both angry and concerned at the extent of her injuries, I swore softly.

"Can we see her?" Dad asked.

The doctor nodded. "Two at time, and just for a few minutes."

"I'm staying with her," I declared.

"Are you her husband?" the doctor asked.

I shook my head before saying, "Not yet, but I will be."

"Technically the rule is only family can stay with a patient," he said.

"I'm not leaving," I declared.

Seeing the determination in my eyes, he nodded. "We'll get you set up with a cot."

Shaking his hand, I said "Thank you."

Turning to everyone, I implored. "Give me a minute."

Understanding my need to see her first, they hung back. I entered Paige's room and walked slowly to her bed. She was hooked up to a monitor that displayed her heart rate and blood pressure. An IV was attached to her left arm. Fresh gauze encompassed head from just below her hairline to just above her eyes. Her left eye had started to turn black and blue.

Her right cheek was swollen and red. Looking down from her face, I saw the deep bruises that encircled her throat. I lifted the blanket and pulled back her hospital gown to reveal the gash just below her belly button that needed fifteen stiches to close it.

I pulled a chair next to her bedside, took her hand in mine and brought it to my lips. I was barely holding it together. Seeing her hurt, imaging what she went through, ripped me apart. If Jaxson hadn't stopped me, I really would've killed Walters. I knew that I had to put aside my anger and concentrate on taking care of her through her recovery. I leaned down and told her how much I loved her. I told her that I needed her. I pleaded with her to wake up. Half an hour later when my parents walked into the room, they found me with my head on her shoulder, eyes closed and begging God to heal her.

Two hours later, everyone had left for the evening. I had just turned down the lights and was going to try to get some sleep. The hospital staff had brought in a rollaway cot and set it up between Paige's bed and the window. I was sitting on the cot to remove my shoes when Jaxson walked in. He came over to the head of Paige's bed and kissed her forehead.

Looking down at her, he muttered, "Fucking bastard." Turning to me, he said "How is she?"

After I relayed what the doctor had told us, he sighed. "Do they have any idea when she is going to regain consciousness?"

I shook my head. "No. It could be minutes or it could be days."

"She's a strong lady," he insisted. "She'll pull through."

"She has to, Jax," I croaked. "I can't live without her."

He walked over to me and put his hand on my shoulder. "I know, man."

After squeezing my shoulder, he sat in a chair near the foot of the cot.

"What happened tonight, Jax?" I asked. "How in the hell did he get into her office?"

"We located his rental house this afternoon. The place was outfitted with various weapons and restraints. As soon as I saw the set-up, I figured Walters was close to putting some kind of plan in motion. I called the patrolman stationed at the front of Paige's office building to let him know I was on my way over to get her and bring her somewhere safe. It wasn't until I was halfway there that the detectives at Walters' place called to let me know they had found receipts for a variety of disguises. I radioed the information in, but by then Walters had already showed up for his appointment with Parker."

My blood had run cold at the mention of what was inside Walters' house. Knowing that he planned to torture Paige in unimaginable ways made me sick to my stomach.

"I'm just thankful that Parker was able to get out and tell you Walters was inside."

Jax nodded. "Yeah. Paige tipped him off with a cryptic message. Luckily, Walters didn't know what she was doing."

I looked down at Paige's face, still unresponsive. "I told her she was a survivor."

"She's a smart and courageous woman. She took a chance in order to escape as well."

"What do you mean?"

"When we entered her office, Walters shoved Paige in front of him as cover. He also had a knife up to her stomach and threatened to kill her if we didn't put our guns down."

I closed my eyes and took a deep breath. "Shit."

"Yeah, fucking coward," Jax continued. "Paige must have really paid attention during those self-defense classes she took. Within a couple of seconds, she stamped down on Walters' foot and headbutted him."

Amazed, I looked down at her. "My brave girl."

"Unfortunately, although her actions caused the bastard to loosen his hold, he was able to stab Paige first. And, as she dodged to the side, she fell into the corner of her desk which is how she got the head wound. I got a shot off at Walters that hit him in the shoulder. One of the other officers hit him in the leg."

"Am I an asshole for wishing at least one of the bullets was fatal?"

He shook his head. "No, completely understandable. But here's some good news. Walters confessed to everything. We're charging him with two counts of attempted murder — one for your dad and one for Paige — stalking, attempted kidnapping, sexual battery, and arson. Even his daddy's money and connections won't be able to keep him from going away for the rest of his life."

"Thank Christ."

Taking a small tape recorder from his pocket, he said. "There's something else you should know. Before Paige passed out, she told me two things. She mentioned to look in her top drawer and she also told me to let you know that she loved you."

I pushed the hair back from Paige's forehead and squeezed her hand.

"In the top drawer of her desk, I found a small tape recorder. Evidently, she had turned it on to record just as Parker was leaving. It may be difficult to listen to, but I wanted you to hear it. Even knowing Walters was going to hurt her, she had the mindset to protect you. She was thinking of your safety in the face of losing her life."

He handed me the recorder. "It's a copy, so I don't need it back. I'm thinking you will probably want to destroy it after listening to it. Feel free."

I stood up and hugged him. "Thanks for everything, Jax."

"I wish I could've gotten to her sooner, but I'm glad we got there before it was any worse. I'll call you in the morning."

I watched him walk out the door, thinking how grateful I was to have him as my best friend. I wouldn't have wanted anyone else to watch over Paige. I knew it was likely that if someone else had been in charge, Paige might not be alive.

Sitting down in the chair at the end of the bed so Paige couldn't possibly hear the recording, I pressed play. As I listened to the assault, I could feel my blood pressure rise and my hands clench into fists. When I got to the part where she lied about our relationship, I felt my chest grow tight with emotion, realizing the depth of her feelings for me. By the end of the tape, I was openly crying. After the recording turned off, I pressed stop and ejected the tape. I ripped the ribbon out of the cassette before cracking it in half and throwing it in the trash can.

I lowered the side rail of Paige's hospital bed and pushed the cot up against it, effectively creating a king-sized bed. I turned on my side facing her and kissed her temple. Wrapping my arm around her upper torso, I gently hugged her against me. I talked to her for over an hour, telling her how much I loved her, how proud I was of her, and how much I needed her and wanted her to come back to me. I dozed off while waiting for any sign that she heard me.

CHAPTER FIFTY-TWO: PAIGE

"You promised you would never leave me again, baby. Please wake up."

Through a haze, I thought I recognized Carter's voice and struggled to open my eyes.

"I love you so much. Wake up so I can tell you how much for the rest of our lives."

Blinking, I finally was able to open my eyes and see Carter next to me, holding my hand with his head bowed down and his eyes closed.

"Hey," I tried speaking out loud, but my throat hurt, so it came out as a whisper.

His head snapped up to look at me.

"Paige?" he asked, tentatively, as if he didn't believe I had just spoken.

I brought my hand up to stroke his cheek. He looked like he hadn't slept in days. His clothes were a bit disheveled and he had several days of stubble on his jaw. He was still the most gorgeous man I had ever seen.

"You're okay," I rasped, grateful.

He gently kissed my lips, his eyes filled with tears. "I'm better than okay now that you are awake."

I frowned. "How long have I been asleep?"

Stroking my hair, he answered, "Four days."

Shocked, I asked, "Derrick?"

"Locked up behind bars where he belongs. The next time he leaves prison, it'll be in a casket."

A few tears ran down my cheek. "It's over."

"Yes, sweetheart. It's over."

He bent down and brushed his lips over mine. I inhaled his scent and delighted in the feel of his mouth. The nurse cleared her throat as she came in the room.

"Well, look who's awake?" she asked, smiling. Turning to Carter she instructed, "I'm going to ask you to leave while I take some vitals and call for her doctor."

Nodding, Carter left the room. While the nurse looked me over and removed my catheter, I took stock of myself. I had a pretty bad headache, my face ached, my throat was sore, and my abdomen hurt. I wiggled my hands and feet and slowly sat up. Other than a bit of dizziness, everything seemed to be working. It took about an hour for the doctor to arrive and examine me. After letting me know that they would like to keep me another couple days until I regained some more strength, he left.

Feeling gross, I asked the nurse to help me shower and change. Someone had brought a few pairs of pajamas, underwear and my toiletries to my hospital room. As I was escorted into the bathroom, I took a look in the mirror. My hair was matted from the gauze wrap they had just removed. My left eye was a disgusting shade of purple and my right cheek was slightly swollen. There were finger-sized bruises on either side of my neck. As I stepped into the shower, I noticed deep bruises on my upper arms and a faint scratching around my right nipple. The wound to my lower abdomen had been closed with dissolving stiches and was an angry red. With the nurse helping to hold me upright, she and I gingerly washed my body and my hair, careful to not apply much pressure to the gash on the side of my head.

I needed assistance to dry both my body and my hair, and the nurse helped me apply a light coat of lotion everywhere. Feeling better, I brushed my teeth and added some balm to my dry lips. Exhausted from my efforts, I let the nurse lead me back to the freshly made bed. After promising to bring me some water and check on me soon, she left the room.

Instantly, Carter entered the room and pulled a chair up next to me. He stroked my face and took ahold of my hands.

"Have you been here the whole time?" I inquired, noticing the cot folded up in the corner and his gym bag on the floor.

"They couldn't drag me away."

Smiling, I kissed him gently. "I missed you."

He gazed at me. "I missed you too, sweetheart. You scared me."

Touching his cheek, I said, "I'm sorry.

Leaning forward, he gingerly took me in his arms. "I'm just so glad you're going to be okay. I don't know what I would've done . . ." he broke off, unable to continue.

"You're not getting rid of me that easily," I joked through my tears.

Drawing back, he looked at me with stormy gray eyes. "I love you, Paige. I can't even imagine my life without you."

"I love you too, Carter."

Kissing me again, he reached into the front pocket of his jeans. Pulling out my angel necklace, he fastened it around my neck.

"You'll always be my angel."

"And you'll always be my first, last, and forever."

He gently tasted my mouth, and I responded in kind.

Behind us, I heard the sound of someone clearing their throat.

"Hey, she's still in the hospital. Keep it in your pants, will you?" Xander joked.

As we broke apart, I saw all of the Sullivans in the doorway, arms laden with flowers and gifts. Smiling, I gestured for them to come closer. I was swept up in hugs, kisses, and tears. Carter filled them in what my doctor had said and that I would most likely be released in a couple of days.

The rest of the evening was spent with visitors. Caitlin, Peyton, and Alyssa came to see me for a few hours and we cried together. Hunter and Grayson stopped in with hugs and flowers. Parker dropped in with apologies. I told him there was no need to apologize. I was just glad he was alive and thanked him for alerting the police. My parents came by, but only stayed five minutes because they said they didn't like hospitals and couldn't stand to look at me when I was not *presentable*. Not surprised at their behavior, I put a restraining hand on Carter's arm when he began to berate them. My parents weren't going to change. I had long since giving up hoping for a deeper relationship.

Three days later, Carter wheeled me out of the hospital. He had insisted that I stay with him until I was completely healed. Mike Perlman had called to let me know he wanted me to take all the time off that I needed and my job would be there whenever I returned. Peyton had gone to my townhouse to pack my clothes and toiletries, then dropped the suitcase off at Carter's.

As we pulled up to Carter's house, I gasped in surprise. The garage was rebuilt, complete with craftsman-style lights and doors. The brand-new front porch looked like my rendering brought to life.

Turning to Carter, I sputtered, "How did you do this?"

Smiling broadly, he admitted, "I can't take the credit, as I was in the hospital with you around the clock. My dad took charge, and Xander, Jarrod, Hunter, Grayson and Jax pitched in. Plus, some of the company's crew lent a hand as well. What do you think?"

I walked up the front steps and strolled the porch from end to end. "It's beautiful. The work is incredible."

Wrapping his arms around me from behind, he stated, "You provided the vision. All they had to do was create it in

3-D."

Leaning back against his broad chest, I sighed. "It's amazing."

For the next four days, I recuperated. Carter made me breakfast every morning. Lunches and dinners consisted of take-out or meals brought over by Colleen or Caitlin. I had plenty of company too. Hunter visited and we played checkers, just like we had as teenagers. Peyton and Alyssa treated me to a home-spa one afternoon, consisting of a deep-conditioning hair mask, waxing, and a manicure and pedicure. Jaxson brought over home movies from our middle and high school years and we watched them, laughing until we cried. Grayson and Xander came over every afternoon and provided color commentary while we watched the Dr. Phil show. Jarrod drove me to an art museum, which was really sweet, because I knew he did it just for me. I laughed at his puzzled expressions and wry comments. Colleen arrived every day at four to have tea together on the front porch. Patrick joined me one morning to sketch out some designs for the Lawrence house. It was nice to get back to working, if only in a marginal way.

Carter took delight in pampering me. He drew me bubble baths. He gave me back and foot massages. He rearranged his schedule so that he could work from home and either had clients visit him there or had Jarrod or Xander substitute for him. When I got tired, he set me up on the couch in the family room or carried me up to bed. We took daily walks around his neighborhood and bundled up against the November chill every evening to sit on the front porch swing. We talked for hours about anything and everything. We speculated on how long it would be before Jax and Alyssa gave in to their ridiculous chemistry and slept together. We also wondered what was really going on between Jarrod and Peyton. He told me he had heard the tape and how that affected him. I described to him, in my own words, what it had been like in my office that night.

While Carter never missed an opportunity to touch me, he hadn't attempted to make love to me. We had enjoyed many kisses, but he seemed to be holding himself back. I knew he was most likely concerned that I wasn't physically ready, which was thoughtful, but I was getting desperate. Sleeping in his arms every night and waking with him every morning was torture. I missed touching him and I yearned for him to touch me.

On Friday night, five days after being released from the hospital, I stepped out of my bath and slathered myself with lotion. I looked in the mirror, assessing my healing. The bump on my head had shrunk, now almost non-existent. The swelling on my cheek was gone. My black eye was now a very pale yellow, as were the bruises on my throat and upper arms. The stab wound on my abdomen was healing nicely, though still bright pink and a bit tender. Overall, I both looked and felt more than ready.

I brushed out my hair until it was full and shiny. Deciding to put on a little make-up, I opted for a dusting of eye shadow and some mascara. I debated on stepping into some fancy lingerie but decided against it. Naked, with only my angel necklace on, I walked into the bedroom. Positioning myself in front of the large picture window as the sun was setting, I called out to him.

"Carter!"

I heard him run up the stairs. He entered the room and stopped short. His eyes appraised me from head to toe and I saw them darken with desire. My nipples pebbled and a warmth flooded my core.

Swallowing audibly, he asked, "Is everything all right?"

Taking a step towards him, I answered, "I need you, Carter."

Breathing deeply, I saw the bulge in his jeans swell.

"Are you sure, Paige? Do you think it's okay?"

Stepping closer to him, I kissed the side of his neck and whispered in his ear. "If I don't have you inside me, I'm going to die."

I could feel the tension in his body as he fought to stay in control. "I don't want to hurt you. I want to make sure your body is healed enough."

Taking one of his hands in mine, I ran it down my neck, over my breasts, and past my belly before cupping it over my crotch. I could feel my own heat even through his hand. I separated one of his fingers and inserted it inside me.

Looking him in the eyes, I stated, "I think I'm all better. Do you agree?"

Groaning, he lifted me in his arms and gently placed me on the bed.

His eyes were stormy as he revealed, "I've been craving you since you woke up in the hospital, but I didn't want to rush you. I take care of myself in the shower every day so I wouldn't ache so much. It's been a poor substitute for making love to you."

As he stripped the clothes from his body, I felt my breasts swell and the dampness between my legs thicken. I had missed seeing his muscular chest and arms, his tight stomach, his strong thighs and legs, and his huge erection that currently pointed straight at me holding a glistening drop on its head. I made a move to sit up and touch him, but he stopped me.

"I want you so much, sweetheart. It's been too long. If you touch me, I'm not going to last."

Carter lay down next to me and brought his mouth to mine. Very gently, he traced my lips with his tongue. Moaning, I opened my mouth and invited his tongue inside. Our tongues tangled repeatedly before he used his to stroke the inside of my cheeks. He moved his mouth downward, kissing my neck before nibbling on my collarbone. Sighing, I stroked his arms and chest, marveling at the feel of him. Heading lower, he gently licked my nipples, causing my upper body to lift off the mattress. Using his tongue, he traced a path down my torso, stopping to plant gentle kisses on my healing stab wound.

As he nuzzled my pubic hair, he growled, "I've missed tasting you, sweetheart. You always taste so sweet."

Whimpering as he licked me, I fisted my hands in his hair. Wincing slightly at the twinge of pain from my lower stomach, I couldn't help thrusting towards his mouth. On edge from our abstinence, I felt my orgasm hit me as soon as his mouth closed over me. He smiled as he brought his face level with mine. Leaning down, he kissed me long and deep. I ran my hands anywhere they could reach — over his chest, down his stomach, over his back. His muscles quivered everywhere I touched.

Groaning, he admitted, "I wanted to go slow and take my time, but it's been so long and I need you so bad."

Wrapping my legs around his hips and positioning him at my entrance, I agreed. "I don't want you to go slow. I need you to make love to me like only you can."

Lowering himself to rest on his forearms, he kissed me savagely, devouring my mouth as he joined us together with one fierce thrust. I moaned at the invasion, digging my nails into his shoulder blades. As he moved faster and faster, my cries mixed with his groans.

"Missed you so much, baby," he panted. "Can never get enough of you."

"You feel so good," I breathed, overwhelmed by sensations.

I tilted my pelvis higher and locked my ankles together. Raising up on his knees, he grabbed me underneath my butt and pounded harder and harder into me. My breasts bounced with the force and my hands grabbed the sheets as my head thrashed from side to side. The angle was incredible.

"Yes! Oh, Carter, yes!" I screamed as the spasms overtook me.

"Paige!" he cried out, throwing his head back as he erupted.

Once our tremors ceased, he withdrew and laid down, pulling me on top of his chest. I lifted my face to his to receive his kiss.

Wrapping his arms around me and holding me close, he said, "I don't know what I would've done if I'd lost you."

Looking up at him, I stroked the side of his face. "But you didn't. I'm right here. And I don't plan on going anywhere."

"You did promise me that you would never leave me again," he conceded.

"See that?" I asked. "You had no reason to worry."

Kissing me gently, he declared. "I love you, Paige. You're mine."

Snuggling against him, I agreed. "I always have been. Just like you've always been mine."

Chuckling, he admitted, "Since the first moment I saw you."

Heart full, I professed, "I love you, Carter. I'm so glad we found our way back to each other."

"I never doubted it for a minute," he stated, smiling.

CHAPTER FIFTY-THREE: CARTER

It was Friday night, December twenty-third. My mom had finally gotten her wish to gather all of us together. Everyone was able to attend before heading out the next day for various family holiday visits. My parents' house was decorated with lights and greenery and the nine-foot-tall Christmas tree looked spectacular and sheltered a multitude of presents. We decided on a Secret Santa gift exchange with a $100 limit. Two weeks earlier, Mom had assigned us all the name of who we would be buying for. I was assigned Grayson and took great pleasure in buying him a set of Jerry Springer DVDs, since he had enjoyed watching Dr. Phil so much with Paige and Xander.

Alyssa was the last to open hers. The present itself was wrapped in elaborate holiday paper and adorned with a huge gold bow. After tearing off the wrapping, she lifted the flaps of the box and took out the items inside. First was a pair of black six-inch spike heels covered in feathers and sequins. Next came a pair of black panties that looked like they were made of rubber.

Not looking the least bit embarrassed, but rather annoyed, she stated, "Wonderful. Thank you, Santa. A pair of hooker shoes and edible panties."

Everyone burst into laughter, though my parents did look a little bit embarrassed.

"One guess who your Secret Santa is!" Xander exclaimed.

Eyes narrowing in Jaxson's direction, Alyssa retorted, "Gee, I wonder . . ."

Jaxson smirked but stayed silent.

I caught Paige's eye across the room and winked at her. She smiled broadly in return.

Over the past six weeks, Paige had fully recovered physically. I was in awe of her resiliency. She had just started speaking to other women who had experienced sexual assault. Jax had been correct with his suggestion. She was a natural at it, and people responded to her genuineness.

Walters had agreed to a plea deal and was sentenced to life in prison without the possibility of parole. The media got hold of his entire background, along with his father's continual cover-ups. More victims came forward and a massive civil suit was filed. Between the financial repercussions and the bad publicity, Walters' company's stock plunged. I can't say I was sorry to hear it.

Paige had been back at work for about a month and we were meeting regularly regarding Hunter's riverfront build. She was also consulting with Sullivan & Sons on some of our residential new builds, having dipped her foot in the water with my dad on the Lawrence house. Her career continued to flourish, and I looked forward to sharing my accomplishments with her and also liked getting her professional opinion regarding my projects.

We saw each other several times a week, rarely spending a night apart. She asked me to spend Christmas Eve with her parents. I didn't know if they would ever have the kind of relationship she deserved, but I would support her decision to try. We were coming back to my mom and dad's for Christmas Day. Paige had volunteered to bring the twice-baked potatoes and was making an apple pie as well.

Every day, though I didn't think it was possible, I loved her more and more. Each time she looked at me and I saw the love in her eyes, I fell deeper. It never ceased to amaze me how much she desired me. She enjoyed putting her hands and mouth on me, which drove me crazy. I couldn't stop touching her or kissing her either. And I definitely couldn't get enough of making love to her. The chemistry between us continued to burn strong with no lessening in sight.

I slipped from the room to get Paige's early Christmas gift. I brought the large package over and set it down in front of where she was sitting on the couch talking to Peyton, Alyssa and Caitlin.

Smiling, she asked, "What is this?"

I kissed her gently and said, "Merry Christmas."

Looking at me quizzically, she argued, "But Christmas is still two days away."

Looking into her eyes, loving her, I insisted, "This one couldn't wait."

Grayson smiled at me and nodded.

Paige shrugged her shoulders and unwrapped the gift. Taking the lid of the box, she was greeted by a small tan-and-black face. Laughing, she picked up the wiggly ten-week-old German Shepherd puppy, who promptly covered her face with kisses.

Giggling, she looked at me. "Oh my gosh, Carter. He's adorable."

Smiling, I said, "I thought you could name him Taylor after Lawrence Taylor."

Eyes narrowing, she frowned. "No dog of mine will ever be named after a NY Giant player, and you know it." Rubbing her face into his fur, she said. "He looks like an Emmitt."

I nodded as I knew Emmitt Smith was one of her favorite Cowboys. "Emmitt it is."

She kissed me. "Thank you, Carter. I love him!"

With that, she held the pup up in the air a bit and looked him over. I heard her gasp.

"Oh my gosh," she breathed. "Is this for real?"

Untying the ring from Emmitt's collar, I bent down on one

knee.

"Paige, from the first time I saw you, I knew I wanted to be with you forever," I began. "You captured my heart. Ten years later, it's still yours. I love you more than I thought it was possible to love anyone. You're the sweetest, sexiest woman I have ever known. I don't want to go another day without letting the world know that you are mine. Will you marry me?"

Crying, she threw her arms around me. "Yes, of course, I will. I love you so much."

As I slipped the ring on her finger, she gazed at it, saying "It's beautiful."

My mom had several pieces of jewelry from my grandmother. As soon as I told her I was going to ask Paige to marry me, she offered me my pick. I chose a three-carat oval shaped diamond from a pendant. I took it to a jeweler who used it as the center stone, flanked by two smaller round diamonds and set in a platinum band.

As I kissed Paige, I heard shouts of congratulations and the sniffle of tears.

Caitlin's voice rang out above the rest. "I told you I was going to be your wedding planner!"

Laughing through her tears, Paige responded, "Was there ever any doubt?"

"Not in my mind," I declared before kissing her again.

You may also enjoy the following from eXtasy Books Inc:

Pen and Ink
Lark Westerly

Excerpt

Pen reached over the dip between Ben's hip and the swell of his ribs and curled her fingers around a warm and familiar shape.

"Mmm," she murmured and gave it a bit of a fondle. They were old friends, after all.

Such an overture used to result in a pleasant interlude that culminated, on the best nights, in Ben telling her to pipe down before she scared the neighbours.

"Good practice for when we have a howling baby," she said when she first went off the Pill. She said it less often as time went by with no sign of a baby on the way.

Ben wasn't interested in tests or treatment, so she pretended to be philosophical too. It wasn't so easy when she noticed he was less than interested in sex. They'd lie in bed relaxed, with Pen stroking him gently, and sometimes he'd respond, but he never made the first move anymore.

"Are you okay?" she asked one night when he caught her wrist and gently but firmly removed her hand from its familiar fondling spot.

"Yes."

"Have I done something to annoy you?"

"No."

She tried for a touch of humour. "Is that your way of telling me I've let myself go, and I have to give up slopping about in slippers and curlers with a fag on my lower lip? Are you going to throw me over for a younger woman?"

"Don't be ridiculous."

She was silent, hurt.

"It's not always about you, Pen."

"But you said you were okay."

He rolled over and put an arm around her. "I'm always tired. Maybe I'd better go to the doctor and get looked over."

"Good idea." She felt a jolt of fear. Ben almost never went to the doctor.

Tests showed Ben had a low-grade virus, which just had to burn itself out. It took a few weeks, but eventually, he was his old self. The only difference Pen detected was in the state of their sex life. After the virus, things improved, but it never did get back to its former frequency. Ben had a clean bill of health, so Pen put the lack of amorous activity down to middle-aged slump. They were well into their thirties and had been together since meeting at art school when Ben was seventeen and Pen, nineteen.

There was no falling out, no fights, and absolutely no estrangement. Since they lived together and worked together from home, and shared most of their non-work interests, Pen thought maybe the togetherness she loved was stifling Ben. She started making the occasional excuse not to go to the Oval when he went to football events and encouraged him to go out with his mates for an after-match beer.

All the while she puzzled over how to recover their former level of intimacy. If she never mentioned it or made overtures, it would decline even further. If she tried to initiate sex or simply caressed him, he might feel pressured or think she was being needy. Could it be that he really disliked the idea of having a family? Would it help if she offered to go back on the Pill or get an implant?

"If we're ever going to have a baby, it'll have to be fairly soon," she said.

"I'm not getting tested."

"I don't expect you to. I just thought we could try the rhythm method."

"Um, isn't that to stop you having a baby?"

"Usually, but we can use it in reverse."

"Reverse rhythm. Does that mean you come and I go, or I go and you come?"

Pen grinned at him. "How about we both come together."

"Sounds good to me. You'll have to make me a roster. Sex by appointment for Ben and Pen. Coming together. Sounds kinky."

She made up the roster and hung it in the bedroom. Initially, Ben thought that was fun, and made a point of presenting himself, naked, shaved and showered, whenever the x of a kiss appeared on the calendar.

They made a game of it, but Pen realised after a while not much had changed; their infrequent encounters had simply been rearranged into rostered clumps.

When these also tailed off, she was worried.

The next month, she indicated the roster, although she too was losing momentum, and Ben stared at it for a few seconds as if he was unsure what it meant.

"Ben, are you okay?"

He blinked and turned to frown at her. "Stop fussing."

It was nothing more than that but just for a moment he wasn't Ben anymore. Then he got into bed and lay down as if nothing had happened. Pen spooned behind him and draped her arm over his hip. He reached up, murmured something drowsy, and pulled her hand to its familiar fondling position. For the first time holding the warm, heavy sac failed to give her comfort or pleasure.

In the night, he rolled over and nuzzled her neck, moved down to her breasts and on down over her belly. Pen let her body take over, and when she'd calmed, she pulled him up to lie breast to breast. "Your go now," she said, parting her legs to receive him, but he just patted her thigh.

"In the morning, I'll be up for a wham-bam before you can say good morning or cock-a-doodle-do." With that odd comment, he turned and went to sleep.

Pen, physically satisfied but emotionally chilled, lay awake and worried.

Ben got up early the next day and went off to the Oval. Pen got down to some sketching. Her concentration was shot, and she was quite pleased to be interrupted by a bang on the door.

She opened the door and smiled at her friend Skye Bakewell. Skye was a hippy-chick, earth mother, and dressmaker extraordinaire, and Pen had known her for years. They saw one another every so often, and Ben got along well with Skye's husband, Si. "Skye! Come in!" She peered over her friend's shoulder. "Si not with you?"

"No, he's gone to visit Honeycomb and embarrass her sculptor."

"Honeycomb has a sculptor?"

"He's called Jake Peters. She's been seeing him for a while."

There was something in Skye's voice that sounded off key. "Don't you like him?"

"I don't dislike him. He seems okay — been married before and has a couple of stepchildren. I don't know him very well, but you know Honey. She makes her own decisions." She looked at Pen. "So, how are you and Ben? Any news?"

"I don't think there's ever going to be any news," Pen said. Then, because Skye seemed lost for words, she added lightly, "It's not easy to get pregnant from muff-diving."

"I suppose not. Do you want Si to give Ben the talk? As in what goes where and how you get it up and in and don't pull it out until it's done its duty?"

"It's about fifteen years too late for that. Unless he's

forgotten the what goes where bit." She shrugged. "We've been together a long time. You have to expect things to get a bit routine."

"We've been together over thirty years," said Skye.

"So, things have slowed down for you two?"

Skye paused.

"Never mind. None of my business."

"I was trying to think how to put it. Si is—Pen, you know what Si's like."

"Affectionate," Pen said, smiling. "Demonstrative?" People did tend to smile when they thought of Skye's husband.

"That's putting it mildly. He's always been like that from the moment we met. It's not all about sex, either. He's probably hugging Honeycomb's sculptor right now while Honeycomb disapproves."

"How did you two meet?"

"Bushwalking. But my point is Si has always been touchy-feely in the nicest way possible. He never oversteps the bounds with other people, but with me, he has no bounds, and I have none with him. I don't think you can compare him with other men."

That didn't answer Pen's question directly, but it gave her the idea Skye and Simon still enjoyed a lively sex life.

"Everything else all right?" Skye asked.

"I'm not sure. Ben had a virus last year, and he's never really been the same. You know how it is . . . it takes ages to get over some of those things."

"So I've heard," Skye said vaguely. "Why don't you and Ben come to dinner when Si gets back from scaring Honey's sculptor with PDAs?"

"We'd like that."

"Si can do a chakra alignment on Ben." Skye caught Pen's doubtful expression. "It's okay. It's just a little cleansing thing he does for a lot of patients at the clinic. He won't start chanting and dancing naked with a black cockerel on his head. Well, he might do a bit of dancing if he decides to add flow movement to the treatment, but I'll tell him to keep his pants on, or else."

It was settled that the dinner would be in two weeks, but although Ben agreed and claimed to be looking forward to it, the dinner never happened.

The muff-diving episode, as Pen thought of it later, proved to be the last of its kind.

A few days after Skye's visit, Pen and Ben came home from a shopping trip and started restocking the pantry. Pen was making coffee while Ben tipped potatoes into the vegetable box when she heard an odd noise. She turned in time to see Ben holding an empty eggbox upside down above the potatoes.

She stepped over and saw the mess of crushed shells, splattered yolks, and whites. "Hey! What are you doing?"

Ben looked at her blankly. "I have a headache. I can't see straight."

"You'd better lie down. I'll bring you a cup of tea and some paracetamol."

He turned and walked straight into the pantry door.

Pen took his arm and led him into the bedroom, and pressed him down on the bed. "Back in a minute, love," she said and kissed his cheek. Then she went out and telephoned for an ambulance. "This is Pen Swan from Number 19 Ridgeway Road. I think my husband has had a stroke."

ABOUT THE AUTHOR

Diane Ziock has been creating fictional narratives for years, including holding court at high school sleepovers where she would entertain friends for hours with fantasy romances. As a young adult, she had stories selected for literary journals, worked as a reporter, and was a contributor and an editor of a travel catalog and various corporate newsletters. She has been married to her soul mate—and inspiration for all of her male heroes—for over 20 years. When not writing, she can be found spending time with her husband, daughter, and mixed mutts, redecorating her house (again), and volunteering at various dog rescue events.